# The White Rajah

# The White Rajah

*Being a true and honest account of my life
with James Brooke of Sarawak
by John Williamson*

## Edited by Tom Williams

jms books

# THE WHITE RAJAH

JMS Books LLC
10286 Staples Mill Rd. #221
Glen Allen, VA 23060
www.jms-books.com

Printed in the United States of America

ISBN: 978-1-61152-033-0

*To Tamara with all my love.*

"When his Biography comes to be written, there must be in it, dark chapters as well as bright ones, but while those who loved him the best, could fondly and sadly wish it had been otherwise, they will ever be able to think of their leader, as the Father and Founder of a nation and as one of England's greatest sons."

*The Monthly Packet*, 14 September 1874

# Prologue

YESTERDAY I SAW THE London papers. I read the death notices first. At my age, you do that. And there was his name: Sir James Brooke. A knight now.

I cried then, for what he had been. And I cried, too, for my lost dreams. But I don't think I have any regrets. He changed my life. But, in the end, I think I had no choice but to do what I did.

I wrote it all down. I never meant to keep it but I did. This morning I took it out and read it and then I made my way to church and I prayed. I remembered his kindness and his gentleness and all that he had been to me, and I prayed God would forgive him his sins and that he might find repose for his soul.

I should destroy this now, yet I cannot. It is a true record of my early life. To destroy it would seem, somehow, to dishonour my recollection. For if we did wrong, we meant all for the best.

I will wrap this safe and hide it away. If, one day when we are all dust and this story can be told, it is found and read then, whoever you are, pray for the souls of John Williamson and James Brooke.

*J.W.*
*June 1868*

# Chapter 1

I CAN STILL REMEMBER the very first time I saw James Brooke.

It was in the Goat and Compasses, a low dive of an inn, even as sailors' taverns go. I was there because I wanted to be alone to drink away the last of my pay and decide what I was to do for the future when the door was thrown open and in he came.

He was so much younger in those days, of course. We were all so much younger. I was scarcely a man, really, for all I thought myself cock o' the walk. He was in his middle twenties, tall, good-looking with dark curly hair blowing untidily. I say good looking but, in truth, he was one of the handsomest men I had ever seen. He was of medium height but slim and swift in his movements, and he carried himself with the easy confidence that comes with wealth. It seemed to me he brought an energy and enthusiasm into the room with him. At first I thought it was because of the red soldier's coat he wore over civilian trousers. (It was the coat of an officer of the East India Company and he had no business wearing it, having resigned his commission the previous year, but all this I was to learn later.) As he and his friends fairly skipped across to the bar, though, his gaze caught mine and the fire that glinted and shone in that glance was brighter than any red coat.

Since that night, I have seen him pass into all sorts of company—joining a seaman's mess, bursting into an Admiral's cabin, being ceremoniously ushered into a throne room—and I have so often seen the way the room lights up, charged as it were by an almost mystical energy he brings with him. By now I hardly notice it, but then I was caught staring in that light the way I have seen rabbits trapped in a lantern's beam on those nights I went lamping back in my farmhood days.

Besides him, the others seemed almost shadows. I am not even sure who was there and whom I met later. Colin Hart, I remember—another lively man of about Brooke's age but more solid and with the bearing of a sailor (which, indeed, he was). John Kennedy was there, too. Kennedy was an older man, dressed carefully in decent but slightly shabby clothes which told of a person in whom taste and ambition outstripped income. His bearing, though, suggested a strong man who saw life as a battlefield on which he marshalled his legions with every hope of success. There were two or three others but they were younger and, I think now, of no account. That is not to say I thought them of no account at the time, for they were clearly gentlemen, both by their clothes and by their manner. I, you must remember, was amongst the humblest class of sailors in the tavern and my experience of gentlefolk was scarce.

The party was well in drink but not, in my book, drunken. They all seemed merry, even Kennedy, in whom a certain caution sat, calculating, even in the midst of celebration. They seemed to be celebrating some good fortune and coins were hammered impatiently on the bar as ale was called for. Someone shouted for food and it was agreed they should eat in the tavern. The young gentlemen, I remember, thought this a great joke, a sailors' inn being apparently somewhat inferior to their usual haunts. Brooke, though, drew Hart and Kennedy to him, an arm around each of their shoulders, and said they should break bread together in an honest meal with honest seamen and this was a fine way to celebrate a venture which would see them dining in many stranger places than this.

I had been quietly finishing my ale as I watched them. They were so alien to the world I inhabited, I was fascinated by them but, at the same time, nervous of having them about me. I decided that once I had supped my pint, I would take myself away to some lodging house and leave the gentlemen to their pleasures with their own sort.

Meanwhile, Mr Brooke's party was calling for a table to be moved and more chairs to be brought up against others who, they said, would follow them. There was a great hustling and bustling and all at once one fellow, turning to gesture to a friend, struck my arm and caused me to spill my drink. I bit back my oath, for it would do me no good to swear at one of his station, and I drew myself together to depart. It was then Mr Brooke clapped me on the shoulder and set his own jug in front of me.

"I will not see a fellow without a drink on our account," he said "Tell me your name."

"Williamson, sir," I said, knuckling my forehead. "John Williamson."

"Well, Williamson, don't mind Richard. He's a clumsy fellow at the best of times."

Richard laughed as someone started a long, disjointed story about a vase Richard had broken in some Chinese temple on a voyage they had undertaken together, and then someone else was telling a story of a Chinese temple *he* had seen, and all at once food was being set out and some other gentlemen were coming into the inn to join them. Someone set a slice of beef before me. I started to push it away, for clearly I was served in error, but Brooke looked up and said I was to eat. "We are celebrating the purchase of a ship," he said. "We are to set out for the Far East on our nautical venture and if we cannot have a sailor join our feast, then I would hazard we are in the wrong line of business."

There was more laughter at this. One or two gentlemen slapped me on the back, saying they should be proud to eat with me. More ale arrived at the table and we settled together to our meal.

Roast beef and ale have a wonderful way of hastening good fellowship, even amongst those who would not expect to keep the same society. Certainly the ale was plentiful, yet the principal actors were never drunk. Kennedy maintained always a reserve of sobriety that watched and calculated as the others talked louder and laughed longer with the passing of the evening. Brooke, although flushed and noisy, was ever aware of what was said by everyone enjoying his hospitality and moved among them with a word here and a smile there, ensuring harmony among all his guests.

I sat quiet at first, minding my station, but as the meal progressed I found myself joining in the cheer. They were, as Mr Brooke had said, celebrating the purchase of a ship, the *Findlay*, in which Mr Brooke hoped to make his fortune as a trader. Mr Brooke had served in the East India Company's army and was something of a hero, having been shot whilst charging at the head of his men. His injury had necessitated his leaving the service but, before he returned to the land of his birth, he had taken ship with some of the fellows met with us in that inn and had sailed the South China Seas, tasting adventure on the ocean. Now recovered of his wound, he declared nothing would suit him so well as to return to that part of the world in his own trading venture. To that end, he had prevailed upon his father to sponsor his purchase of a brig and had assembled together some of his old comrades who would be his officers.

I understood Mr Hart was a particular friend of his and beery toasts were drunk to him. Then Mr Brooke rapped sharply on the table with his tankard and proposed a toast to Mr Kennedy. "For he is to be our Master and the success of our venture is in his hands. Let us, then, drink to Mr Kennedy's success!"

Mr Kennedy stood and bowed slightly. There were cheers and much banging of tankards but, it seemed to me, Mr Kennedy was not overly impressed with the company—soon after, he made his departure.

While Mr Kennedy had been with us, the mood had been excited enough, but with his departure, it was as if the schoolmaster had abandoned his charges and riot was the result. Jugs of ale were passed ever more quickly around the table, bawdy songs were started and forgotten in mid-verse, and quarrels flared and died, ending in laughter and mock blows. Most of what was said was of no import but at one point Mr Hart fell to complaining that none of his colleagues in the venture was ready to dirty himself with the menial work of a ship. Several voices rose to deny this, but Mr Hart would have none of it.

"What man is there here who can loose a top-mast halyard in a gale?" he demanded. At this, there was a quietening from those who had declared themselves handy, and Mr Hart laughed. "I'll give ten guineas to any of you who can tell me they've run a spar when the ship is pitching more than enough to spill a jar of ale."

He had spoken without thought and at least partly in jest but, as no one spoke up to respond to his challenge, there was an uncomfortable pause in the talk around the table.

I looked about at the flushed faces of these gentlemen and thought that, for all their money and fancy clothes, none of them could hold a candle to me aboard a ship. My experience was confined to the North Sea trade, carrying piss to Whitby and coals to London, but I believed myself one hell of a fellow in those days. I had left farming for the sea just two years earlier but I had every confidence in my ability to sail any ship in any ocean. You must remember, too, that like them, I had taken drink. This made me more forward than I would otherwise have been for, clearly, his money was not intended for me. Still, ten guineas was a lot to be had for the asking.

"I will take your money, sir," I said.

As the words left my mouth, I realised I had spoken out of turn. But then Mr Brooke laughed and told Mr Hart to give me my money. At this everyone else fell to laughing and the moment passed and the talk turned to other things. As the night's drinking drew to its close, though, Mr Brooke took me aside from the others.

"You are handy aboard a ship, then, lad?" he asked.

"I have not travelled the oceans like you, sir," I replied, "but I have been a sailor these past two years and am as handy afore the mast as any other of my age."

"Mr Hart is correct in his complaint," said Mr Brooke. "We are all enthusiasts here but most of us know all too little about the practicalities of ocean life. Mr Kennedy is a good master and, of course, he will procure us a good crew. But I would like to think that I, too, can spot a good man and have someone aboard who can be my own choice. Would you work for your ten guineas, Williamson?"

So, from a chance meeting in a tavern, I found myself on the crew of the *Findlay* and favoured by the man who owned the best part of her.

※

WE SAILED IN MAY.

It was a fine spring day as we eased our way from St Katherine's dock and started down the Thames to Tilbury. By dusk we were in the Channel, with fresh winds filling our new canvas. For the canvas *was* new. Everything about the *Findlay* that could be improved had been improved. Every detail had been gilded, every rail burnished, the decks themselves scrubbed until it seemed a shame to step upon them. A great deal of money had been spent on the *Findlay* and she was a vessel of which any gentleman could be proud.

And therein lay the germ of all that followed. For the *Findlay* was to be no gentleman's pleasure yacht but a working ship, paying her way on the short but busy passages between the islands of the Indies. With all her pretty paint, her toil would be much the same as that of the colliers I had sailed forever to and fro between Newcastle and London. Such work could well be handled by a schooner, but the *Findlay* was a brig. The square rigging took a full crew to handle. There were thirty-two seamen and a full complement of officers and officers' servants, making the *Findlay* an expensive ship to run.

To start with, at least, the *Findlay* was a happy ship. The officers were, with the exception of Kennedy, gentlemen, and they saw the venture as an escapade. The ship was their toy; they took pleasure in her and their pleasure was reflected in their treatment of the crew. We were lucky, too, in that the weather was kind and the ship made good way. Gibraltar passed, then for weeks Africa lay to port. We would lounge at the rails, watching the dolphins playing alongside or the flying fish breaking the water ahead. Life was easy and the pay was good.

It was not until we came to round the Cape that the reality of life on an ocean-going ship was brought home to me. Remember that, save for the odd run to France, all my experience had been in the coastal trade. Life aboard the *Findlay*, ploughing its way through a blue ocean under a tropic sun, was for me the essence of romance. Now, for the first time, I was to face the Southern gales.

We were a day out of Cape Town when the storm hit. We were running before the wind, strong westerlies carrying us toward our destination with all the speed we could wish. The waves were rising higher—twenty or thirty feet, often breaking across the deck—but we kept our canvas on in the hope we could outrun the foul weather.

When the storm clouds arrived, rushing toward us faster than anyone could imagine, we had hardly time to prepare. We furled the sails on the main mast but kept enough canvas on the fore mast to hold our heading, for if we were to lie at the mercy of such a storm, the wind would turn us side on to the tempest and we were sure to founder.

As the sails were furled, we started scrambling down the rigging. Already the rain was beating at us with such force, it was as if we climbed down a waterfall. The rigging was slippery with the rain; it beat against our faces so we could hardly open our eyes to see. We grasped at the lines as the deck swayed perilously below us. I jumped the last ten feet and fell, careering across the deck until I crashed against a hatchway and finally had a chance to stagger to my feet.

Although it was but mid-afternoon, the clouds all but blocked the sun . We were sailing through a perpetual gloom that was now and again relieved only by stabs of lightning. All those with no immediate business on deck ran to shelter below, but Mr Kennedy shouted to me and three others to stand by lest we needed to trim sail. So we stood, holding desperately to anything we could grasp as the world turned about us.

There was a crack as the topsail canvas stretched past breaking point. There was no time to think of the danger. I scrambled upward as if the devil was at my heels and, reaching the yard, tied back the loose sail and unfurled the canvas below to let us keep our headway.

The rain was blowing near horizontal and the *Findlay*, with not enough canvas to control our direction, was beginning to swing around for all the efforts of the helmsman lashed to the wheel forty feet below me.

I fumbled at the rigging with numbed hands. I worked on one side of the mast while another seaman—a big chap called, I think, Malcolm—worked on the other. The strength of the wind and the noise of the storm meant we could not hear each other, however hard we shouted, but we both knew our work and, by each watching what the other was about, were able to complete our business safely.

With the extra canvas spread, the ship was brought more steadily under control, but she still pitched from side to side with the motion of the waves, which now broke steadily across the bulwarks. Malcolm and I struggled to make our way down the rigging, but no sooner had he reached the deck than a wave knocked him off his feet. He was carried to the rail before I could move to aid him and would have been lost overboard but for a figure roped to the rail who threw himself forward to catch him up in his arms.

I struggled across the deck toward them, slipping on the wet timbers and terrified I would lose my footing and be swept away as Malcolm so nearly had been. I came safe to them, though, and saw Malcolm's saviour had been none other than Mr Brooke himself. Although he had no business on deck, he had roped himself up and joined us there. Looking at his face, his eyes sparkling, his teeth glinting white as he opened his mouth to laugh, it seemed he was there just for the thrill of it.

Whatever his reason for being there, he had saved Malcolm's life.

Mr Brooke put his head to mine. His mouth was just inches from my ear, but still he had to shout for me to hear him over the storm.

"Get him below. Mr Kennedy will send someone up to relieve the two of you."

I nodded my assent and wrestled open the door to our quarters. As we collapsed into the warm fug within, I glanced back. Mr Brooke was still on deck. And he was still laughing.

WE SURVIVED THE STORM with remarkably little damage and no loss of life or limb. It blew itself out the next day. We sailed on in suddenly calm waters, northeast to India.

Mr Brooke was visibly excited as we drew nearer to the subcontinent. His father had been a judge in the employ of the East India Company. He had been born in Madras though he had been sent to school in England for his education, returning to India as a young man. He loved the East and his enthusiasm transmitted itself to the crew. By the time we finally arrived at Bombay and docked to re-provision, we were all desperate to get ashore and see India for ourselves.

My first experience of the Orient gave me some idea of why men like Mr Brooke were so taken with the place. I was amazed at the sight of so many people, at the smells and sounds of their markets—or bazaars, as I was to learn to call them. It was the first time I had been among natives whose skin had been darkened by the harsh sun of those regions and I found them strange but beautiful. Some of the men, as is too often the case after a long voyage, entertained a good many of the women of the poorer sort and were loud in praising them by comparison with other women they had known. It is not my way to take my pleasures in this manner, so I cannot speak from my own observation, but I did notice that both the women and the men were more graceful than Europeans.

From Bombay, we sailed South and then directly across the Bay of Bengal to Singapore. The City of Lions, for that is what the name means, was already established as a thriving European settlement where but a few years before there had been only swamps and wild beasts. It was a busy port, full of all types of vessel from Chinese junks and rickety Malay dhows to the latest clippers, with the majestic bulk of British men o'war standing offshore on their regular patrols. Singapore was a gateway for all the commerce of the region and a natural base for our enterprise.

Although Singapore was a European city, the Chinese were to be seen everywhere, for they were cunning merchants who had established themselves well with the native people of the islands thereabouts. Several of the *Findlay*'s early ventures were therefore taken on the part of Chinese merchants, carrying out huge vases which the natives greatly value, simple tools, and some dyed cloths, then returning with rice, tapioca, and sugar cane.

These trips took us to various of the islands that fill these seas. Each voyage would last only a few days, and usually ended with the *Findlay* feeling her way uncertainly up some muddy creek to find a few ramshackle huts clustered at the water's edge. Even to the crew, it was clear that the few such commissions we received could not be profitable and, for a square rigged vessel such as ours, this coastal trade would never make a sensible return on the costs of running her. Life on board, though, remained pleasant enough. I may have been an impudent rascal to boast of my prowess in London but, as the weeks passed, I was turning into a true sailor and proved as handy in a tropical storm as I had been rounding the Cape. We saw nothing else as fearsome as that night at the Cape, but there was many a time I would be near washed overboard by the waves. I grew used to falling asleep in my hammock, my clothes still soaked with salt water, for there was no way to dry them till the storms abated.

As the *Findlay* made more and more runs for less and less profit, the officers began to scowl and mutter amongst themselves. Carelessness was more likely to receive a rebuke from the poop deck than had been the case in the past. My efforts, though, seldom gave any cause for complaint. I even felt I earned the grudging respect of Mr Kennedy.

As to Mr Brooke, although he was the principal in this adventure and thus the person with most to lose, still he seemed less troubled than the other gentlemen. He would often leave the poop and move among the men at work on the main deck, stopping every now and then to exchange a word or even to put his hand to a line, hauling in a way that showed a raw strength under the easy charm.

I came to feel he would look out for me especially. He would call me over to enquire as to how the men were feeling— were our victuals adequate? Was the crew satisfied with their conditions? True enough, it was in his own interests we were happy with our lot, for we were forever in and out of port and any man who was unsatisfied could easily jump ship and find another craft to work his passage home. Even so, Mr Brooke's concern with the welfare of his crew seemed real enough and I felt, also, he took a true interest in my own well-being.

It was in October the tensions among the officers first became clear to the crew. I was, indeed, witness to some of the warning signs of the tempest to come. I had been given the task to wait on the officers at table, as their steward was ill. (The steward was a servant of one of the gentlemen and had not sailed before. He was careless of himself with the native women and died some months later from the pox.) One evening—it must have been a Friday, for we served fish—I entered the cabin as Mr Kennedy was speaking. His tone was, as always, precise and his manner condescending, but there was a tinge of colour in his cheeks that suggested he was as near as he ever came to passion.

"I tell you again, sir," he was saying, "we can make no decent profit from such limited commissions as these. We must seek the sort of work we might find from Jardine Matheson who—"

Mr Brooke had been lounging back in his chair affecting a casual air that failed entirely to mask his irritation. At the name of Jardine Matheson, one of the largest and most respected firms amongst the Singapore merchants, he was unable to control himself. He leaned forward and interrupted Kennedy. "I did not leave the East India Company, sir, to be the servant of another cabal of old men with no greater ambition than to exploit their position in the service of avarice."

Kennedy gave Mr Brooke such a look as a schoolmaster might cast at a particularly stupid pupil. "Avarice has much to recommend it, when the alternative would appear to be penury."

"For God's sake, man! I am not offering penury but a chance for glory. I have come here to find adventure in new and undiscovered lands and you would have us simply plying for hire from one established trading post to another. I could have found more interest driving a hansom cab around London." He paused, visibly trying to control his temper. "John, I know you are worried about the money. But if we lay in a mixed cargo—opium, muskets, gunpowder, broadcloth, even some of these damned vases—then we can make a profit by trading on our own behalf. We can dash into the Straits and find vast returns in the remoter islands where the people are yet barbarous and have not been cowed into trade agreements with the Chinese…or Jardine and Matheson, come to that."

The other gentlemen had been sitting quietly watching. From their manner, it was clear this was an argument they had heard before. Now Colin Hart winked at the man next to him and in a stage whisper, behind his hand, intoned one word. "Smuggling."

Someone sniggered and Mr Brooke opened his mouth to reply, but Kennedy was the first to speak.

"Smuggling seems to be a very fair word for it, sir. I have been a sailor for thirty years and have not attained the position of Master to see my command running contraband. You may have a share in the ownership of this vessel, sir, but I would thank you to remember I am her captain."

I had stood quiet near the door, waiting for them to finish so I might start to serve. Several of the gentlemen now looked pointedly at me. Mr Brooke and Mr Kennedy fell silent and I served them their fish. No more was said on the matter—or no more while I was in the cabin.

In the years to come, I heard much from Mr Brooke about the differences he had with Mr Kennedy. At the heart of the problem was the difference in the character of the two men. For Mr Brooke, the venture was the chance to explore new lands, meet with the uncivilised inhabitants, and build trade with them upon his own terms. This, he argued, was how the great merchant dynasties of the Empire had all started. I think he saw himself alongside these merchant princes, carving out his own little kingdom in the archipelago. Mr Brooke was a gentleman and knew he would inherit money. For him, commercial success was incidental.

For Mr Kennedy, things were very different. Older, perhaps wiser in the ways of the world and, most important, with no prospect of wealth other than that he created by his own efforts, Kennedy saw the voyage as a straightforward commercial enterprise. The *Findlay* was a fine ship, but expensive to run. Therefore, he reasoned they must find a mercantile house big enough to be able to charter the vessel for regular work and thus recover their investment by steady toil.

The argument between the two came to a crux some five or six days after the incident I have just related.

None of the crew was present in the officers' quarters, but Jeb North—one of the older hands—was scrubbing the deck aft and said he heard a deal of shouting followed by a crash as if something had fallen. That afternoon, the officers were little seen on deck and, when they were, they were abrupt about their business. Mr Kennedy kept to his cabin and when he appeared the next morning, his face was marked. The officers put it about that he had fallen with the movement of the vessel, but it had been calm all that day and no one believed this for a moment. Instead, the word spread about the ship that Brooke and the Master had quarrelled violently and Brooke had struck him.

I do not know how the story got about, but I know now it was true. When Mr Brooke talked about the incident, he would say only he had lost control of himself and had been very wrong. It left him feeling he could no longer argue with Mr Kennedy; the Master now carried an absolute moral authority aboard. James Brooke knew his plans for adventure and glory on the *Findlay* were now in tatters. The little brig that had been his pride and joy was now an irksome reminder of his failure.

Mr Brooke stuck it out for three months after that fight. Three months which, I see now, must have been misery for him. At the end of that time, he came down to the low-beamed mess deck that I and the rest of the crew called home. Gathering us around him, he told us he was to leave and return to England.

We heard the news in silence. Then Malcolm called, "Huzzah for Mr Brooke!"

We cheered and sang, "For he's a jolly good fellow," and he smiled—although it was obvious the smile was an effort. He thanked us and wished us well. Then he moved among us, shaking each man by the hand. He had some private word for every one of us. He told me he would remember me kindly and I should seek him out if I ever needed employment back in England.

I mumbled some reply but, in truth, had trouble in speaking for I was so distressed. When he offered me his hand, I clasped it as if holding fast to all that could save me from drowning. He released himself, moved away among the hammocks, and was lost in the gloom. That was my last memory of him for the next five years.

# Chapter 2

JAMES BROOKE TOLD ME, years later, he had thought of leaving the *Findlay* to rot in Singapore, but his sense of honour acknowledged that Kennedy should be allowed the chance to make a profit. The ship, together with her crew, was chartered to Jardine Matheson and Co., as Kennedy had wished. Most of the officers left her and returned to England with Mr Brooke, but Kennedy stayed on as Master. I stayed on with him. The *Findlay* was never the same ship after the others left but I did well enough.

I crewed on her for two years. She worked mainly on the China coast, making occasional voyages south, back to Singapore, but we rarely ventured into the archipelago. The work was, as James Brooke had complained, dull trade, but it was profitable and Kennedy eventually saw the return on his capital he had so desired.

For myself, I found I shared Mr Brooke's feeling that there should be more to life than a dull berth and a safe profit. I remembered the villages we had seen in the islands, the sense of wonder as we worked our way up the muddy rivers to the jungle settlements, the cries of the monkeys shrieking their defiance as we passed in the morning mists. I wanted to go back to the archipelago.

With money saved from my pay, I decided to leave the *Findlay* on one of her increasingly infrequent visits to Singapore. With two years' experience of the seas of East, I had no trouble getting a position on a little schooner, the *Lady Irene*. She ran from island to island carrying rice, cloth, knives, tapioca, sugar, spices, the occasional small chest of gold to settle a debt, letters, tea and, from time to time, merchants with business at one out-post or another of their enterprises. The crew was mainly Malay and the Master, an elderly Scot named Paterson, gave me au-thority over them. I had already picked up a smattering of their language and, in my time on the *Lady Irene*, I learned to speak fluent Malay.

Life on board was far from ideal. The ship was small but under-crewed. We worked at full stretch in all but the calmest weather and, in the sudden tropical storms that were the bane of Far East shipping, we were often in real danger of wreck. Paterson, though a decent enough man, was distant and could be surly.

Paterson and his mate were the only two officers aboard. We had discharged our surgeon as an economy and Paterson himself gave such medical attention as the crew needed. As I became better acquainted with the ship and its crew, so I found myself increasingly given the responsibilities of an officer. I still messed with the men and had no particular privileges to attend my responsibilities but, nonetheless, it was pleasant to be in-vested with some measure of authority. Without an education, I could not get regular papers, so this position was as good as I might reasonably expect. Indeed, when I looked about at other vessels, I saw I would not find such a good berth elsewhere, so I stayed with the *Lady Irene*, for all her faults.

In June of 1839, almost five years after I first arrived at Sin-gapore in the *Findlay*, James Brooke came back into my life.

I heard the news almost as soon as I stepped ashore after

three months of shambling from island to island in the *Lady Irene*'s everlasting attempts to sail at a profit. Mr Brooke, it seemed, was still the charismatic figure he had been when I first knew him and, only days after his arrival, he was already the talk of Singapore. Though he was now in his early thirties, all the evidence was that he still retained the enthusiasms of his youth and, apparently, his latest enthusiasm was for Borneo.

The mysterious island of Borneo was a nine day wonder in Singapore just then because of the behaviour of the Sultan of the place, one Muda Hassim. Only a few months previously, a British brig had been wrecked there. She was called the *Napoleon* and any British crew sailing in a vessel with such a name deserved all they got, I shouldn't wonder. But this Sultan Hassim had treated them with every courtesy, fed and clothed them at his own expense, and arranged for their safe return to Singapore.

In a part of the world where piracy was still widespread and where a lost sailor was an easy victim for all manner of thieves and rascals, this was more than a common politeness. It reinforced suggestions that the Sultan was tired of the way the Dutch were lording it over the South China Seas as if they had a divine right to colonise the place. If he were cooling toward the Hollanders and turning toward Britain, as the rumour said, then Borneo offered wonderful opportunities for trade…opportunities the merchants of Singapore would be anxious to exploit.

At just this moment, Mr Brooke arrived on the scene, claiming he was there with the primary purpose of exploring the island of Borneo. He would, he promised, raise the Union flag in some remote jungle settlement and spread the benefits of civilisation to the most benighted corners of the globe. And, as if as an afterthought, he promised a good return on any trade conducted through such an enterprise. No wonder, then, that though he was but one man with a small vessel, he seemed to take Singapore by storm.

To me, the exploitation of Borneo was a matter of indifference—although, like all British sailors, I welcomed the chance to give the Dutch a bloody nose. The return of Mr Brooke, though, stirred feelings I thought I had forgotten in the years of his absence.

There is no harbour in Singapore and shipping must lie to in the Roads, an anchorage just off the shore, with Chinese junks scurrying back and forth with their cargoes. So it was that, travelling to and from the *Lady Irene*, I could see his vessel, the *Royalist*, bobbing on the waves but a quarter of a mile from our station.

He had obviously learned something from the disaster of the *Findlay*, for the *Royalist* was not a brig but a schooner and as trim a craft as you could wish, ideally suited to trading in these waters. As if to demonstrate she was no mere merchant, though, she mounted six six-pounders and a number of swivel guns. Most important, her mainmast carried the White Ensign, for though she was a private vessel, the *Royalist* belonged to the Royal Yacht Squadron and, in foreign ports, she had all the privileges of a man-of-war.

I started to enquire amongst the idlers around the port if anyone knew of Mr Brooke or his plans. I had no difficulty in finding out all I might want to know, for it seemed everyone from the harbourmaster to the local whores had a tale to tell of him.

He had arrived in Singapore with a total complement of just nineteen hands, but this was more than ample for the handling of such a vessel. The Master was the same Colin Hart I remembered from the *Findlay*. His adventures then had given him a taste for the sea and he had spent the past few years gaining his papers. His new status, it seemed, had not changed him; the reports I heard suggested he was still the competent officer and kindly man I remembered.

At first, I thought I might just report aboard the *Royalist* and ask Mr Hart to take me on. More than once, I set out to find a boat to have me rowed across to her, but every time I stopped and turned back. Why should either Mr Brooke or Mr Hart remember me? And, if he did remember me, why would Mr

Brooke show me that same consideration he had when I was younger? Better to mind my own business aboard the *Lady Irene* and leave the *Royalist* alone.

About a week after the *Royalist*'s arrival and my incessant havering, I told myself I should, once and for all, try to forget about her. The easiest way to do this seemed to involve drink. So I found myself in the ramshackle shed where the English sailors would congregate in Singapore. It was run by a Chinaman and should, by rights, have been known as Lee Foo's or Lung Fut's or whatever, but we all knew it as the St George. This distinguished it as the English bar, as against the Clogs, where the Dutch sailors would meet and drink, or one of a dozen other grog shops, each with their own style and their own favoured customers.

Harry Flood, a crewmate from when I had first joined the *Lady Irene*, pushed his way over to where I was sat minding my own business and jerked his head toward a bully, red-haired fellow who had just sat himself down with a mug of what passed for ale in Singapore and, a wiser choice, a tot of rum.

"That's Will Spence, off of the *Royalist*."

He raised his eyebrows at me, sipped his ale, grimaced—not surprisingly, for it was foul stuff—then stared before him as if he had said something of great moment and now waited for my reply.

I remembered Harry Flood as a provoking shipmate who could never come straight to the point of anything. So I remarked that it was a fine day, that the weather was as ever as hot as Hades, that the *Lady Irene* was still afloat and that trade was good, so long as the Dutch didn't establish a foothold ahead of you. Then I bought him a drink.

He sniffed at it, as if daring it to taste as foul as the last jug. It did, of course. He took a swig, then grimaced at me again and said, "He's been asking whether there be anyone around who sailed with the *Findlay*."

When I did not reply immediately, he grunted and, after another pause, added, "Mentioned your name especially, I hear."

That was pretty well it. I introduced myself to Spence and was told Mr Brooke was looking for a reliable man who spoke the local lingo. He wanted someone who could handle dealings in those smaller ports where Dutch, not English, was the language of commerce and where we, having no Dutch would have to get by in Malay. There were clear advantages to rehiring someone he knew from the *Findlay*, assuming any of his old crew had stayed in the region and learned the language. And, yes, he had let it be known he was particularly anxious to learn of my own whereabouts.

The next day I presented myself to Mr Hart and officially joined the company of the *Royalist*.

❄

WE LAY AT SINGAPORE for some weeks. Mr Hart had command of us aboard and his governance remained far from harsh, although he did indeed seem somewhat more reflective than I remembered him. Perhaps this was because of some unhappy romance, as the rumours claimed. If so, I never heard him speak of it, then or later, but Mr Hart has always been a man who keeps his own counsel, and it may be his heart was broken. I suspect, though, it was more that he now had the responsibility of his own vessel.

Whatever the truth of it, the only concerns he allowed expression to were those immediately relating to the care of the *Royalist*. The deck was always immaculately clean, the lines neatly coiled, and the brass work shining in the tropic sun. For all that, it was an easy time, with plenty of shore leave and good food aboard when our pay was spent on drink and there we had no money left for food ashore.

I did not see much of Mr Brooke in those first weeks. He would rise early to carry out an inspection of sorts, greeting each man by name and always finding a kind word about the state of the ship or the turnout of the crew. We would stand to and smile and nod but, even after his experience with the *Findlay*, he knew practically nothing about the running of the craft and the real inspection would be carried out by Mr Hart once our owner was safely off the ship.

In those days, I had never seen Mr Brooke in Society. I can only imagine how he must have charmed all those who met him. Even today, with all that has passed, he can still infect an audience with his boyish enthusiasm. He must have swept through the stuffy atmosphere of Singapore society like a tropical storm, tumbling everything about him and leaving the place sparkling and refreshed by the memory of his passing. Men would have thought him daring and wished they had his confidence and ready wit. Women would have been charmed and many a friendship will have foundered as merchants' daughters vied for his attention. Mr Brooke would have moved from serious meetings with the great merchants of the Colony to dances organised by their wives. He was a welcome guest at the meanest tavern and in the Governor's mansion. In less than a month, Mr Brooke learned more of Singapore life and politics than some who had lived there half their lives.

All of Mr Brooke's researches, as I learned later, confirmed his belief that Borneo would be the right setting for the adventure of his life. It was an as yet unexplored jungle paradise, but one that offered plentiful opportunities for trade, coal to attract the new generation of steam vessels, and a favourable political situation.

Knowing Mr Brooke as I now do, I think it was the Sultan's kindness to the wrecked sailors of the *Napoleon* that finally decided him. His whole voyage was, I now see, built on the purest romantic whimsy, and the tale of the noble Sultan dealing honourably with poor British tars was irresistible to him. He came up with the idea that the Sultan should be thanked in a formal letter, beautifully penned by one of the Governor's clerks on the finest parchment available—which in Singapore, in those days, was probably not saying much.

The letter was produced and ceremonially signed by the Chairman of the Chamber of Commerce and half the nabobs of the European community. Mr Brooke undertook to deliver it personally and, on the strength of the goodwill generated, persuaded the Governor to produce an official introduction for him which, taken together with the White Ensign fluttering proudly from the *Royalist*'s mast, was likely to suggest his expedition had more authority than an impartial judge might understand to be the case.

I write now with an understanding I did not have then. In those days, when it all began, there was an innocence to all of us. We did not think of politics. If Mr Brooke may sometimes have given the appearance of cunning, it was the guileless cunning of a child who, seeing some sparkling gee-gaw so tantalisingly close, will by some innate understanding, say and do simply that which is required so that those in authority move it within his reach. For Mr Brooke, the island of Borneo— mysterious, rich, and fantastical—was as sparkling a toy as he could wish. He had longed for it from even before the disaster of the *Findlay* voyage. Now it was within his grasp.

Five weeks after I rejoined the *Royalist*, all shore leave was cancelled. Half a dozen chickens were brought aboard and stocks of fresh fruit were re-provisioned. Of dried food, we already had more than enough in our hold, but the water casks were all checked and refilled as required.

This all happened on a Thursday. On the Friday, Mr Brooke had the men assemble on deck so he could address us. I can't recall much of what he said, but I know there was some stirring stuff about "noble purpose" and "great adventure," and then there was a rum issue. The men all cheered and I remember Mr Brooke, done up in the green uniform jacket of the Royal Yacht Squadron, grinning like a little boy and waving as the men cheered and cheered again.

On Saturday, 27th July 1839, the *Royalist* slipped quietly away from Singapore and headed East to Borneo.

\*

WITH A FAVOURABLE WIND, the *Royalist* made good speed across the South China Sea. The Sultan was not at his capital in Brunei but almost at the other end of the island, in a province called Sarawak.

I remember now when I first heard Borneo described as an island, I thought of it as like the Isle of Wight or, at most, like Ceylon, Madagascar, or even our own dear British Isles. Better to think of it as an island in the way Australia is an island, for Borneo is vast. If I had realised then how big Borneo is, I would have understood the jokes the officers made about the Sultan's reasons for being in Sarawak.

Officially, he was in Sarawak simply because of some mild unrest and misunderstandings between the local populace and his government. Knowing more of the geography of Sarawak, I see now this made as much sense as saying Queen Victoria, God bless her, was to pay a personal visit to the British community in Athens to deal with a minor dispute about local taxes.

In truth, the Sultan was in Sarawak to deal with an uprising among the locals. To many on the *Royalist*, anyone who was not a white man was just a 'native' and the distinctions between them appeared unimportant, but my time sailing in these waters had made me understand the significance of some of the differences. Sultan Muda Hassim was a Malay, one of the rulers of Sarawak and a race that was, by its own standards, sophisticated and cultured. The locals were Dyaks—true primitives living largely in tribal groups in the jungle, hunting pigs and monkeys and, so it was said, each other. That some of the Dyaks had risen up against their Malay masters was unsurprising. Mr Brooke's genius was to recognise the opportunity the conflict gave for him to obtain some influence for himself and the British.

None of this was known to me that August morning when the *Royalist* first started to nose her way cautiously up the Sarawak River toward the tiny settlement of Kuching.

We entered the river soon after dawn and my first view of the country that was to be my home for so many years was just a grey blur. The morning was a quiet one with the everyday sounds of life aboard strangely muted in the early fog.

The *Royalist* felt her way up the river on the tide. We carried no canvas. Indeed, with no breath of wind to clear the mist, we could not have gained any advantage from the use of our sails. Having no business in the rigging, I leaned out over the rails trying, like most of the crew, to make out some details in the haze. Will Spence came and stood next to me. He seemed to make himself responsible for me, having introduced me aboard, as it were, and he would often seek me out.

We stood together, watching the jungle slide silently towards us through the mist. There was a wall of timber, solid as any palisade, stretching on beyond anything we could see. Stretching, I was to discover, beyond anything I could imagine.

Will chewed steadily on a quid of tobacco, occasionally spitting a stream of juice over the side, careful that not a drop fall on Mr Hart's precious deck. Although he was normally a talkative man, there was something about the immensity of the jungle around us that reduced him to just the odd remark.

We would hear the occasional cry of birds but we could not see them—except when a sea eagle appeared, circling over the river ahead of us. It dived once, emerged from the water with a fish glittering silver in its talons, and wheeled away and out of sight.

Will jogged my arm and pointed at a branch on the water's edge. "There!"

A great lizard was balanced on the wood. As I watched, it slipped from its hold and vanished into the murky water. Later, we heard the noise of a troop of monkeys nearby and saw dim shapes moving through the branches on the jungle's edge, but mostly there was a tranquillity and a silence that left us strangely subdued without being in the least melancholic.

The mist cleared slowly. By noon it had melted away entirely but it made little difference aboard. We were already well on our way upriver. The forest pressed close on either side while the continual twists and turns of the waterway meant we could scarcely ever see more than a hundred yards ahead or astern.

In the afternoon, the jungle drew back from the water's edge. The riverbanks showed a strip of clear land, some of it crudely cultivated, lying between the water and the trees. We began to see figures in ones and twos working in the fields. Will hollered toward the first few but they just turned and stared so he gave up, relapsing into silence.

Finally, after some miles, we rounded yet another bend in the river to find ourselves at our destination.

I must confess I was disappointed. Although my experience of a hundred miserable ports in the region should have left me prepared, I had still expected better of Kuching. The place, after all, was the provincial capital and, when we arrived, the seat of the Sultan's court. I had hoped to see great palaces of marble or beautiful fountains and statues. In reality, Kuching was the familiar jumble of semi-derelict buildings, tottering on their piles along the river's edge. Where I had expected to see busy wharves, a single, rickety jetty jutted precariously from the bank.

There was life in the place, though. Behind the riverfront, lanes of shophouses wriggled away toward the jungle beyond. Here and there were glimpses of strong walls, which I guessed would surround the home compounds of the greater families of the place. Brown shapes hurried between the buildings, emerging to stand on the trampled earth at the river's edge and then vanish away again into the huddle of the town. Figures pointed excitedly at us. Several brandished weapons: wooden spears, a sword or two, even the odd musket. Despite these martial signs, their expressions seemed friendly enough and, there being no indication we faced any form of danger from them, Mr Brooke decided we should immediately go ashore.

Whilst we were in Singapore, Mr Brooke had had white uniforms made up for us so we could put on a good show anywhere he intended to impress. The crew of our gig, the *Lily*, were ordered to get changed sharpish and I was told to dress myself as well, an interpreter obviously being required.

A quarter of an hour after we had dropped anchor in Kuching, we were clambering aboard the *Lily* for the row to what passed for a wharf. Mr Hart had been left aboard to make the vessel secure so Mr Brooke was accompanied by Mr Murray, the surveyor. Mr Murray was a Scot and held a good opinion of himself, as I have noted many of that race to do. He had kept himself to his own quarters on the voyage from Singapore and I had little to do with him, but I did not like the man. He had dressed himself in a dark suit with a heavy waistcoat and he was pouring sweat almost before he was in the boat. Mr Brooke himself had changed into his Royal Yacht Squadron uniform of green, a neckerchief loose at his throat. With the two of them dressed as gentlemen and the crew dolled up in their fancy whites, we made a good showing on the short row to the pier.

As we bumped to a halt against the rotting wood, we raised our oars vertically, smart as any admiral's barge, while Frank, the ship's boy—promoted to honorary bo'sun for the occasion—managed to produce some sort of sound from a twopenny whistle so the officers could be piped ashore.

As soon as we were on the wharf, some of the natives, better dressed than the others and apparently men of substance, pushed their way through the small crowd already gathering and gave instructions that we should follow them.

We were led through the ramshackle mess of huts to a building distinguished by its slightly larger size and comparative isolation. Like the others, it was supported on tall piles with the entrance well above our heads, but where other buildings had ladders lashed from bamboo leading to their doors, here planks had been crudely pegged to make a serviceable staircase.

Our guides gestured us to wait and hurried ahead into the building.

We stood for some time. After a while, the crowd tired of staring at us and drifted away. Some chickens appeared, pecking half-heartedly in the dirt. A pig snuffled its way from under the building, stared at us, and vanished back into the shadows.

It grew hotter and the men began to get restless, but we remained standing in the roadway. It might have been more sensible to shelter in the shade, but somehow it seemed most important to maintain our dignity. In truth, we had little but our dignity to protect ourselves. It was as if we knew instinctively we would be judged on our bearing.

The men were a credit to Mr Brooke and the *Royalist*. It was only Mr Murray who, after almost an hour, began to let his irritation show. He started to fidget from one foot to another and finally started to grumble, as much to himself as anyone else. "I don't know why we're waiting around for this tin-pot ruler. His town's naught but mud huts and his palace is little better than a cowshed on stilts."

I noticed Mr Brooke's knuckles whiten as he gripped the letters of introduction he held like a child clutching to a blanket to reassure himself all will be well. I felt it best, as I was their interpreter, that I interpret the situation for the edification of Mr Murray.

"Begging your pardon, sir," said I, "but this is not a palace. By custom, the Sultan cannot receive us in his home. This is an audience chamber only. Also, the dwellings are of wood, not of mud."

Murray was not one to take kindly to correction by a social inferior, but I had judged my tone so he could not claim insolence on my part, and he was dimly aware any reply he might make would simply show him more of a fool. Most important, Mr Brooke had listened to the exchange and a corner of his lip was twitching in what might have been taken as the beginnings of a smile.

Fortunately, Mr Murray was spared any further embarrassment. A figure appeared at the door above us to beckon our party in. We trooped up the steps in as good an order as we could and took up position in two neat rows behind our officers.

Inside, the building was as splendid as the exterior was unprepossessing. We were in a single large room, three walls of which were hung with tapestries of red and yellow. Where the fourth wall might have been, the room was open to the river so we could see the stern of the *Royalist* swinging at anchor a hundred yards upstream. Huge brass plates had been set in the wall; from time to time one would flash as it caught a reflection from the water outside.

The brilliant sunlight at one side of the room had the effect of making the other side seem sunken in shadow. It gave the impression of a great solemn hall in which we could see dark figures moving about the business of an ancient house.

A semicircle of chairs had been arranged in the gloom, looking out over the river. In the centre sat the man we had travelled so far to see—the Sultan of Brunei. In truth, he was not a particularly impressive figure. He was a small man and, in that line of seated nobility, easily overlooked. He wore a red velvet jacket and a pretty cap on his head, neatly woven and fitted with a rim of gold. He sat stiffly, as if conscious of his dignity, but his face was kindly and intelligent. He kept glancing from side to side as though embarrassed to be the centre of so much attention.

Around him sat a dozen or so nobles of his court. They wore similar caps, or coronets, with a sarong round the waist, bejewelled daggers—the famous wavy *kris* of the region—tucked into the fabric. Their chests, though, were bare. Lesser officials and servants stood behind them.

Chairs were hurriedly arranged for Mr Brooke and Mr Murray. The rest of us took up our places, standing facing the Sultan's court, determined to put on as good a show as we could muster. Mr Brooke, though, ordered me to sit beside him, the more easily to make use of my services as interpreter.

There was much bowing and muttering and I had to introduce myself as Mr Brooke's interpreter. I found myself a little flustered, for it is one thing to deal with dock labourers or local merchants but another to be standing before a ruler and translating in his court, even if the man was only a native. However, Mr Brooke smiled at me and I made as best a start as I could.

First there was some great formal welcome with flowery phrases about his noble visitors and the usual nonsense about how his humble home was not good enough for us. I wouldn't have minded so much except we weren't actually in his humble home. The audience chamber was there especially to keep us out, as we were not really considered good enough for it.

Finally, he got to the bit where he wondered aloud why we might have made such a journey to visit so unworthy a ruler. They were his words, not mine. I translated his meaning for Mr Brooke. "He wants to know who we are, why we have come here. He will ask no direct questions but he is uneasy."

At once, Mr Brooke was all smiles and easy gestures. When he wanted to, my master could inspire confidence to an almost unnatural degree. Now he made a great show of reassuring the Sultan. His letters from the Governor of Singapore were produced with a flourish.

"Tell the Sultan," he said, "we have come to strengthen the ties of trade and friendship so that our countries may be bound together."

I told him and he was, doubtless, duly impressed. Perhaps Mr Brooke had not properly explained he brought the Governor's letters not as an envoy but merely as a messenger. Possibly the Sultan did not understand the White Ensign hanging from our jack mast was there simply because of the *Royalist*'s registration with the Royal Yacht Squadron. On the whole, it was probably best not to dwell on the fact that Mr Brooke was simply a private individual with one ship, twenty-eight men, and a capital of just £30,000.

"And tell him, too, that we have some trifling tokens of our esteem aboard the *Royalist*."

I duly translated this and the Sultan visibly brightened. "He says you are too generous to one who seeks only to do the will of Allah." There was the slightest of pauses. "He says he will be pleased to visit you aboard."

The Sultan smiled slightly, bowing toward Mr Brooke before, resuming his bland expression, he clapped his hands and a troupe of musicians filed in from the balcony where they had awaited their cue. They seated themselves on the floor in the middle of the room, setting out drums, gongs, cymbals, and a variety of native instruments I could not at once identify. Even before the last of them had finished arranging his instruments the orchestra, such as it was, burst into cacophonous life. In the years to come I grew to love the sound of the *gulong* but on that first hearing, it seemed merely a din in which any two surfaces that could be knocked together were, with little interest in anything except obtaining the maximum possible amount of noise.

Mr Brooke leaned toward me, shouting to make himself heard. "Ask him why he is in Sarawak. Tell him the merchants of Singapore cannot understand why he is not holding court in Brunei."

I turned to the Sultan to relay Mr Brooke's question but it was impossible to get his attention. He watched, smiling, as servants came forward with tobacco rolled in leaves almost a foot long and distributed these among the crew. Then he turned toward his orchestra, apparently oblivious of everything but the music. I began to realise the value of native music in the diplomatic process.

Mr Brooke tried again. "Tell him I have heard rumours of war. See if he can hear that."

This remark, apparently, could not be ignored, for the Sultan turned and replied animatedly. I translated as best I could. "He says there is no war. It is merely a little child's play among his subjects."

Mr Brooke looked uncertain and I added hurriedly, "You do realise he's lying, sir?"

THAT EVENING, THE SULTAN arranged an entertainment for us. It was a shadow play—a tradition of his country. The Sultan and the *Royalist*'s officers sat before a screen of bleached cotton behind which was a line of spluttering oil lamps. In the light of the lamps, the performers held up stick puppets and the shadows, cast on the screen, acted out the drama of whatever legend the actors were portraying.

To a Western eye, it was a strange procedure. The crew of the *Royalist* sat with the commoner elements of the court on the puppeteers' side of the screen. There we were able to admire the puppets close to. Each was a flat figure cut from leather, stiffened with gorgeous painting. The red and gold robes were decorated with tiny cuts. Diamonds and circles in elaborate patterns that would show up as beads of light on the screen ahead of us. It seemed odd that, as the less privileged audience, we saw the colour and detail of the beautifully made puppets, while the grander folk saw just the wavering shadows. But perhaps the shadow puppets reflected the truth of the Sultan's court. The gaudy show counted for nothing. It was the darker shadows that told the real story.

SO BEGAN WEEKS OF patient negotiation. The custom of the country dictated we should pretend to believe the lies, however preposterous they were. I would accompany Mr Brooke as he received the Sultan on board the *Royalist* or as we made our way to another meal at what Mr Murray still insisted on calling 'the palace.' Mr Brooke would suggest we might explore the interior of the country. The Sultan would respond that the weather was too wet or too hot or he would like us to be accompanied by guides who would not be available for several days. Each day there would be another excuse. Mr Brooke made a sport of it with the officers and wagers would be placed on the reasons that would be advanced for prevarication. As I was always present at the meetings, Mr Brooke said I should be allowed to wager with them. My knowledge of the ways of these people meant I had more than my share of winnings.

When I was not escorting Mr Brooke, I was excused any duties about the ship and told to mingle with the people of the town to find out what I could of the real situation. I was sent ashore to buy goats for the ship or to trade for fresh fruit and vegetables.

I found this a pleasant task, rising early every day to visit the market as the industrious Chinese were starting business, and staying to talk to the Malays, with their more relaxed approach to trade. I could have bought all we needed in an hour or two but I would take my time, examining goods I had no intention of purchasing and talking all the while about inconsequential matters. In this way, I not only came to know more of the traders but I was more readily accepted by them, for this approach to doing business was the norm in their country.

Indeed, when Mr Murray would appear, as he did from time to time, demanding supplies (usually drink), his abruptness and unwillingness to linger annoyed people enough to at least double the prices they charged him. I, on the other hand, would find myself favoured with the best cuts of meat and the fattest chickens. Murray would complain of what he saw as my idleness, but Mr Hart pronounced himself more than satisfied with the way I used my time.

Most of those I talked with were Chinese for here, as in most of the ports I had visited on my travels, they dominated the merchant community. They had the habit of industry. They lived cheaply, even to their clothing. They generally wore white, loose jackets and wide trousers, usually of dark blue but both of the same thin cotton. Their shoes were cut of felt. Their staff were members of their extended families and expenses thus kept to a minimum, meaning they were almost always able to sell their goods more cheaply than Europeans.

The Chinese were easy enough to talk to—as traders, they were all fluent in Malay—but they were a poor source of information. They had little interest in the revolt, as their position seemed secure whichever faction won. Their business acumen was fabled and the ceaseless clicking of their abacuses a constant reminder of the stranglehold they had on local trade.

I met with fewer Malays in the course of my business in the markets, for they generally felt themselves superior to such commercial activity. Those I did have dealings with were generally more forthcoming about the realities of the political situation. They soon became used to my presence, and the various small gifts I would take whenever I visited them helped form friendships with them. After a week or so spent cultivating their acquaintance, I was able to keep Mr Brooke informed, day-by-day, of the progress of the revolt.

It soon became clear the revolt, though involving only a handful of men, was not easy to put down. The uprising had started four years earlier. The Sultan had been in Sarawak for months and nothing seemed to have changed since he had moved his court there. Hassim left the actual conduct of the war to his general, one Makota. Village talk suggested Makota was both idle and a coward and would do little to bring things to a conclusion. Rumours were soon flying around the marketplace, claiming the *Royalist*, with her six guns, was to carry the British into battle on the side of the Sultan. Certainly, the Sultan was anxious to keep the *Royalist* at anchor in Sarawak.

As the weeks passed, we came to recognise that Mr Brooke would never get permission to explore the country while the war continued. The Sultan made constant half-promises of the possibilities of friendship and trade between Britain and Sarawak that could come about were British sailors to help him. The hints were obscure, for he would never go so far as to admit there was a war for us to help him in, but they were clear enough for all that.

Despite his politicking and his duplicity, the Sultan was a

kind and considerate host. He made sure the *Royalist* was always well supplied with such culinary luxuries as Sarawak could offer. The men grew familiar with lychees and bananas in their rations as often as they cared to eat them. There were plentiful supplies of sugar cane and some of the crew tried their hand at making their own rum. They were extraordinarily merry for a while and then piteously sick for two days.

Every few days I would be called upon to interpret at another meeting between Mr Brooke and the Sultan. The two men were as different as could be, the tall, dashing Englishman and the small, quiet-spoken Malay. Yet they seemed to have an understanding of each other that verged on friendship. The Sultan even presented Mr Brooke with a ceremonial *kris*. The hilt and scabbard were covered in gold and studded with red stones. A gilded dragon was etched into the wavy blade. Mr Brooke was delighted with the gift, which he properly saw as having some symbolic importance, and he swore the weapon would be forever at the service of the Sultan.

So the weeks passed with courtesies on both sides but no activity to speak of. We could have continued indefinitely in this stalemate but the crew, idle aboard the *Royalist*, grew restless. Worse, two of them were taken ill and, for a few days, there was a real fear the sickness might spread. Fortunately they recovered and no lives were lost, but the incident made us all aware that this little expedition could not forever remain marooned in Kuching.

It was clearly a difficult decision for Mr Brooke. He had spent many hours with Hassim and truly seemed to like the man. Sometimes he would leave the *Royalist* with me in the morning to stroll among the people gathered in the Kuching market-place. He took pleasure in the bustle, the smell of spices, and the casual beauty of the natives. Further, the whole purpose of his voyage—the opening of Borneo to British influence—hung on the success of his negotiations in Sarawak and failure here would send him back to England with nothing accomplished. He had started with such brave hopes and now stared failure in the face.

The situation looked likely to provoke one of the black moods that would, from time to time, displace his normal good humour. These sudden changes in his character could be accounted for, in part, by the effects of the wound that had ended his service with the East India Company. He had been shot in the chest, and though he was generally in the rudest of health, his injury would trouble him when he was low in spirits and then he would plunge into the deepest melancholy.

The surgeons had removed the bullet from his lung and he kept it in a glass jar in his cabin. Once, when he was out of sorts, he had gestured to where it sat on a shelf alongside an Indian dagger and some other souvenirs of his time as a soldier. "Don't find fault with me for my temper, Williamson," he said. "There's the fellow to blame."

IT WAS WHILE WE were stuck in Kuching, waiting on word from the Sultan, that my relationship with Mr Brooke began to change. He had always treated me with an openness that one of my station would seldom see from a gentleman like him and, in some small way, I felt the seeds of a friendship. On one occasion, I presumed on this so far as to ask him how he had come to be shot. He had laughed and clapped me on the back. "By my own foolishness, Williamson. That and damned bad luck."

He explained how, as a lad of sixteen, he had been commissioned as an Ensign in the Company's Army. "The 6th Native Infantry. I ended up in the Commissary-General. Counting ammunition pouches and haggling over supplies. I ask you, is that any sort of life?"

But then came the war with Burma and suddenly he had the opportunity to see real action.

"The great thing about the Commissary," he confided, "is

you get into the company of Staff officers. One day I heard the general complaining that he had no light cavalry to scout for him. By the next afternoon, I had found enough infantry volunteers to form a troop, and the day after that, I was officially a cavalry officer."

He smiled at the memory of it. "By God, Williamson, for a bunch of infantry, we made damn fine riders. We would push on ahead of the main force, scouting the ground and clearing out any enemy remnants we might discover." He pulled a rueful face. "Not that all of them were that easily cleared."

It had been late in the afternoon. The army was moving through an open valley and James and his troop were returning to join the main column when they saw a company of rebels riding from the cover of rocks on the hills to attack the advance guard below them. Yelling to his men to charge, Lieutenant Brooke had drawn his sword, dug his spurs into his horse, and started toward the enemy.

His troop's intervention broke the Burmese attack but, as they turned and fled, they fired a ragged volley toward the cavalry. "And that was the end of my army career," he concluded. Abruptly, he turned away from me and busied himself with orders to the rest of the crew.

As if reviving the memory had awakened the old wound, Mr Brooke's chest seemed to bother him more in the following days and his temper suffered for it. I was sorry to see him so but it was not my place to say anything. I went about my duties and gathered such intelligence of the country as I could.

After another week or two of diplomatic intransigence from Hassim and growing irritation from Mr Brooke, an evening came when I reported to his cabin to bring him the latest news from the Court and found him in the blackest despair.

Though I had seen him in dark moods before, I had never seen him sunk as low as this. There were marks of tears on his face. It was then I began to realise just how set he had been on the success of his Borneo venture. More, seeing him alone in his distress, I realised that, for all his easy ways, there were none on board who could come close to him and comfort him. Among the others, he always played a part: the gallant captain, the good comrade, the diplomat, or the man of business. To none was he simply a friend and, though there were many who would say they loved him, there was no one to whom he could turn for simple comfort when he needed that above all else.

In England he had no position, no friends, no purpose in life. The *Findlay* expedition had been an attempt to fill these lacks but the voyage had ended in disaster. Back in England, he had returned to his family home in Bath, surrounded by old men who had served in India and now sat out their days, like his father, waiting for death. With nothing to do, he could but sulk and fret until, in time, his father passed away, leaving the young Mr Brooke sick with guilt and sadness but a wealthy man. All his inheritance was spent on the *Royalist*, and now this venture was to join the *Findlay* in failure.

Yet, for the sake of his position on the ship, he could never show his fears. Instead, he would always endeavour to be cheerful, encouraging the men in any wild venture that might cheer their spirits.

At that time, I knew nothing of this. I saw only a man who had been good to me, sitting alone in the twilight gloom of his cabin, his face streaked with his tears.

I do not know now what made me do it, for it was not my place, but I knew where the brandy was kept and the glasses. I poured a healthy swig of drink and placed it before him. He looked up at me and smiled. "Pour one yourself, John."

It was the first time he had ever called me by my name. Later, he was to joke about us as James and John, the disciples of Borneo. "We are the sons of thunder, John," he would say. "Look it up in the Bible."

That evening, though, I had not been certain he knew my baptismal name until he said it.

I poured myself a drink. I was nervous, the situation being

unusual for me, and my hand may have shaken. Perhaps I poured myself rather more brandy than I had intended.

Mr Brooke told me to sit down at the table with him. I did as he asked and we drank, and as we drank, he talked. He told me of his hopes when he had come out to the Far East, of how he had heard tales of Borneo, a land of rhinoceros and elephant and strange, man-like apes. Above all, he had heard of the native people, the Dyaks, living in the jungle in a state of nature.

"They are like children, John," he said. "I had thought I might do some good if I should meet them."

We drank some more. Now his discourse turned to the rule of the East India Company and his experiences in its employ. "They are not men. They are machines to calculate profit and their rule is naught but a means to enrich the plutocrats of the City."

He scowled at his glass, raised it to his lips once more and, after drinking, suddenly looked me in the face and almost shouted, "But they are Englishmen. As are we, John. And we English have a great duty. We are privileged, but our privilege brings a responsibility, for if we cannot help these people, who can bring them help?"

Then, his mood changing and the liquor working on him, he started to laugh and to sing *Rule Britannia*. When I did not join the song, he cursed at me and swore I should sing with him. I joined him in a chorus distinguished for its enthusiasm rather than its tunefulness. As I drew breath for another verse, he fell silent, set his head on his arms, and slept.

I remember standing for a moment, watching over him. Then, closing the door quietly behind me, I withdrew.

✳

THE NEXT DAY, MR Brooke had me called early to his cabin. He made no reference to the night before. Indeed, he gave no sign he had been deep in his cups only a few hours earlier. He was sombre, but the black dog of depression seemed to have released its grip on him, at least for a while.

He wasted no words in setting out my task. "We have to leave. We can lie here no longer. You are to tell the Sultan we will sail tomorrow with the tide."

"Yes sir."

I stood, waiting for more instructions.

None came. Instead, Mr Brooke appeared to consider that he had said all there was to say on the subject and my remaining there was tantamount to querying his orders. "It is a simple business, man. There is no need that I should visit the Sultan myself."

I was given no instruction to withdraw. Mr Brooke seemed to be struggling within himself as to whether to speak further or no, so I stayed in my place until he should give me a clear order. "The Sultan has come to rely overmuch on our presence. He will feel I am betraying him. It is bad enough this venture would come to naught without my calling on the Sultan to tell him the *Royalist* is to abandon him to this wretched, interminable squabble they call a war."

Mr Brooke looked up at me as if I might make a reply but I knew not what to say. Finally, emboldened by the events of the previous evening, I made my own suggestion. "Perhaps, sir, if I were to break the news, as it were, in the morning, then you could see him once more in the afternoon. Sort of to say your farewells, sir."

And that is how Mr Brooke decided it should be. Which, I suppose, changed the history of that part of the world. Or perhaps not, for if the Lord had intended to see the people of that land delivered from ignorance and superstition, would he not have found some way to achieve this end, whether James Brooke had stayed or no?

However it may have been, what happened was this. I called at the audience chamber in the morning and sent word with one of the courtiers there that the *Royalist* was to leave and the news should be given to the Sultan. I said also that Mr Brooke would present himself in the afternoon and, if the Sultan were so gracious as to permit it, Mr Brooke would be pleased to make his farewell. I was kept waiting the better part of an hour before a message came that the Sultan could not see me that morning but would be pleased to receive Mr Brooke in the afternoon.

The two of us went alone. I think Mr Brooke felt the meeting would inevitably be a painful one and did not want to have it witnessed by more of his officers than was absolutely necessary. Perhaps Hassim had a similar feeling for, when we arrived, he was almost alone in the audience hall. For once, he was unable to maintain that bland expression with which he was wont to conceal his true feelings. His face revealed his dismay that the *Royalist* was to leave and he started to speak as soon as we entered the room. I translated as fast as I was able. "He says his heart weeps that you would leave him."

"Tell him my heart weeps, too, but I cannot remain here forever. We have had sickness aboard. We are achieving nothing here. I have a duty to my crew. Explain this to him."

I explained as best I could, but the Sultan replied with a torrent of words. I was used to hearing him speak slowly and calmly, so I was unprepared for this outburst and could not catch every word, but the gist was clear enough. "He says he does not ask you to stay forever, only until the war is over. He says you are an English gentleman. You would not desert a friend when he has need of you."

Mr Brooke gave an impatient sigh. "Tell him I have been kept here with this nonsense too long already. The war has been going on for four years, damn it! If I wait for peace, we will all be buried here."

I translated this as best I could, substituting more appropriate phrases for those Mr Brooke had offered. The Sultan's reply was again a torrent of impassioned speech.

"He says that is not true of you but of himself. He cannot return to Brunei without first defeating the rebels. The shame would be too great. If you leave, he says he will never be victorious. He will spend his life in Kuching and die here. He begs you not to desert him."

Mr Brooke heard this out in silence, merely shaking his head as I translated. Before he could formulate a reply, the Sultan was speaking again. "Now the war goes well. Many of the enemy surrender. He says they are surrounded on all sides and, if you stay, he will be victorious. He asks you to visit the army. He says that if they see you there, it will finish in a week."

I watched James Brooke's face as he struggled with his conflicting emotions. On the one hand, he knew the Sultan was lying. The war was going no better now than it had for over a year. If any of the enemy had surrendered, it would have been the talk of Kuching and my own enquiries had heard no such thing. On the other hand, he felt a real sympathy for the Sultan and it was pathetic to see Hassim's unfeigned distress at the idea the *Royalist* might abandon him.

Hassim, too, was watching James carefully. He sat cross-legged, as intent as a cat before a mouse hole. Then he played his masterstroke. "You swore that the *kris* I gave you would be at my service. Is the word of an Englishman not to be relied upon?"

The appeal moved James Brooke in any number of ways. He was jealous of his honour as an English gentleman. The possibility of joining in the battle resonated with the impetuous adventurer who had brought his crew halfway round the world on little more than a whim. The opportunity to lead his men to victory in a jungle war stirred the romantic in him. And, after all the talk of honour and glory and romance, he could be relied on to recognise the opportunities for exploration and trade that would be opened up if he intervened decisively on the Sultan's side of the conflict.

For a long moment, there was silence. Then Hassim reached out his hand to Mr Brooke and James took it. Both were laughing and Hassim ordered tea to be brought in. There was a bustling of servants, and over sticky cakes and fruit and with many toasts of sweet liquor and cups of Chinese tea, the future of Sarawak was decided.

# Chapter 3

WHEN MR BROOKE ANNOUNCED to his officers he intended to travel to see the war with his own eyes, Mr Murray was quick to object. "You can't seriously be risking the crew in a journey to the interior. It's madness."

Mr Brooke seemed more amused than annoyed by his navigator's complaint. "There's very little point in coming all this way if we are to confine ourselves to the capital," he said. "What insuperable problems do you see in the way of further exploration?"

Mr Murray bristled with irritation and started to lecture his commander as to the impenetrability of the jungle. He pointed out the mountainous nature of the terrain. It was true, he conceded, most of the hills appeared quite small, but they formed a network of rocky ridges that interrupted communications and made travel difficult beyond the immediate environs of the town.

Mr Brooke let him run on in this vein for a while before remarking mildly that he intended his expedition to be carried along the river. "For you are quite right, Andrew. Any overland exploration must be limited. I understand that even the natives here will scarcely travel any distance along the jungle paths. Fortunately, Sarawak is blessed with an abundance of waterways, which serve as the highways of the land. There are few settlements that cannot be reached by river."

The *Royalist* was too big to manoeuvre in the twisting waterways of the interior, but, as Mr Brooke pointed out, the ship's longboat, the *Skimalong*, was an ideal vessel for this task. Less than a week after the fateful meeting between our Commander and the Sultan, the *Skimalong* set out from Kuching toward the centre of the little country's conflict.

The first day, the banks remained clear. A reassuring strip of open ground separated us from the immensity of the jungle beyond. There was something awe-inspiring about the mile after mile of trees, stretching farther than eye could see or brain encompass. A hundred different kinds of timber crowded together, though none even faintly resembled the honest oaks and yews of England. They were all tall, rising a hundred or two hundred feet into the air before they shot out a mass of branches holding their leaves out to the sun blazing above them in the flat, pale sky. The tallest lived; the rest fell into the shade and died.

Mr Brooke passed his telescope among us so we could share his excitement. Although my travels with the *Lady Irene* had taken me to many smaller islands, I had seen nothing before to compare with this and was impatient for my turn with the glass. When at last I raised it to my eye, I saw the tangle of bushes that grew at the forest's margins crushed here and there where one of the giant trees had fallen. These gaps gave a view of the interior. There no scrub grew, no bush could survive. The great leaf canopy smothered all other vegetable life. The place was silent, the stillness broken only by the sound of our oars and the occasional cries of unseen birds.

After a while, as if uncomfortable in that quietude, Will Spence began to chant a shanty. The rest of the crew joined in to keep the pace of the rowing. The crew of the native craft that was our guide struck up their own song. The Malays kept to a faster rhythm than was our wont, but the Skimalong's crew would not admit to being bested by the natives and struck at the pace they set. All I remember of the afternoon was the ache in my arms and the songs we sang, ever faster and faster in our crazy race.

Night comes on suddenly in the tropics. The sun dipped below the trees but the river shone silvery in moonlight. On either side, the darkness of the jungle was suddenly filled with the noise of night creatures. Somehow, we had no more heart for singing. We rowed on in silence.

That first night, we camped in a Malay village, or *kampong* as they called it. There were twenty or so houses perched on piles at the water's edge. I knew no more than what I could make out in the darkness as we staggered wearily from our boat. Mr Brooke himself issued everyone with a tot of rum and, as soon as we had drunk, we collapsed on the ground to sleep till dawn.

We were on our way again at first light and had left the village several miles behind before we breakfasted. The river was still wide but we kept near the bank to avoid the rush of the current. The jungle grew right to the water's edge, and the nearest trees abandoned their struggle upwards to grow outward instead, reaching almost horizontally across our path. Sometimes we were inconvenienced by the necessity of ducking under a branch, but at least the vegetation provided a welcome shade from the heat of the day.

We began to see monkeys hurling abuse in their jabbering tongue as they frolicked in safety far above us. We would round a bend to surprise a family of wild pigs, which would flee their watering place with agitated squeals, running Indian file into the trees. Once we saw a tiny deer, no more than a couple of feet in length from head to tail, start shyly from the trees and then, at the sight of us, vanish back into the shadows. Most of the time, though, we saw nothing. There was something uncanny about moving past a jungle you knew to be teeming with life and yet to see so little. I imagined I was watched by hundreds of invisible eyes and I bent to the oars with a will, anxious to be out of the place.

We rowed throughout the day and darkness had again fallen by the time we reached the place where the Sultan's army was encamped. The river moved from jungle darkness to a clearing lit by scores of flickering torches, illuminating a great fleet of native craft lying under the shelter of a riverside fort. On the banks, defensive earthworks stretched into the distance; across the river, a boom protected them from surprise attack.

I had seen native fighting ships in the past, of course, but only at a distance. The South China Seas were dangerous waters and if we saw a fighting craft on the horizon, our policy on the *Lady Irene* was to move rapidly in another direction.

Close to, I was impressed by the deadly efficiency of the Malay craft. Long and slim, the lower parts were made of timber but the upper parts were kept light by being made of bamboo, rattan, and dried palm leaves. The savings in weight were important, for the vessels carried no sail. They were propelled by oars, the rowers sitting on galleries suspended either side of the vessel, just a foot above the water. The craft carried little artillery, although a few might have a small bow gun. Instead they were surmounted by a strong, flat roof, upon which the warriors would assemble to fight. Their tactic was to use their speed to close with the enemy, then the fighters jumped down from the platform deck to board their foe, overwhelming them in hand to hand combat with *kris* and spear.

The *Skimalong* bumped her way through the native craft as Mr Brooke ordered us to make for the biggest we could see, a giant war *prahu* with room for forty men at the paddles and a score more warriors on the deck. He had learned enough about Malay protocol to know where he could expect to find the Pangeran Rajah Makota, Governor of Sarawak, Panglima of the Grand Army, and the Sultan's chief lieutenant in that part of his domain.

As we scraped alongside the vessel, a figure splendidly dressed in robes of crimson and gold, appeared on the deck. I rightly supposed this to be Makota himself. He was shorter than most of the Malays we had met heretofore and inclined to plumpness. He bustled toward us, somewhat self-importantly, and greeted Mr Brooke. We were, he said, to sleep aboard his vessel that night. He would not need his quarters as he would be ashore, inspecting the fortifications. It was only much later we discovered the sacrifice he had made on our behalf, as this was to be the first night inspection he had ever made.

When I think of that cabin, I can understand why Makota was reluctant to spend time tramping the shore in the night air. His quarters took up most of the stern of the boat and were fitted with every luxury. The walls hung with tapestries, and plates and bowls of gold lay on the mahogany tables scattered about the cabin. Although the *prahu* was nominally a vessel of war, the accoutrements were far from martial. I think it was while he was resting on Makota's down-filled mattress that Mr Brooke first realised the Sultan's general was not committed to the military life and the rigours of a successful campaign.

The *Skimalong*'s crew were left to make shift as well as they could on shore, but, as interpreter, I was allocated a bed in these quarters. After our days of rowing and a night spent on the hard earth, I slept deeply and, with Mr Brooke, woke early to go ashore and greet Makota.

We spent a fruitless half hour enquiring of one gorgeously attired captain or another where the grand commander might be before we were sheepishly informed he was still asleep and not to be disturbed. Around us, though, Makota's troops were preparing for another day. Besides the Malays, who strolled about in their brightly coloured *sarong* skirts, there were many darker, tougher looking men wearing nothing but loincloths. Their bodies were covered with elaborate tattoos that rippled as they walked on the margins of the jungle with an easy grace. James Brooke watched entranced. These were the fabled Dyaks, the savage men of the Borneo jungle. It was common knowledge they were headhunters. Some said they were cannibals. Yet to many Europeans, they represented a purer, more innocent race than those corrupted by the artificial ways of the modern world. These were a people who knew not the poorhouse nor the lockup, whose lives were not blighted by working in great factories. They knew nothing of steam locomotives or spinning machines but led a simple life at one with nature.

These were not my thoughts, you must understand, for as a common seaman I saw nothing but savages—and savages with swords who I therefore reckoned as probably dangerous savages. But since those days, as Mr Brooke taught me to read and explained the ways gentlemen viewed the world, I have come to hear of Mr Rousseau who wrote about the "noble savage," and I see how Mr Brooke may well have thought these people wonderful. There was much that seemed noble in their bearing. Here, on the fringe of the jungle, they were in their home and did not defer to their Malay captains, knowing their masters relied on them and had no power over them in their native place. Indeed, as the Malays fussed and scurried around and the Dyaks moved with stately calm about their business, it was hard to recognise the former as the more civilised of the two races.

Makota eventually arrived, accompanied by a retinue of bodyguards, and we set off to inspect the camp. The Grand Army was bivouacked for more than a mile along the river. Every few hundred yards we would reach another cluster of men in their separate encampment. The Malay camps were quite large, but each group of Dyaks jealously guarded a space reserved to just those few who had joined the army from a single tribe. When we asked the reason why they did not make larger and more defensible camps by joining with one another, we were told relations between many of the tribes were poor and they often settled their differences by warfare. Each group, therefore, kept apart from the others, sleeping with weapons to hand, not in fear of the rebels but lest they be attacked by other groups within their own army.

The bulk of the army was made of Malays and Dyaks, but there were also a few groups of Chinese. We did not spend long with these people. Mr Brooke made no secret of his dislike for

Chinamen. He would complain of their godlessness, their greed, and their duplicity, but these same characteristics were found in many of the races he admired. The Chinese seemed to me to have many virtues. The Chinese troops, drawn up in neat lines before their hutments, showed an orderliness surpassing that of any other part of the Grand Army. Perhaps it was their virtues, rather than their vices, that worried Mr Brooke, for they were the only troops in the army who could measure up to the disciplined presentation of his own men of the *Royalist*. Indeed, the habits of industry and organisation, which Mr Brooke was forever trying to inculcate in the Malays, were always perceived as a threat from the Chinese.

"A plague on John Chinaman," he would growl when supplies were expensive, labourers could not be hired, or Hassim appeared unduly distracted. The Chinese were to blame for everything from the weather to pain from his old chest wound. "They are cunning, base, yellow men, Williamson," he would say. "Never trust a Chinaman."

Whatever underlay his antipathy, it was all too clear to Makota that Mr Brooke wished to spend as little time as he could inspecting the Chinese troops. We were therefore moved rapidly past their encampments and toward a rocky knoll that rose from the plain about halfway between the river and the jungle. The landscape, we observed, was dotted with such outcrops which served as useful vantage points. A short, if steep, climb brought us to a point where we could look out across the trees and gain some impression of the lay of the land. From here Makota, for all the world like some brown Napoleon standing at a place of vantage above the battle, sought to explain to us the main points of his campaign.

As I stood beside Mr Brooke on that vantage point, I was surprised to see how many clearings there were in the jungle. Some, from their artificial, rectangular appearance, were clearly cultivated fields, though even from this distance I could tell they were slipping back into a state of nature, presumably abandoned because of the war. Others looked more natural; irregular patches where the trees could find no purchase in the rocky ground. Here and there, among the nearer clearings, we could see small stockades, the only signs of any military activity.

The land sloped away, jungle interspersed with clearings either natural or artificial, with occasional rocky outcrops such as that where we stood. In the distance, the outcrops seemed more prominent and the ground generally hillier. Makota gestured toward the twin peaks of one mountain that rose clear above the rest halfway to the horizon. "That is Sarambo. At the foot of the mountains runs the river. On the river is the town of Siniawan. There the rebels have their army. It is defended by their great fort of Balidah and they have other forts on the mountain and on both sides of the river."

Mr Brooke shaded his eyes from the already brilliant sun and stared toward the distant mountain. "It must be almost ten miles! I can't even see Siniawan or any sign of it. If that is where the rebels have taken their stand, why does the army wait kicking its heels here?"

Makota rattled off an explanation with the satisfied appearance of a master-strategist outlining a winning ploy to a novice. "The enemy are surrounded. They grow hungry. Then they surrender."

Mr Brooke again gazed out over the scene. Makota, we knew from Hassim, had some five hundred men. It was absurd to suggest one could effectively besiege a town miles away in heavily wooded country with a force that size.

Makota continued to explain his strategy while I translated as best I could. "He says the enemy are led by Malays who plot against the Sultan, but most of their forces are Dyaks and that the Dyaks desert them as they see they are trapped. On the top of Mount Sarambo there are forts held by a Dyak tribe that has changed sides. Our men are now on the mountain and the enemy are attacked from all sides."

"Attacked?"

I questioned Makota and turned back to Mr Brooke. "He says attacked but he also says they stay always in their forts and if the enemy moves, they are shot."

Below us, the army was stirring, men gathering in groups to break their fast. Each received some rice and salt. At the end of the day, he would receive some more rice and salt. It could go on forever.

Mr Brooke stood for a long while looking over the scene. Finally, he turned to me. "Tell Makota we need to gather his officers together. It is time for a council of war."

IN THE END, IT took the better part of a month to get the meeting Mr Brooke had proposed. Makota, it appeared, was kept very busy with inspection visits. Then he was, regrettably, forced to be absent from the Army for a few days. He was travelling, we were told, to one of the tribes whose loyalty was wavering. On his return, though he would have been happy to meet us immediately, it was necessary to see each of his commanders alone before there was any general assembly.

Another week passed and we learned Makota was building a special hut to act as our council chamber. Only when this was finished was the meeting finally to take place.

When I accompanied Mr Brooke to the council hut, I had to admit it was a splendid structure, though I had my doubts it justified the delay. Like most of the buildings, the walls were of rattan panels, but they had been covered with silks from Makota's quarters. The floor was of bare earth scattered with gorgeous carpets, woven in reds and blues. Low tables were set with sweetmeats and bronze cuspidors for those who chose to chew the betel nuts displayed in silver boxes.

As we entered, most of the commanders of the various tribes and groupings that made up the Grand Army were already present. To my surprise, they seemed eager to begin the meeting. Their martial ardour contrasted with the languor that so often characterised Makota, and Mr Brooke responded warmly to the atmosphere he perceived there. In a room full of warriors, he was himself full of energy. His eyes sparkled as he strode from commander to commander. I was scarce able to keep up with him as I translated his words of greeting to each. Even the Chinese general received a few polite words, but Mr Brooke was especially careful to talk to each of the Dyak chiefs, enquiring which part of the country their tribe came from and asking as to the condition and health of their men.

By the time Makota himself entered, there was an air of excitement in the room even his visible lack of soldierly enthusiasm could do nothing to quell.

While Makota sat sulkily on the only chair in the room, the Malay generals arranged themselves cross-legged on the floor, the Dyak chiefs squatting beside them. Mr Brooke and the Chinese general were the only ones remaining standing. This lack of courtesy, however, rebounded to Makota's discredit for, standing surrounded by the chiefs, Mr Brooke appeared even more the natural leader he was and support for his demand that the army move forward became so strong that Makota was forced to acquiesce. He claimed, of course, it had been his intention all along to proceed in this way but, as we filed out into the brilliant sunshine of mid-morning, it was clear to all that the initiative was with Mr Brooke.

With agreement on a positive plan of action, the leaders of the army proved more able than we had had any reason to think them heretofore. The meeting was on a Tuesday. Just two days later, the Grand Army struck its camp and began to move. The defences were cut down. Timber and bamboo stockades were transformed into rafts, ready to be propelled up the river. Three hours after dawn, only some mounds of trampled earth showed where Makota's camp had stood, while in the river a fleet of Malay *prahus* and Dyak war canoes, the *Skimalong* among them, began to move slowly but steadily upstream.

That night we bivouacked uneasily at the water's edge, all too aware we were in enemy territory. The next day, the crews were on board at first light, moving to their final destination under cover of the morning fog. These early fogs were characteristic of this region and a great aid in military planning.

This was the first opportunity we had had to see the troops of our ramshackle army about their manoeuvres. Mr Brooke insisted we move amongst them to get their measure, so I found myself near up to my waist in water as we joined the Dyaks in slipping ashore. It was an eerie experience, for the natives seemed to vanish in the mist, their presence disclosed only by an occasional splash. Their long, heavy swords slashed into undergrowth already taking over the abandoned rice fields where we had decided to make our new base. Mr Brooke took me by the arm, hurrying me away from them and moving toward the Malays who, as the mist began to clear, were dragging the rafts of timber and bamboo from the river. Already some of the men worked to drive poles into a square to form the foundations of their fort. Earthworks appeared with miraculous speed; watchtowers grew before our very eyes. Dark bodies busied themselves within the earthworks, raising sheds that would provide shelter for the garrison while, outside, Dyak warriors erected a defensive palisade of timber, bristling with sharpened points of bamboo.

Soon after noon it was finished, and the army reassumed its customary air of indolence, leaving us to explore the lie of the land.

Less than a mile away, on the other side of the river, lay the town of Siniawan, the domestic cluster of houses incongruous behind a serviceably stout palisade. A little farther, on the same side of the river as our encampment, was the enemy's strongpoint of Balidah. A rebel *prahu* moved slowly from fort to town, proving their control of the river remained undisputed.

Mr Brooke drew a spyglass from the pocket of his jacket, which he still wore despite the heat. For some time he examined Balidah's defences. Smaller forts were hidden among the trees but were insignificant in comparison. At Balidah, a wooden breastwork of some six or seven feet in height enclosed a central thatched building on the higher ground within. A smaller lookout house was built into the palisade itself. A few swivels and some light cannon comprised the enemy's total artillery.

At length he turned to me. "Williamson, this is going to be easy. The cannon have not the field of fire they need to cover an attack and the swivel will be too slow to get in more than one or two shots in the time any force would take to cross from the trees to the palisade. They've mounted it too far back to bring the fire down onto troops immediately below their walls. In this heat, the thatch is vulnerable to fire and we can smoke them out. The place will fall to an assault whenever we choose to make one."

He set off back to our camp with the jaunty walk of an assured victor.

It did not take long for him to lose his illusions. When he arrived at the gaudy awnings Makota had erected before his headquarters, he was first kept waiting for no less than two hours. When Makota finally condescended to see him, he was allowed just five minutes to present his plan while the Panglima put his signature to a pile of papers ostentatiously delivered by a servant a few seconds after we were allowed to enter. Mr Brooke's plan called for a limited number of casualties—perhaps, if the swivel gunners were accurate and fired quickly, as many as two or three. Makota flatly rejected it. He could not, he said, putting the papers aside for a moment, countenance anything that led to the prospect of deaths in open battle. Instead, a series of small forts would be built, moving our lines ever closer to those of the enemy without exposing our troops to the dangers of a frontal attack.

So we settled in our new camp. The enthusiasm Mr Brooke had kindled in the army dissipated as Makota refused to move. Indeed, several of the generals who had most enthusiastically supported Mr Brooke at the council of war were now sent away from the army on one pretext or another. Each morning we woke to see Balidah before us but for all the difference it made, we might as well have stayed in our old camp. The crude wooden huts we had set up when we first arrived grew with the passing weeks until they were miniature forts. From their shelter, we watched the enemy, who seemed to spend most of their time simply watching us. Occasionally, for no apparent reason, one side or the other would send out a working party to build another little strongpoint. Troops would move forward to the new position and the stalemate would resume.

After something over a fortnight of this, there was a flurry of activity from the opposition when, with much shouting and clashing of cymbals, a group of warriors emerged from their lines, apparently offering to meet us in open combat. Mr Brooke had ordered his men forward as the Malays and Dyaks around us reached for their weapons.

Some of the Malays had taken up positions with their pipe muskets, a weapon so crude I was always astonished to see it kill anyone other than a man so foolhardy as to fire it. The gun was no more than a length of pipe sealed at one end with a small hole drilled for lighting the charge inside. The loader poured down gunpowder and rammed a ball on top, then resting the tube on a palisade—or, in the field, on the shoulder of a companion—they would point in generally the direction of the enemy and put a light to the touchhole.

On this occasion, before any shot could be fired or blow struck, it started to rain. The enemy immediately withdrew. On our own side, the natives went back to such shelter as they could find while Mr Brooke had us stand our ground and get wet.

Our soaking was a futile gesture. Neither side was prepared to consider conflict in the rain and by the time the sun came out again, the opposition had apparently thought better of their plan and remained firmly ensconced behind their fortifications.

If the situation then had been ridiculous, it had at least been at the expense of the enemy. Worse came the following night.

Mr Brooke suggested the Sultan's men slip forward to start a fort right under the noses of the enemy, working under cover of darkness. It would at least have moved the two armies into something approaching the European idea of battle positions. The plan was eventually agreed upon and a working party set out from the foremost fort.

Meanwhile we set off in another direction, firing a musket at the trees and making as much noise as possible. Behind us everyone left in the fort set to banging their gongs, raising the din with which they habitually indicated their readiness for battle.

For a while, I thought the plan would succeed. The enemy duly beat their gongs in our path and we promptly turned back for the fort. Meanwhile, from the direction of the other party came absolute silence. Mr Brooke broke out the rum kept on board the *Skimalong* and success was being toasted when the building party slipped shamefacedly back to the cover of our fort. It had been a very dark night, they said, and they were sleepy; the building would wait till the morning.

Mr Brooke was so angry, he came near to striking the captain of the building party, and it seemed best not to translate some of the things he said.

The sense of the ridiculous that often permeated our undertaking was increased by the battle dress of the Malays. They protected themselves with great padded coats to absorb the impact of their enemies' wooden spears. The sight of the little Malay warriors inside their huge coats always made me think of an army of scarecrows going into battle. Absurd as they looked, the coats were certainly effective, as was demonstrated in one of the few bits of real fighting we saw. An enemy skirmishing party appeared out of the jungle as a group of Malays worked on yet another fort. Several of our force were struck by spears, but protected by their coats, they were able to reply to the attack. They fired off the pipe muskets that looked so futile but, this time, with deadly effect. Two of the attackers were killed, though the Malays admitted this to be an unusually successful effort with these weapons.

Mr Brooke stayed altogether almost a month at this siege, chafing every day at the futility of it. He was never the most patient of men and it was remarkable he allowed the situation to continue for so long. As the weeks passed, though, he decided to act to break the deadlock. He returned to the *Royalist* with half of the men to row the *Skimalong*, leaving the remainder to maintain a presence with the army. He told me I was to be in charge of our position in his absence.

This was a very great thing for me, for it meant I was treated as an officer, which had never been the case before. I was nervous of the responsibility, but the men were very good humoured about it and made no trouble for me, so things passed well enough until Mr Brooke's return.

When the *Skimalong* arrived back at our camp, she carried three of the six-pound cannon from the *Royalist*. These guns were, by European standards, small things—how else could we have transported them in the longboat? But it was the fiercest artillery yet introduced to Sarawak.

The *Skimalong* ran straight onto the riverbank and we were soon busy carrying the cannon from the boat and getting them safe ashore.

The next morning we started to manhandle the guns from the riverbank to the farthest forward of the forts. Mr Brooke was very jealous of these guns, which accounted for half the cannon on the *Royalist*. He would not let any of the natives lay hands on them, which made a heavy labour for us. Each gun weighed almost two hundredweight and the little wheels on their carriages were designed to move over the smooth deck of the *Royalist*. It was impossible to push the weapons along the path the Dyaks hacked out for us. We had to dismount the cannon and haul them to their new positions in slings.

The task took almost all day and we were mightily glad when it was done. But Mr Brooke had not done making us labour yet. We rested for the night and the next morning we had to build gun platforms to give us a clear shot over the walls of the fort. Once we explained what we were to do, the Malays helped somewhat with the digging and setting of timber to hold the carriages, but the bulk of the work fell on us.

By now speed was of the essence, for the enemy had seen the activity around our fort and belatedly recognised it could pose a real threat to them. They began to fire at us with muskets and the swivel gun that was their main defensive artillery, but Mr Brooke had had the foresight to mount our own swivel on the palisade. Will Spence volunteered to man this weapon, for he had fought in the old King's navy in his youth and was anxious to prove he still held some skill as a gunner. He had been accustomed to firing from one moving vessel to another and he found the work of an artilleryman on *terra firma* posed no great challenge. As he said to me when it was all over, "If you've holed an enemy when you're firing from a vessel yawing in a heavy sea, then knocking off a few darkies from that palisade is a piece of…" Well, he intimated it was no great difficulty and, indeed, silencing the enemy's guns was the work of barely a quarter of an hour. By then, the platform was completed and we were fixing our six-pounders in their places.

We had drilled with the guns before, as there was always the danger of attack by pirates and it was necessary all the crew be prepared. This was the first time, though, I had ever seen a cannon fired in anger, as you might say. Not that there was any sign of anger, or even of much excitement, as we prepared— priming, ramming in the ball, and adjusting the elevation before, on Mr Brooke's orders, lighting the charge.

The first shot fell short and the second was lost in the jungle behind its target, but the third struck home.

Once we had the range, the rest was purely mechanical and soon the damage wrought by our guns was clearly visible. At first there was a crack in the palisade one man might climb through, then a passage for two, and finally a gap that might be stormed by six men together.

At this point, Mr Brooke gave the cease-fire and went in search of Makota to give the good news that the fort could now be stormed with but minimal risk to life. I, of course, accompanied him to interpret.

Makota, though seldom seen near our camp, kept himself informed of our activity. He already knew Balidah's defences had been breached and expected our visit. He was still based at the first fort we had built upon landing, now some half a mile distant from the possibility of any fighting. There he received us, surrounded by his senior commanders.

Mr Brooke's artillery had clearly increased the respect in which Makota held him, and he greeted us with great ceremony. He listened gravely while Mr Brooke advanced his plans for an assault on the fort. With the walls breached and the *Royalist*'s guns in a position to provide covering fire, the capture of the fort was a foregone conclusion. An immediate assault would see the enemy's position in our hands by the end of the day. The war as good as won.

Makota smiled, nodding his agreement. The plan, he said, was a good one. There remained, of course, some risk, and there would be some casualties. If, on the other hand, the army continued to advance by building forts, the risk would be much less and there would be fewer casualties. He smiled again.

While I listened to his temporising, I recalled his last refusal to bring the war to any conclusion and expected he would again dismiss Mr Brooke's ideas out of hand. In the event, though, it appeared our status had grown sufficient to require a more sophisticated approach.

Makota explained that he, of course, was prepared to take any risk to end the war. However, his army was drawn from many tribes and it was only right he should consult his captains before the men were ordered to hazard their lives in this way. He could not directly order it, if the tribal war leaders were unhappy with such a course. The decision must be theirs.

Makota smiled quietly and gestured at the nearest of the

commanders. It was a Malay, a man whom I had seen about the lines chastising any of his troops who showed the least carelessness in their work. He was, I thought, a good captain, and I had assumed him a brave man. Yet he stood and announced he could not possibly commit his men to such a reckless attack.

Another Malay echoed his view, then one of the Chinese captains and then a Dyak warrior. The Dyak was the most clearly uncomfortable, mumbling his excuses and refusing to meet our eyes.

One by one, each of the captains in turn stood to declare their readiness to die for their Sultan but the impossibility of leading their men to certain death.

When it was over Makota smiled quietly, assured us of his eternal regret at the decision of his commanders, and withdrew.

As Makota was leaving the room, and without any pretence of ceremony, Mr Brooke made his own departure. He strode through the lines at such a pace, I was hard put to match it.

Returning to our own camp, he threw himself into a hammock lashed up to the gun platform. There he remained the rest of the day, volunteering no comment on the proceedings and glaring at any who came near in a manner that made us keep our own counsel in his hearing.

For myself, I had some small sympathy with the captains. Certainly Makota had drilled them in their response and some would have been happy to join an assault, but many were unhappy with the plan for reasons not wholly political. In the time we had been there, I had observed the way the Dyaks would slip into the shadows of the trees to skirt the very footings of the enemy's forts, ready to take the life of any men foolhardy enough to venture forth alone, and I have already recounted an ambuscade the enemy carried out on our force in a similar fashion. There was no doubt as to their readiness for battle but warfare to them was an affair of skirmish and ambush, of hand-to-hand combat between individuals. The European notion of a mass open assault was an alien notion.

By now, no one seemed interested in the realities of the battlefield any longer. All was politics and Mr Brooke felt he had suffered such a reverse as made it impossible for him to achieve anything of use. That night, he announced we were to withdraw our force, small as it was.

The next day was spent in returning the guns to the *Ski-malong*. Makota would get his way. We would leave him to his eternal war and quit Sarawak.

# Chapter 4

O F COURSE, IN THE end, it came about quite otherwise. Mr Brooke and I went, once again, to Hassim to tell him we were leaving, and again we listened to his impassioned pleas that we should stay. This time, though, even calls on Mr Brooke's honour as an English gentleman failed to move him. I had to explain to the Sultan, as tactfully as I could—and the choice of words was mine, for Mr Brooke lacked discretion in this area—that while Makota commanded the army there would be no victory, and the *Royalist* could not wait in Kuching for the rebels to surrender of their own free will.

It was an uncomfortable meeting and we were pleased to escape back to the ship.

We had not been aboard more than a couple of hours when a procession of Malays arrived on the quay, escorting a man wearing a splendid gold and red jacket over his sarong. He was clearly a figure of importance and I was summoned from my quarters to find out what he wanted.

His name, he said, was Budrudeen. I realised from the two ceremonial *kris* in his sarong that he was a *pangeran*, as they call their nobility, and held a high rank, but I was surprised when he announced himself as Hassim's brother, for he was very little like him. Where Hassim was short and seemed self-effacing, Budrudeen was tall and his personality dominated the room. He had large eyes of soft brown, but any suggestion of weakness was more than compensated for by the firm line of his lips. His jaw, too, betokened strength of character, and there was none of the fleshiness of self-indulgence that prevailed amongst so many of those in Hassim's court. Indeed, Budrudeen was every inch a prince and would have shone in even the most civilised of company.

He bowed to Mr Brooke and explained his mission as I translated. "He says the Sultan has appointed him to negotiate with you concerning your position in Sarawak."

Mr Hart raised his eyes to heaven and Murray made a sound of disgust. Mr Brooke looked as if he would have spoken, but Budrudeen raised his hand for silence and continued to speak. "The Sultan Hassim offers the command of his Grand Army to his friend and adviser, James Brooke. The Sultan asks once again that his friend should not desert him."

There was a crash as Murray dropped the glass he had been holding. Brooke stared at Budrudeen. Everyone else was still. "What about Makota?"

"Makota will remain with the army but will answer to you."

"That's an impossible situation. With Hassim in Kuching, Makota will do what he wants—just as he has done so far."

Budrudeen smiled and replied quickly, as if he had antici-pated this point. I translated his answer for Mr Brooke. "He says the Sultan will remain in Kuching, sir, but he will accom-pany you. He is confident Makota will then make no objection to your commands."

Brooke looked at Hart and Murray who, in their turn, were staring at Budrudeen. The Malay continued to smile quietly. He exuded authority. There was no doubt Makota would step into line if Budrudeen accompanied us.

It had been a long day. Brooke desperately wanted an excuse to stay in Sarawak and pursue his dream. Budrudeen's appeal was direct and honest. We could all feel him weakening, preparing himself to change his mind, yet again, about leaving the country.

It was Murray who broke the spell. "For God's sake," he said, "it isn't as if it were his own country."

Budrudeen turned to me for a translation and, without thinking, I simply told him what the Scotsman had said.

The moment had passed. Mr Brooke would say nothing now. Budrudeen saw it too. He bowed, said he would convey our views to the Sultan, and left.

Mr Brooke did not look a happy man and I could tell that a row was, yet again, brewing between him and the surveyor. They would need no interpreter there and I left for my own quarters as quickly as I decently could.

The next morning I had plans to be in the market early, as we needed to buy new provisions, ready for our setting sail. Mr Hart was just ordering the gig to be readied to take me ashore when a boat came alongside and a native shouted up a request that Mr Brooke should call again on the Sultan.

James Brooke made no secret of his irritation, but he decided he could not refuse a direct request for another meeting and I, perforce, must accompany him. The meeting, he assured me, would not take long and we could use the necessity of my being free to negotiate our supplies to cut things short if Hassim attempted to prolong it. So, with orders to Mr Hart to start his preparations for our departure that week, we set off once again to the audience hall.

We found Hassim there waiting for us. Budrudeen stood at his side with a few of the nobles who advised the Sultan on matters of state, but no one else was present. It was clear this was to be a business meeting and, for once, Hassim wasted no time. As soon as we were settled, he turned to me and said I was to tell Mr Brooke that he agreed to our terms.

I did so, but Mr Brooke and I were as confused as each other as to what terms Hassim was agreeing to.

Budrudeen understood our confusion and spoke quietly to

me. "Your Mr Murray has explained the problem very clearly. If *Tuan* Brooke is to stay in this country, it is right he should have a stake in its future."

This was the first time Mr Brooke had been addressed as *Tuan*—a word I would translate as 'Lord,' and the first inkling we had of what was to come.

"If *Tuan* Brooke would be content to stay and subdue the rebellion, he should be rewarded. The Sultan would be pleased to grant *Tuan* Brooke the rule of Sarawak."

❄

OF COURSE, IT TOOK some time to arrange the details. Mr Brooke, as a loyal citizen of Her Majesty the Queen, would also have to swear, in his role as ruler of Sarawak, that he would be a loyal vassal of Hassim. Finding a form of words both men were happy with fell to me and proved a difficult undertaking. In the end, I fear my translation may have been inexact and it is possible the version I gave to Mr Brooke in English emphasised his continuing loyalty to the British Crown rather more than the Malay wording might have expressed.

Even here, though, Hassim saw clear advantages in having Sarawak under *de facto* British protection whilst remaining nominally a vassal state under his rule. You must remember Sarawak was but a small province governed by a Sultan who controlled much of Borneo. The war in Sarawak forced him to absent himself from the capital. He could not leave Kuching without the rebellion being crushed, as the loss of face this would involve would mean he would risk control of the rest of his country. Yet by staying in Sarawak, he was losing control anyway as other factions in the capital conspired to gain power while their master was so far away. Ridding himself of the day to day rule of Sarawak cost him little, but the end of the war would bring immediate and substantial benefits.

The confusion of the negotiations was heightened by Mr

Brooke always hurrying from one task to another. At the same time as he prepared to take on the rule of his own country, he was planning, with Mr Hart, the campaign that had to be won before the country was his to rule. And he had to persuade his men—and the irascible Mr Murray—they should be happy to stay in Sarawak indefinitely.

The men were the least of his difficulties. When Mr Brooke and I had left the *Royalist* for our adventures with Makota, Mr Hart had properly reckoned that the ship would be in Kuching for some time and, rather than have idle men aboard, had given the crew liberty to go ashore. I fear that, as is all too often the way with sailors in a foreign port, they had been quick to take advantage of the local women and, though Mr Brooke would surely not have approved of such a state of affairs, Mr Hart had not seen fit to take any measures to put an end to these goings on. With good food and drink readily to hand, the men were in no hurry to depart. Only Mr Murray complained, with typical irritation, that the stay would waste his talents, though Mr Brooke assured him he would be able to do all the surveying he wished once the war was won.

As for winning the war, Mr Brooke was convinced success would be ensured by our possession of artillery. The three cannon were again painstakingly lowered into the *Skimalong* and the *Royalist*'s other two boats. The two smaller boats were precariously low in the water with the cannon aboard, and the three set off slowly and cautiously toward Makota's camp. Meanwhile, Budrudeen hurried ahead in his own vessel to break the news of his dismissal to Makota and to smooth the way for Mr Brooke to take command.

I AM NOT THE best man to talk of the days that followed. It is a tale that should be told by those like Will Spence, who were at the forefront of the fighting. For there *was* fighting, and Will and the others showed themselves to be such as has made the British Empire the power that it is. They fought bravely and won in honest warfare.

I wish that were how I remember what happened. I wish I could write of the charge toward the fort; of men running forward, ignoring the shot from the swivel, deaf to the crack of muskets as the defenders made a last stand behind their splintered palisade. Spence should be telling the tale but—as you shall learn—Spence has already told his tale before the last Great Judge to whom, in the end, we must all account for ourselves.

My abiding memories of those days are not of glory and brave men fighting on an open field but of politics and intrigue and betrayal.

We arrived to find Budrudeen still trying to impose his authority on the army, with Makota at best surly and, increasingly often, given to open contempt for Hassim and his orders.

Budrudeen had brought with him a number of his own men to form a retinue, reflecting his status. Over the days that followed more of his followers appeared, until there were thirty or so. Clearly they had no purely ceremonial purpose. Half a dozen would always remain around Budrudeen, while the others camped near our gun emplacement. I noticed their line was set not to face the enemy but to protect our rear.

My duties meant most of my time was spent in conferences with Mr Brooke, Budrudeen, or Makota. It was all too clear that, while Makota could no longer openly refuse to support Mr Brooke, plans that involved him or the chiefs in his party would mysteriously fail to come to fruition. When men were ordered to positions ready for any planned assault, not only would they not appear but we would all too often learn the next day that they had vanished altogether from the Sultan's army, returning silently to the jungle.

We could all see that Hassim had let his control of Sarawak slip almost to the point where he would lose the country entirely. His offering the place to Mr Brooke was less an act of generosity and more a calculation that it was better to have it controlled by an Englishman than by Makota and his allies. Not that Makota was in open rebellion. If our ambushes were thwarted, there was no evidence the rebel camp had been fore-warned. If a raiding party slipped through our defences as if they already knew the position of every watching guard, there was no proof it was to be explained but by their woodcraft. Even so, James took to moving about the place with his own armed escort.

Makota was allied with some of the leading men of the area and had strong links with the local tribes. Above all, he was a favourite of the Chinese. The Chinese were, first and foremost, traders and, Budrudeen assured us, they could be bought by anyone who promised them more and better opportunities to trade. Whether Makota had suborned them in this way, I truly cannot say, but Mr Brooke was happy to have Budrudeen con-firm his prejudices against the Chinese and he believed they were not loyal.

I was puzzled as to what Makota's motive could be. He was, after all, already the governor of the province and, with the re-bellion over and Hassim back in Brunei, he would effectively rule Sarawak in any case. It was not until Budrudeen had been at our siege of Siniawan for a week that I came to understand. The men had built a small hut, which Mr Brooke used as his headquarters, and Budrudeen had fallen into the habit of calling on Mr Brooke in the evening. While his religion meant he did not serve alcohol in his own quarters, he was happy enough to take a drink with his British allies. That night, his guard re-mained outside the hut and he had, perhaps, drunk more than usual. Mr Brooke had by now picked up enough of the language to get by but I was there, partly to interpret if needed but mostly, I think, because it had become a matter of habit for us both.

Thinking Budrudeen might be minded to talk of politics, I asked him about Makota and he explained the governor was related, both by blood and marriage, to some of the chief families in Brunei. "His heart is in Brunei. He wishes to return there."

I was confused, as well I might be. "Then why doesn't he allow us to act and finish things here?"

Budrudeen gave a tired smile. "It is not so simple as that. His family in Brunei are strong but they want more power, as all who live in the shadow of the court want more power. Yet Hassim is placed above them. They can rise only as he falls. So Makota is sent here to see that Hassim will fall."

I had already come to suspect the struggle we were caught up in must be part of some larger cause, stretching far beyond Siniawan. Yet Mr Brooke seemed shocked at Budrudeen's calm acceptance of Makota's duplicity. "You mean Hassim's general is conspiring against him?"

Budrudeen shrugged. "The longer Hassim is in Sarawak, the stronger Makota's family grows in Brunei. How can Makota act when to do so must damage those to whom he is tied by blood?"

For a moment, I thought Mr Brooke would choke on his rum. He had distrusted Makota from the first and knew he could not rely on him as an ally, but only now did he realise how desperate Makota was that the war should not come to a conclusion. It seemed that, even with Budrudeen's help, we might find it impossible to force Makota into any active steps against the rebels. Yet again, we stood on the brink of success and yet might prove unable to seize victory.

This situation continued for weeks. Mr Brooke began to let his irritation show. He would retire late, often having drunk well. He slept badly and, when he woke, he was sometimes waspish with the men, although I was spared his tongue.

Budrudeen was better at disguising his emotions, but he took to drinking longer in the evenings and his criticisms of Makota grew more barbed. He formed the habit of leaving his guard outside on every visit that he might talk more freely. In those evenings, drinking together with no guards or servants around us, we grew to know each other. Budrudeen would share his frustration and anger at Makota, and Mr Brooke would curse the war and the whole ridiculous situation.

Thus was formed a friendship between the English gentleman and the Malay prince, which was to serve both well in the years ahead. And I, simply by being there, was encompassed in their friendship.

After Budrudeen had left, Mr Brooke would often detain me for another drink and we would talk together of our lives and our hopes. For all the difference in our stations, we had much in common. We had both been lonely as children, loved by our parents yet somehow feeling apart from those around us. We had both been restless at home and both of us had found an escape from the land of our birth in ways suitable to our respective positions in the world—I as a common sailor, Mr Brooke as a gentleman adventurer.

"I doubt, though, I would have had your courage," he confided one evening. "I had my father's money and my experience with the East India Company. Yet you set out to see the world with no knowledge of other lands and with nought but the clothes on your back."

Then he smiled and added, "And, of course, your bonny good looks." He leaned across toward me and ruffled my hair.

It was the first time he had touched me with a quiet affection of that sort and it fixed the evening in my mind. I had known before, of course, that I was handsome, for there had been girls enough to tell me so, though none who had ever come to mean anything to me. But, somehow, after that evening, I found myself paying more attention to my appearance. When my business took me to his cabin, where a small mirror hung upon the wall, I would, if unobserved, check my appearance, smoothing my hair and rubbing with my sleeve to remove any visible dirt from my face. I would compare my smooth brown hair with his tangle of black locks, which always made him seem somehow piratical—an impression quite at odds with the gentleness of his features.

So the weeks passed in growing intimacy among the three of us until one night Budrudeen arrived in an unusually sombre mood. When Mr Brooke enquired as to the reason, he explained he had just had news of his family in Brunei. His sister was unwell and he wanted to visit her but could not do so because he could not be spared from Sarawak. For the first time in my experience, Budrudeen allowed himself to get visibly the worse for drink, and by the time he left, he was cursing Makota to perdition.

The next morning I went to wake Mr Brooke, expecting to find him in a particularly gloomy state, for he had drunk enough to render most men incapable for much of the following day. Instead, to my surprise, I found him already up and shaving and more sprightly than he had been for some days.

"Ah, John!" he greeted me. "Let's get Budrudeen over here. It's time we got a move on."

I hurried over to Budrudeen's encampment. Once I arrived, I had to wait some time before the pangeran finally emerged. One glance proved his capacity for alcohol was more limited than Mr Brooke's. As his people were not meant to drink, I supposed he could claim the excuse that he had had less practice. In any case, he was in no condition to attend a meeting that morning, but he arrived with us in the afternoon, smiling gamely at me, though I'll wager he had a headache he wouldn't forget in a hurry.

It seemed an inauspicious start to the meeting: James Brooke full of enthusiasm and vivacity, and Budrudeen clearly wishing he was at home in bed. But Mr Brooke poured tea into him, encouraged him to eat some cakes and honey, and gently coaxed him into a state where they could talk sensibly about what they were to do. For he had decided he could tolerate the present situation no longer—it was time to take the initiative.

I do not know the details of that meeting. I was kept running back and forth to find things to tempt Budrudeen's palate or to fetch herbs from his encampment, which he swore would ease his head. It seemed to me, too, that the pangeran welcomed the chance to speak privately to Mr Brooke. Though the two of them struggled to talk without an interpreter, Budrudeen was anxious that no ears, not even mine, should hear him plotting behind Makota's back.

Early the next morning, a messenger left Budrudeen and set off to Kuching with instructions to the pangeran's household and a letter for Mr Hart on the *Royalist*. Mr Hart was instructed to leave Mr Murray and three men alone to guard the ship, and to bring the rest of the crew together with another twenty from Budrudeen's household to join us at dawn four days after receiving the message.

While the messenger travelled to Kuching and we waited for our reinforcements, we continued to give the appearance that we were settled for an extended siege. James Brooke and Budrudeen met daily with Makota to draw up elaborate plans they knew would never be carried out. Meanwhile, our men and Budrudeen's split into two groups. While half lazed around, ostentatiously idle, the others, hidden in our little fort, drilled until they were as disciplined a body as any commander could wish.

On the night before Mr Hart was to join us, we were in no mood for sleep. I remember sitting up with Will Spence, swapping stories of our experiences in different ships and sharing a quid of tobacco, chewing rhythmically and trying not to think of what the day might bring. Before dawn, our forces were ready at the guns and in place behind our palisades. Scouts had slipped out in the darkness, checking that the ground between the forts was clear of obstacles. Most of our force fought barefoot and both sides would protect their positions with sharpened stakes concealed in hidden pits.

We had extended our palisade, facing the enemy, but we had constructed it so it could be thrown down to allow our men to advance from cover with the minimum of delay. We knew the greatest danger would be in the first few minutes as we covered the open ground. Mr Brooke planned to make as much as possible of his advantage of surprise.

As the sun rose on the morning of the attack, there was a thick mist hanging over the river. Mr Hart was able to disembark our men and Budrudeen's reinforcements without either the rebels or Makota's watchers knowing they had arrived.

With the additional men, there were some seventy of us ready for battle. Of this number, barely twenty were white men and ten of these had to man our artillery—nine on the six-pounders and a tenth on the swivel. Will had asked to be relieved of this position so he could join the main attack and Mr Brooke had agreed. This left a less experienced hand to man the swivel gun, but Will had spent the previous day drilling him and we were confident he would do all that was needful.

With the gun crews about their business, just a dozen Britons remained to assault the enemy once our artillery had done its work.

As I crouched behind the palisade with the others, I felt myself shivering. I told myself it was the cold, for the early morning was often chilly, even though the days would bathe us in sweat. I knew, though, that it was fear. I was no coward—I had proved that, scrambling among the ratlines in a storm, the mast swinging from side to side with the surge of the ocean. But I was no fighter. Several of the crew, like Will, had served in the Navy. Sailors generally could be a rough lot and there were few who did not carry the scars of drunken fights. Yet I avoided such quarrels. I had no desire to hurt my fellows, even with my fists. Could I, then, strike a man down with a sword and be the cause of his death in battle? How would I respond when I faced the enemy hand-to-hand?

To keep my mind from dwelling on my own position, I watched the gunners preparing to open hostilities. With only three men to a gun, they would be working at the limits of their strength. They prepared their positions carefully so they would be able to fire as fast as possible in the first minutes of the engagement. Piles of cannonballs were neatly stacked near the muzzles, buckets of water were at hand to dampen the mops that would ensure no embers from the last charge remained alight as fresh powder was rammed in. The powder cartridges themselves, stored in small casks to lessen the damage should an accident occur, were to hand. I watched the battery captains ram in the first balls and stand by the touchholes, tapers lit. Their men were ready at the ropes to haul the cannon back into position after the recoil of the first shot.

As the sun warmed the ground before us, the mist began to clear and the enemy's fort started to take a ghostly shape half a mile across the open scrub. I saw Mr Brooke nod sharply toward the captains. Three tapers moved together to the touchholes and the world seemed to explode into noise and smoke.

I did not see where the first shots fell, but I heard the captains shouting their orders for the repositioning of the guns. It seemed but a few seconds before the guns roared again and I saw earth rising ahead of the fort as at least one round fell short.

The gun teams moved smoothly, the captains swabbing and reloading while the others pulled their heavy charges back into position straining on the ropes. The noise of the firing seemed continuous, the shouted orders and the smell of powder overwhelming my senses. Where but a few minutes earlier I had felt my bowels gripped with dread, now I was seized with the excitement of the moment, ready—nay, anxious—to rush forward into the charge.

By now the battery had established the range. At a command from Mr Brooke, some of our men showed themselves, as if by chance, above our palisade, drawing the fire of the rebels' swivel. When the rebels had fired and before they could reload, we threw down the palisade, revealing our main force. Mr Brooke and Budrudeen, running side by side, led our charge across the open space before us.

I had never thought to find myself in such a situation but all there was for it was to put on as good a showing as I could. We poured from our defences, running and screaming but, after our initial rush, we advanced at an easy trot, line abreast. The enemy's cannon were of little use to them. Their gunners could not range them fast enough and, in any case, they could not protect themselves against an attack on such a wide front as we offered them. Even so, we would hear their balls passing over us or see them striking up great clods of earth where they struck the ground ahead of our line.

For the first half of our charge, our own cannon maintained their fire on the fort. The noise of the artillery almost drowned out the war chants of Budrudeen's men and the fearsome howling of our own lads. Again and again, the swivel gun spat from the rebel ramparts. Twice I saw one of the Malay figures ahead of me stagger and fall screaming to the ground. In the noise and excitement, I thought nothing of it. Though I felt a ball pass me by only a yard or two, still I ran on, caught up in the wild enthusiasm of the charge.

After the first couple of minutes, we began to slow and the enemy came close to finding our range. Mr Brooke shouted for us to move faster and we forced ourselves to start running again, stumbling on the uneven ground as Balidah seemed to stay frustratingly distant from us.

Suddenly we were on them, running the last few yards to their walls. By now the swivel could not bear down because we were too close below the fort. There was some ragged shooting from pipe guns but, although their noise and smoke added to the confusion, they offered no material threat. More dangerous were the spears hurled down from above as we pushed through the gap our artillery had made in their defences. I saw another two or three fall and then we were in and engaged in fighting hand to hand with the enemy.

There must have been at least a couple of hundred natives in the fort but our lads carved their way through them. We had no muskets, judging that the fighting would be fast and furious and a sword would be of more use than a bayonet. Indeed, some were armed only with belaying pins. Yet the force of our assault, combined with the unpreparedness of the enemy, meant those opposing us fell back before our charge. Indeed, after all my concerns about how I would conduct myself, I found there was no one for me to fight. Budrudeen's men were ahead of me, stabbing and slashing at all in their path and, as I ran behind, my main danger was that I might trip on one of the bodies the Malays left in their wake.

It took only minutes for the enemy to break. Taken by surprise, terrified by the speed and fury of the assault, and unused to open warfare in the European manner, they fled toward the river. A dozen or so lay dead or dying in the fort and a few more were killed as they ran but most, I think, reached the river and swam for the safety of the town. Less than a quarter of an hour after our first shot had been fired, Balidah had fallen, Siniawan was defenceless, and the war was effectively won.

＊

BUDRUDEEN ACCEPTED THE FORMAL surrender of Siniawan that afternoon. Twenty of the leading men among the rebels gave themselves up as our prisoners. We disarmed the warriors we found and left them to escape into the jungle. Mr Brooke ordered the *Royalist*'s crew to stand guard as the women and children took their possessions and slipped into the trees to find their menfolk, but we stood aside as Makota's forces looted whatever had been left behind, then burned Siniawan to the ground.

Makota was ready to have the prisoners marched away to his lines but Budrudeen intervened. They had surrendered to the Sultan, he said, and as the Sultan's representative, he would have charge of them. So they were housed in our fort and our men and Budrudeen's guarded them. The guard was as much for their protection as to prevent their escape and they knew this was so. They gave no trouble and when we fed them, or showed them any little kindness, they were pathetic in their gratitude.

It was two more days before Makota was ready to leave. Many of the troops were already moving off to return to their homes but his own men and those from Kuching or thereabouts were to sail back with us and the prisoners.

In the event, it was a spectacular return. A fleet of twenty or thirty war *prahus*, accompanied by smaller canoes and the *Royalist*'s boats, arrived in Kuching with flags flying and cymbals crashing. It was after dark when we arrived and torches had been mounted on the prows while the people of the town, forewarned of our coming, had built bonfires on the banks of the river. In the flickering firelight, with victory chants filling the air, it must have looked most impressive from the shore. Even Mr Murray, watching from the *Royalist*, was moved to comment, "Ye made a fair show, for all your savage noise."

There was little ceremony that night, for all the men were tired from the day's rowing. Budrudeen had the prisoners escorted off under a guard of his own men, and the rest of the Grand Army found its way to its various quarters and there, I should imagine, fell into blameless sleep. The next morning, though, we were all awakened early and fallen in to be inspected by Mr Brooke, then paraded to the Sultan's audience hall to give an account of ourselves and our exploits.

As we marched from our berth, it became clear all the captains had had the same idea and the streets were full of parading men. The space before the audience hall was crowded with Malay warriors and our men were left there as Mr Brooke and I joined the other captains inside. Budrudeen already waited in the hall and, as we pushed our way through the crowd, the prisoners were brought before the Sultan.

Budrudeen was dressed in his best. His jacket was stiff with gold embroidery and the gilded hilts of his two ceremonial *kris* could be seen above the white silk sash he wore around his waist. He was speaking as we entered and it was clear this was a formal report to Hassim.

The Sultan appeared rather overawed by the display of his

own power filling the audience chamber. Budrudeen had brought his personal escort with him, as had Makota. Other chiefs and their advisers left their guards waiting outside, but all were in their finery. The prisoners, dressed only in loincloths and bound with their hands behind them, were escorted by more of Budrudeen's men with spears at the ready. Hassim's own guards stood silently along the walls, while his servants moved through the throng carrying trays of tiny cakes.

Budrudeen was describing the fall of Siniawan and the surrender of the leaders who were, as he spoke, abasing themselves on the floor in front of the Sultan.

Mr Brooke turned to me. He almost had to shout to make himself heard above the din. "What's he saying?"

I was hardly surprised he could not understand. With the wails of the prisoners, the insults hurled at them by the soldiers, and all the excitement outside the hall, it took all my concentration to make out what was going on.

"He's giving the prisoners into the hands of the Sultan. Hassim will decide their fate." Even as I translated what was happening, the courtiers around the Sultan burst into a renewed frenzy of shouting. "They're demanding the prisoners be executed."

"But why? They have been content to have these men foment unrest for years. Why are they suddenly so concerned to see them put to death?"

"It is the custom of the country. And besides, their enthusiasm for the death of the Sultan's enemies will be taken to show that they are themselves the Sultan's friends."

Mr Brooke was clearly unhappy with the turn events had taken but seemed at first disposed to hold his counsel.

Among the prisoners there was one who was much younger than the rest. I think he had stood substitute for his father who was incapacitated by injury and in no state to leave Siniawan. In any case, this lad stood out, not only for his youth but for his beauty. He was very tall and well formed and his skin was the soft brown I had often observed in Malay youths. His face, too, was handsome, and I was not surprised Mr Brooke noticed him among the others.

This young man felt Mr Brooke's gaze upon him and called out, crying for the Englishman to save him. And, above all the row, James heard him.

He turned to me, his face set. "I cannot stand by and watch this barbarity. Tell the Sultan these men surrendered after a fair fight. He cannot have them killed now that they lie bound and helpless before him."

I translated as best I could, shouting to make myself heard. Makota and his men pretended to be horrified anyone could suggest sparing the lives of the rebels while Mr Brooke, seeing his argument was not being heard, started to shout himself, half in English, half in Malay. He spoke of honour and decency, and I must say I paid little heed for it was clear Makota's allies saw in our interjection the opportunity to argue that we were not truly to be trusted as defenders of the Sultan's cause. Mr Brooke's scruples were turned against us, and it was all I could do to stand my ground in an argument that was becoming ever more fierce.

Fortunately Budrudeen, whatever his private opinion, recognised the importance to our standing that we should win the argument and he, too, pleaded for mercy. The men had fought honourably, he said, and had surrendered so their people might be spared. They were acknowledged leaders in the jungles of Sarawak, where Hassim needed loyal followers who would carry his rule to those who lived far from Kuching. If they were spared, they would owe their lives and their loyalty to the Sultan, and they could be relied on to ensure there was no more talk of rebellion.

I tried to flatter Hassim by reminding him of the favourable impression created by his treatment of the *Napoleon*'s crew. I assured him—and, if it were a lie, it was in a good cause—that the European community valued mercy almost above all things and his standing with the British would be considerably improved if he could show magnanimity in victory.

As so often, when caught between rival groups in his court, the indecision on Hassim's face was all too clear and quite pitiful to watch. I do not know what finally decided him. Budrudeen said afterwards it was his love for James but I think it may rather have been a calculation that by snubbing Makota thus publicly, he might weaken a man whom he must have recognised as an enemy.

Whatever the reason, the prisoners were spared. Three remained as the Sultan's guests—hostages in all but name. The others were allowed to return to their people, having first pledged their loyalty to Hassim.

Mr Brooke had taken a stand over the prisoners not for some grand reason of policy but because he was sorry for them. His was an honest concern with the well-being of his fellow man and not a cunning piece of politics. But Makota could not see it as anything other than a move against him, and this clash signalled the start of an open dispute between Mr Brooke and the governor. Until now, Makota had sought to thwart us by stubbornness and guile, but now he came out in public opposition to Mr Brooke and his plans. The British, he said, had no business in Sarawak. Mr Brooke's desire to see the rebels spared showed he was not truly loyal to the Sultan. Makota claimed that, as an Englishman, Mr Brooke could not understand the customs of the country. The Governor denounced him alternately as a coward for his reluctance to shed blood and for his recklessness in battle, as demonstrated in his assault on Balidah.

Now, as at Siniawan, Mr Brooke and Budrudeen took to spending their evenings together. Often Mr Brooke would suggest I escort him to Budrudeen's palace, ostensibly in case an interpreter was needed but more, I think, as a kindness to me. The palace was quite luxurious and Budrudeen's hospitality was always generous. Food would be served in one of the dozen or so buildings enclosed within the compound that made up his residence. There was housing for himself and other houses for his servants. A separate kitchen stood near the reception hall which he could use on formal occasions or for feasting. There was even a small, covered enclosure where the instruments of the *gulong* orchestra were set out ready in case the prince required music for his entertainment. All these were enclosed within a stout wooden fence with gates guarded day and night by the men of his bodyguard.

Although Budrudeen enjoyed the opportunity to play host to us at his home, he would more often join Mr Brooke aboard the *Royalist*, where they could talk without servants to spy on their conversation. Aboard the ship, Budrudeen could speak frankly about Makota's treachery.

"He whispers against you every day," he told us. "He is determined my brother should not honour his promise to give you the rule of this place, for he thinks of Sarawak as his own. When the Sultan returns to Brunei, Makota will be free once again to plot against him and without a strong ruler here in Kuching, who can stop him?"

Budrudeen made it clear he was all for handing rule to Mr Brooke as soon as possible. Like Hassim, he had a wife and children in Brunei. He wanted Sarawak under, as he saw it, British protection so he could return to his life in the capital. The Sultan, though, was again torn. On the one hand, he had made a promise to James Brooke. On the other, it now transpired the chiefs had not been consulted and they were challenging Hassim's right to make such a grand change without formally taking counsel of them.

Every evening Budrudeen would depart, promising he would try to persuade his brother to make up his mind. And every afternoon, Mr Brooke and I would take tea with the Sultan, and he would agonise between breaking his word to his friend and alienating so many powerful men in his court—men who all had friends and family embroiled in the intrigues of Brunei. He would twist his arguments this way and that, trying to escape the dilemma he found himself in. For example, on the third or fourth afternoon we spent with him, he presented Mr Brooke with a silver box like that in which many of his courtiers would keep the betel nuts they were forever chewing.

"It is a token of my friendship, James," he said. "The friendship in which I promised you so much. And much, alas, I now find it is not in my power to give you."

His argument, teased out a step at a time, was that his promise was given as Hassim the man and was honestly meant. As Hassim the Sultan, though, he was unable to do what Hassim the man had pledged.

Mr Brooke would sit stiffly uncomfortable in the jacket propriety made him wear on these occasions, perspiring in the sticky heat of the tropical afternoon and politely sipping tea while we listened to Hassim's endless protestations of good faith. Once aboard the *Royalist*, though, he would unburden himself of his true feelings in a tirade that could last a full quarter of an hour. "What has changed is that when the promise was given, there was open rebellion in the country and I was needed. Now that I have put down the rebellion, Hassim sees me as less important than the so-called nobles who spend all their time plotting against him. They may look well in their gold thread and their fine silks but they are as dirty a bunch of scoundrels underneath as any that ever lived."

He would storm at Makota and threaten to tax Hassim directly with his lies. Then, it was my task to soothe him and remind him nothing could be gained by such an insult. So, instead, Mr Brooke would return to the Sultan and insinuate that, by failing to fulfill his promise, Hassim lost face with his courtiers. They would think him weak, we argued, and thus his position in Brunei, which was at the core of his concerns, would be undermined.

So the talks dragged on. The discussions were wearisome but I could not afford to relax my guard. Every phrase had to be interpreted not only for its overt meaning but for all the subtleties it concealed. Nothing was ever said straightforwardly.

Everything was dressed in fine words and flowery speeches. On some days we would even have entertainers who would sing or tell ancient tales of the country—each song or story would be in some way related to our situation. In case we failed to appreciate the point, Hassim would carefully explain his position was like that of the mythic ruler in the story, who had been forced to send his best beloved friend away and give the throne to another, or that Sarawak was like the land in a song which chose its own ruler through magic and prophecy.

As the days passed into weeks, Makota became more confident he would prevail. He would ostentatiously ignore Mr Brooke if the two met at Hassim's audience chamber. His guards would jostle the *Royalist*'s men aside when the two groups encountered each other on the street. The slights were petty but were designed to show publicly that his party was in the ascendant and Mr Brooke was a spent force.

On one celebrated occasion, Mr Murray was somewhat the worse for drink— as seemed often to be the case—and became embroiled in a dispute with one of the Chinese traders regarding the efficacy of some powdered rhino horn. He had been promised the medicine would make him more attractive to women and, despite his frequent complaints as to the lack of entertainment offered by Kuching, he had apparently felt he might be able to test this native potion. Unfortunately for him, the local women, though proving very susceptible to the charms of many of the crew, were not anxious to be wooed by a large, noisy Scotsman smelling of whisky. Mr Murray, perhaps unaware of exactly *how* powdered rhino horn was supposed to increase his attractiveness, complained the medicine had been no use and demanded his money back.

A small crowd gathered and one of Makota's men, sensing an opportunity for mischief, demanded Mr Murray show them his male member, claiming it was necessary for the merchant to see if there was enough material for the magic to work on.

The result, as one might well imagine, was an extremely angry Scot in a street brawl with half a dozen Malays which left him with a black eye, torn trousers, and a reluctance to show his face in the town that lasted a full week.

While I enjoyed the surveyor's discomfiture, the sinister purpose behind the incident was all too clear. For Mr Brooke, in particular, such insults against his men—and, by implication, himself—were difficult to bear. He was, and remains, a proud man, for all his easy ways. Yet he had no choice but to accept the situation. For Makota was right; he was in the ascendant. Every day the Sultan prevaricated, James saw the prize slipping further from his grasp. Even when Makota extended his campaign and attacks on British sailors about the town became an almost daily event, there was little he could do. To appeal for the protection of the Sultan would be to admit he was weak and further damage his claim.

So we doubled the watch aboard, refused shore leave for overnight visits, and ensured our men travelled in groups when they had business in the town. And still Mr Brooke and I, though now escorted by a guard of half a dozen armed men, would make our way to the audience hall for yet more talk.

It was about two months after the victory at Siniawan that things came to a head. For several days we had attended the Sultan and then been joined by Makota, ostensibly for social pleasantries but, in fact, so the Sultan could try to negotiate simultaneously with Mr Brooke and his enemy. We feared it was significant that Budrudeen was not invited to these gatherings.

Makota would always be accompanied by two or three men of his and so we had decided Mr Brooke, too, should have an escort in the hall, as well as the men who would wait outside, exchanging suspicious glances with Makota's bodyguard. Our escort was to be Will Spence, on the grounds that he was one of those who had been foremost in the charge at Balidah. Will was to be the guest of the Sultan, alongside Mr Brooke and myself, and this was something of an honour.

On this occasion, when the Sultan called for tea to be

brought in, Makota rose to his feet and raised a stoppered gourd in his hands. "Your Highness," he said, bowing to Hassim, "today I would have James Brooke drink something special. Today, I have brought rice liquor, distilled by the people of the forest: a suitable drink for a mighty warrior. Today, I would have the Englishman drink to the future of Sarawak in the liquor of her people."

Mr Brooke and I both smelled a rat, for this was hardly like Makota, but we could not see what the trick was. But James thought he saw a way to avoid whatever Makota was planning and to do Will a good turn at the same time. "I thank you for your kindness, sir," he replied, very stiff and formal. "Yet I was but one of those who oversaw the destruction of the Sultan's enemies. The task was accomplished by our loyal followers, such as Will here. It should be his honour to raise the toast." And he passed the gourd to Will.

There are those who say James knew what was to happen and Will was sacrificed to his political ambition, but this is to wrong the man I know. Remember, this was in our early days in the country. Mr Brooke was still entranced by the romance of it all. He was like a boy playing in a new nursery. Sarawak was his toy cupboard and Hassim, Makota, and the rest were toys to be played with and admired. Yes, Makota could be wily and deceitful, but it never occurred to Mr Brooke he could present a real danger.

As the gourd was passed to Will, I saw a look of fury on Makota's face. For an instant I was uneasy, but I reassured myself this simply showed that James had done the right thing. There was clearly something tricky about the toast, but if Will were to put a word out of place or cause offence in any way, it would be easy to explain he was but a common sailor and his error should count for nothing. The Sultan would have to overlook it. Of course, if Mr Brooke made any mistake, Makota would insist it was further evidence of his ignorance of the country and that he was unfit to rule.

Will came forward, blushing scarlet, and took the gourd. He raised it with a simple toast: "To Sarawak and all who love her." The Sultan beamed, Makota scowled, Will tipped back the gourd, took a deep swig...and fell to the floor in convulsions.

Immediately all was confusion. James knelt at Will's side, calling me to run for Hart, who had some simple skill in medicine. The Sultan's guards rushed forward, Hassim himself shouting that his physician be brought. Servants screamed, messengers seemed to be rushing everywhere...and in the chaos, Makota and his escort quietly slipped away.

❋

WILL'S BODY WAS BURIED that very afternoon. It is a hot country and there seemed nothing to gain by delay.

Budrudeen arrived on the *Royalist* in the evening. He met alone with Mr Brooke for an hour. Even I was not allowed to join their deliberations, but all aboard knew what must have been discussed. When I was summoned, the decision had been taken. Makota's attempt on Mr Brooke's life had been a step too far. If we did not strike back, Makota would act openly against both James and Budrudeen. If it came to fighting, Makota could summon more men than could Budrudeen and we would be beaten. The only hope was to strike immediately, while Makota was still unsure what we would do. Further, Will's death had provided Mr Brooke with the perfect opportunity to act decisively in his own interests whilst ostensibly avenging the murder of one of his men.

Although it was late, the crew waited on deck. The men were angry after the murder and they sensed the day's doings were not yet over. Mr Hart, Mr Murray, and myself were each told to gather four men we could trust and to join ourselves each to one of Budrudeen's most trusted lieutenants. Mr Brooke joined Budrudeen himself.

Budrudeen had brought with him a substantial bodyguard

and, it now transpired, twenty or thirty more armed men waited ready at his own compound. So, an hour after our conference ended, four groups of Malays and Englishmen together moved quietly through the night toward the homes of Makota and his three principal allies.

My own part in that night's work was easily enough accomplished. The fellow we had been sent to secure was the least of the conspirators and had not even thought to put an armed guard at his door. A couple of his men tried to prevent us from seizing him and were soundly beaten for their pains. We returned to the *Royalist* with our prisoner still half asleep and by no means certain what was happening to him.

Mr Hart apparently had almost as easy a task. The sole guard at the door was silently disposed of by one of the Malays who slipped up behind him in the shadows and slit open his throat. Apparently he had a wicked little knife, useful for such exercises, the *kris* being more suited to stabbing and thus a weapon of open warfare. With the guard dead, and the household taken by surprise, the second of the conspirators had been easy enough to capture.

Mr Murray's night was more eventful. Unfortunately, as Mr Murray explained at length, no decent Scot could fall upon an enemy without fair warning, so he had insisted they openly challenge the gate guard at Mupata's compound—Mupata being the conspirator it was his part to apprehend. The result was the household had fallen to arms and our raiding party was forced to fight its way in.

Despite Mr Murray, we had the advantage of surprise and Mupata's men, woken from sleep by our assault, were overwhelmed with only a few cuts sustained on our side, though at least two of them were killed. Mupata himself fought alongside his men and his bruised and bleeding countenance showed he had not been taken easily.

It was Mr Brooke's party, though, who had the greatest tales of martial valour to relate. James, for all the deadly earnest of the night's activities, returned in the greatest of good spirits. He held court in his cabin, reliving the events of the previous hour. "You know how big Makota's place is," he started. "There's half a dozen houses in there and the palisade must be fifty yards on each side. Which makes it difficult to get to the gate without being seen. Makota must have been worried we'd try something because there were two guards on the gate and both keeping a good lookout.

"Well, we got two of the lads to roll along toward the gate, feigning drunk, while the rest of us kept back out of sight, but the guards were having none of it and called for a couple of men from inside to see them off. There's nothing for it but for our lads to draw their dirks while the rest of us started running for the gate screaming like billy-o and waving cold steel like something out of a storybook. Some of Budrudeen's men were carrying spears and by the time we reached the lads, one of Makota's chaps had a spear sticking out of his thigh and was squealing like a stuck pig. Our lads saw the other villain off, and so the whole pack of us charged for the gate, which someone had the sense to try to close—it having been left open for the guards to go to and fro."

Makota's men had been too slow to realise the danger they were in and at first thought they could make a stand in the gateway. By the time they started to close the gate, our rush was already on them and, as it swung to, a dozen men were already throwing themselves against it from the outside.

It must have been a strange sight—European seamen and the tall brown bodies of the Malays, pushing against the gate in the flickering light of the torches Makota kept burning beside his palisade. In the crush, none could make real use of their weapons, but they were pushing and striking with their naked fists as our force first blocked the door from closing and then, inch by inch, pushed it back.

Mr Brooke's eyes sparkled with excitement. "Once we were in the compound, it was a free fight, each man for himself." He seemed to hear again the ring of steel on steel as *kris* and dirk were brought into play. The torchlight made the whole scene seem unreal. The blood, suddenly welling from the chest of one of their foes, showed black, not red and, despite the screams of the wounded and the cries of the dying, it was almost like a dream. "Makota himself held back but we fought our way through to him."

In fact, it had been James himself who was the first to reach the architect of Spence's death. He had armed himself with a sword, rather than the shorter dirk used by most of the men, and cut his way ruthlessly across the compound. I learned afterwards he had slain two of Makota's followers himself and wounded three others.

"We had brought ropes but when we reached him, he sank to his knees and ordered his men to cease resistance. Then he allowed us to march him away with no struggle. All his pride seemed to have left him—he was quite pathetic, really." Mr Brooke smiled and raised a glass, and we went on to talk of the other captures we had made.

I think Makota was almost forgotten by the others, full of excitement as they were. But I slipped out as soon as I decently could and looked forward to where a Malay guard kept watch over our four captives. Makota sat against the port bulwark, hunched into himself. Even across the deck, I could see his shoulders shaking and I knew he was weeping. He was dressed in the plain robe he had seized when he leapt from his bed, awakened by the fighting. I remembered the gorgeously clad, self-important figure we had met when we first joined the Grand Army and, despite Will Spence, despite all he had done, I felt a pity for the man.

EARLY THE NEXT MORNING, before Makota's faction had any opportunity to react to the night's events, Budrudeen arrived at the quayside with an escort of warriors, dressed in their padded coats, spears and *kris* at the ready. The four prisoners were bound at the wrist and led from the *Royalist* to join their escort. Most of the crew fell in behind Budrudeen's men and we marched smartly toward Hassim's audience hall.

The Sultan was obviously already aware of what had happened. There were more guards than usual standing at the foot of the stairs to the hall, but we were passed through without delay, Budrudeen's men using their spears to prod the prisoners, none too gently, into the hall.

The Sultan was waiting, visibly tense. Around him, those of Budrudeen's faction looked more confident than we had seen them in weeks while the majority, who had backed Makota as the victor in this struggle, were clearly terrified by what had transpired.

Mr Brooke and Budrudeen had agreed Makota and the other captives were to be formally arraigned before the Sultan for their criminal actions. As Budrudeen was familiar with the forms of the court, it was left to him to address Hassim. He stepped forward, bowed to the Sultan, and started his speech.

"Brother! I come before you as my Sultan to seek justice for myself and *Tuan* Brooke, for we have been much wronged. Yet the wrongs done to us are of no significance to the wrongs you yourself have suffered at the hands of those we bring before your judgement."

He gestured at the prisoners, who were promptly pushed to the floor by their guards. Makota opened his mouth, as if he were about to speak, but a kick from one of Budrudeen's men apparently made him think better of it.

"These men conspired together to kill *Tuan* Brooke," Budrudeen continued. "They killed one of his loyal followers, Will Spence, who fought nobly and bravely for you, my Sultan, against the rebels of Siniawan. But their blow was not aimed at *Tuan* Brooke alone. For these despicable villains," (and I swear those were, as near as I can translate, the words he used) "these ungrateful dogs intended, by striking at my friend, to strike at me. And by striking at myself, however unworthy I may be in my own person, they struck at the Royal household and at you."

Now this, in essence, was true but coming on a bit thick. For Budrudeen was implying open revolt, where Makota had sought only to strengthen one faction against another, with no intention of overthrowing the Sultan directly. Why should he, after all? A weak Sultan under the control of his allies in Brunei left him free to do what he would.

I waited for Mr Brooke to intervene, for this was fast turning into a trial for treason, but he stood impassive. Nothing being said came as any surprise to him.

I remembered Budrudeen and James had been closeted alone for an hour the previous night. Now I knew what they had been plotting. Makota and his allies were to be crushed absolutely.

Makota, too, could see the way the wind was blowing. He knelt not ten feet from Hassim and again and again would raise his head to interrupt Budrudeen's indictment. Each time he was kicked or struck with the butt of a spear until he dropped his head again. Sometimes he cried out, but Hassim looked coolly past him, nodding as Budrudeen continued his speech.

"Makota has been honoured by you. He was the governor of this province, yet he was not loyal. He led your Grand Army, yet he was not true. He was welcome in your court, yet he plotted against you. Yesterday, he brought poison to kill the man who would shield you from your enemies. He sought to destroy the man you would have take his place to rule this country. *Tuan* Brooke is loyal. *Tuan* Brooke is true. *Tuan* Brooke has sought only to further your interests and strengthen your rule."

Budrudeen had got into his stride and was larding it on, but Mr Brooke stood there looking stern and Hassim seemed content enough with the turn of events, a small smile playing about his lips. Makota had given up any effort to speak and crouched on his knees, moaning continuously.

Budrudeen allowed himself a few more minutes to remind

the court what a splendid chap James Brooke was and how he had won the war, and how the *Tuan* Brooke deserved every honour. Then he turned to Makota and his co-conspirators.

Budrudeen had done his homework. He didn't just talk of what had happened over the past few weeks. He told the court Makota had been creaming off revenues that should have been passed to the Sultan and keeping them for himself. This was not news, of course. Even Hassim knew it was happening—it was the way of the country. But now Budrudeen told everyone how much Makota had stolen this year, last year, and the year before. I have no idea if the figures were true but Makota was in no position to dispute them, grovelling on the floor, with blood running from a cut on his cheek where the guard had pummelled him over-enthusiastically with the spear butt.

Everyone gasped at the figures and all put on a great show of shock and astonishment, especially those who had been close to the disgraced governor and now had every reason to display their surprise at learning of his crimes.

Budrudeen then listed every legal dispute Makota had judged where it was claimed he had taken bribes to influence his verdict. As everyone who lost a court case in Sarawak would claim their opponent had bribed the judge, this was a long list. It was ridiculous—no evidence was presented but it was clear the court was satisfied Makota's guilt was being established.

The governor's failings as Commander of the Grand Army were described in detail. I knew from my own experience these were legion, but whether all stemmed from corruption or whether most simply reflected his incompetence, I could not say. In this court, though, all were presented as proof of his treachery.

Finally, for good measure, Budrudeen accused him of beating his wife and sleeping with his daughter. Then he demanded the Sultan order all four conspirators be put to death.

Makota was dragged to his feet and asked what defence he could offer. By now, the wretched man could see it was hopeless. He had been accused of so many things, some true, some not, many too vague to respond to. He had been dragged from his bed and spent the night in mortal terror aboard the *Royalist*. He had been beaten throughout Budrudeen's speech. The wonder of it was he was able to make any coherent reply at all.

"I kneel before you, your Highness, as one who has sought always the best for this land. I have been in error but I have never intended you any harm. The *Tuan* Brooke is a great man and he is known for his mercy. My life is forfeit to him. Let him speak for me."

It was Makota's last throw…and a cunning one. Mr Brooke had already shown himself, in that court, to favour mercy over strict justice. Makota was humbled, his power destroyed. Mr Brooke could beg the Sultan for his life and Makota would be forever in his debt. Hassim could be seen as both just and merciful. Everyone would be satisfied and no more blood need be spilled.

We all turned to James to hear him speak.

He looked straight at Makota and spoke in Malay. He was word-perfect and I knew he must have practised beforehand what he was to say. "Makota is a traitor and a murderer. I cannot speak for him or those who follow him. Your lives are truly forfeit, not to me but to your Sultan. Let him take that from you which you no longer deserve to hold."

There was a hush, broken by a long piercing cry from Makota and the despairing sobbing of the other three prisoners who, until this point, had reasonably expected to escape with their own lives, even if their leader did not.

Hassim looked at Mr Brooke as if he could hardly believe what he had heard. He seemed suddenly older. Then he nodded and pronounced sentence. In the circumstances, he had no real choice.

The four men were dragged to the door, all wailing now. There was a pool of urine where one had lost control of his bladder.

They were pushed down the steep steps. Mupata tripped and fell. I think he may have broken his ankle, for he could not walk from the steps, however much he was beaten, but in the end he was half-carried into the middle of the square to join the other three.

Our men were still there, as were Budrudeen's, and they had been joined by crowds of others as news of what was afoot had spread through the town. The conspirators were prodded into a row and knelt facing the audience hall. Four of the Sultan's guards stood behind them.

Hassim appeared at the top of the steps, looked down at Makota, and nodded to the guards.

Each of the guards carried a *kris* of unusual thickness. These did not have the familiar wavy blade but were straight, vicious daggers. In their left hands, each guard carried a wad of cloth. On Hassim's nod, they put the wadded cloths against their victims' backs and stabbed through the cloth, between the back ribs and into the hearts of Makota and the other three.

The men pitched forward to the ground and the blades were withdrawn.

The wadding soaked up the blood.

THAT AFTERNOON, HASSIM FORMALLY announced that James Brooke was to be honoured with the title of Rajah and he and his heirs were to be set in rule over Sarawak for all time.

# Chapter 5

THERE WAS NO TIME over the next few days to dwell on the detail of how Mr Brooke had finally achieved his goal. He and Budrudeen were both determined to see him formally installed as quickly as possible but with the greatest ceremony we could manage. So all of us were kept busy, cleaning, drilling, planning, and sending messengers—or being sent—all about the country to drum up a crowd for the great day.

Mr Brooke did have the sense to see I was troubled about what had happened, but he simply said it was inevitable. "I had to do it, John," he said. "I owed it to Will Spence and his memory." Which is as close to an outright lie as I ever heard him come. He did it because he wanted Sarawak. That's all there was to it.

If anyone had any doubt about how much being made a Rajah meant to him, they had only to see him rushing from place to place, preparing for the day of what was, I suppose, his coronation.

He wanted to see representatives of all the parties in the country there at the ceremony, so Budrudeen's *prahus* were pressed into service to spread the news from village to village. The *Skimalong* travelled to Siniawan so the leaders of the people there could attend the investiture of the man who had saved their lives. Messengers were sent to those of Makota's followers who had slipped quietly away from Kuching, guaranteeing their safety should they return for the celebration. He even overcame his antipathy for the Chinese, making sure the word went out in their community that their presence would be appreciated.

For some days before the event, Kuching was busy with strangers travelling in from all over Sarawak. The ordinary natives, the Dyak people of the forests, came in ones and twos in their dugout canoes or in groups of warriors in feathered headdresses, rowing war canoes big enough to take out to sea. Chinese traders arrived from their outposts along the rivers of the country, while all the important Malay families made sure to send representatives to demonstrate their loyalty.

Hassim was organising a feast to mark the occasion and the streets were full of the sounds of pigs, chickens, and goats. The news that there was a growing market for foodstuffs brought more traders, and Kuching was bursting at the seams by the time the great day arrived.

The ceremonies started in the morning with solemn speeches in the audience chamber. Documents were brought out, signed, sealed, and witnessed. It was at that moment, strictly speaking, Mr Brooke started his rule. It was very quiet and dignified. It didn't seem real. Afterwards, we all took tea and then Rajah Brooke retired to the *Royalist*.

The afternoon saw the public inauguration, which was more like what I had in mind as a coronation. We started in the audience hall again. As this was to be the public ceremony, the place was packed. James had dressed in formal European clothes, his dark suit looking strangely out of place amongst the loin-clothed Dyaks, the robed Malays, and the Chinese in their embroidered shirts and loose trousers. Budrudeen led him into the room and formally presented him to the Sultan. The new Rajah knelt and bowed his head.

A scribe handed Hassim a roll of parchment. The Sultan unrolled it and began to read. Mr Brooke, still kneeling in a suit made for a European climate, struggled to remain still and dignified while the Sultan spoke. "People of Sarawak! I, Sultan Muda Hassim, ruler of all Borneo, guardian of the Faith, liege lord of the peoples of Brunei, of Sarawak…"

He read quietly, but not one of the list of titles was missed and all listened in silence as Hassim carefully spelt out his right to the province. "And, therefore, having regard to the interests of all my subject peoples of the country of Sarawak and making such provision for their better governance as seems to my judgement most right and necessary…"

James told me afterward he thought he would stifle in his high collar and had to fight a desperate urge to yawn. This was Hassim's last act of rule in Sarawak and he seemed determined to enjoy it for as long as possible.

"…make over the entire government and revenues of the country of Sarawak and its dependencies to my beloved friend, James Brooke…"

Hassim was still speaking but not a word could now be heard above the cheering in the room. Outside, the crowd packing the square joined in the shouting. From Hassim's palace came the crash of guns sounding their salute and I heard the *Royalist*'s artillery echoing their congratulations.

Budrudeen stepped up to Mr Brooke and took his arm, moving him toward the door where he would be seen by the crowd below. As they passed I heard Budrudeen say, "Seize your chance. They will cheer anything, if you but put it to them now."

Mr Brooke stepped into the doorway, raising his arms for silence. Below he saw hundreds of his new subjects. Some cheered because they hated Makota and celebrated his destruction. Some cheered because they had served at Siniawan and would follow their victorious leader on whatever path he chose. The Chinese cheered because they saw firm government as allowing them to flourish. The Dyaks cheered because they hoped for an end to the corruption of Malay rule. Most, though, cheered simply because it was a holiday. There was a new leader; at an official celebration, it was safer to cheer.

Standing within the hall, looking through the door to the crowd below, I think I realised for the first time the enormity of what we had done. I think it was then, too, James first recognised the task he had set himself. Up to that moment I think he had convinced himself running a country would be easy—a grand experiment, whether it should succeed or fail. It was only now, with the crowd waiting for him to speak, that he felt the full weight of the responsibility he had taken on. In towns and villages, in longhouses and tiny huts, thousands—he had no idea even of how many thousands—of men, women, and children must turn to him as their leader. Here was no parliament, no constitution, no check on his power. Everything these people had, even their very lives, was his to command.

For a moment, I saw—or felt I saw—a flicker of uncertainty, an uncharacteristic self-doubt on his face. And then it was as if he had accepted this as his destiny. His dark eyes seemed to grow luminous with the intensity of his desire to take these people to him and love them and be loved by them in his turn. And he looked beautiful. As I saw him, standing there, I think I realised for the first time that I loved him.

I know he had prepared a speech. He had tried it out on me and it was a good speech. But the speech he made was not the speech he had rehearsed. He never knew where the words came from, but I heard him speaking with a quiet new confidence, a consciousness of power, of rights and duties, that seemed to lead him on, scarcely even pausing to think.

"People of Sarawak! We are joined in a great enterprise. Our country has been riven by war; many are on the brink of famine. Sectional interests have been allowed to prevail over the good of the whole." There was a nervous shuffling from the pangerans behind him and he hurried on. "Your customs and religion I am sworn to protect."

This was more straightforward. The crowd recovered from its initial confusion enough to manage a cheer, but James hardly paused. "I have seen your lives here in Sarawak and, in a small way, I have shared your lives with you. I have seen how you toil to raise your crops. I have joined your feasts when you have, with strength and cunning, brought pig or deer or monkey home from the hunt. And I have seen you are a great and noble people."

Before him, the crowd cheered again—and the almost naked Dyak savages, many of them in Kuching for the first time in their lives, cheered most of all.

James paused, looking at the crowd, and every man there felt he looked at them. That he spoke to each one of them. "Yet you live poorly, who should live well. The mineral wealth of this country lies unmined in its rocks. You do not trade. When you have dealings, one with another, you do not seek to build together but to dominate or exploit. A land that could give wealth to all becomes a land of war and want."

The crowd was silent now, responding to the change in his tone. Budrudeen repeated his words in Malay and there was some sombre nodding. Then he continued, positive and enthusiastic again, with the boyish charm that belied his years.

"I come to you as your new ruler, not to take from you but to give to you. I will guide and protect you so you may trade freely amongst yourselves and with the wider world. I will be your envoy so the produce of this country can be sold across the globe.

"With your courage, the natural wealth of the land, the nobility of your Sultan, and the vision we share for the future, I pledge myself to a better life for all who share Sarawak."

Budrudeen finished his translation and the crowd went wild. James bowed to Hassim, bowed again to the crowd and, escorted by the men of the *Royalist* and a guard from Budrudeen's household, he made his way back to the ship.

❋

THAT NIGHT WE WATCHED from the *Royalist* as the Chinese welcomed their new ruler with a spectacular display of fireworks. Afterward, I dined in his cabin with the officers, as had become our custom. James drank well but I swear he was not drunk and I remained talking with him a while when the rest had noisily departed.

He was so happy, like a child who at Christmas finds all the gifts he could ever have desired given him in one glorious heap. He told me he had everything he could wish. That he would build himself a home in Kuching and would reign over the people there for the rest of his life.

"And you, John," he asked, "will you stay here with me?"

I thought of how he had looked at the moment of his triumph and of how I had found myself moved by him. He had roused feelings I had never felt before or, if I had, I had not seen them for what they were. "Of course I will stay with you," I replied. "I will be for you whatever you want me to be."

Suddenly we were both laughing in sheer delight at this moment and all that had led to it, and he wrapped his arms round me and then he kissed me.

It seemed the most natural thing in the world.

Afterward we looked at each other a moment, in silence, then I made some remark about having things to attend to and I left.

The next day we did not speak of it. But it was real. And neither of us was sorry it had happened.

IT WAS A SIN. I know that. It is an abomination in the eyes of the Lord. And I pray I may be forgiven.

Yet if we sinned, why was it that those first weeks and months of Rajah Brooke's rule were so full of hope and happiness? Hassim set off back to Brunei. He had appropriated Makota's *prahu* and my last meeting with him was in the luxuriously appointed cabin where we had first met Makota. It was the morning of his departure and he was happier than I had ever seen him, grinning like a monkey now his troubles in Sarawak were over. He made his formal farewells to Mr Brooke and then turned and spoke directly to me for the first time in all the months I had known him. "I can see that you love my friend," he said. "Look after him."

And he gave me a ring, with a great ruby in it. I have it still.

Budrudeen stayed on for a while so he could ease any difficulties with the pangerans. He, too, was swept up with the enthusiasm of the moment. He had decided James must have a palace and the two of them would spend hours planning it together. Budrudeen insisted he would see it built as his gift, leaving James to get on with the business of rule.

Even Murray came out of himself. For all his faults, the man was a good surveyor and now, at last, he had the freedom of the country. James was anxious to travel and find out more about the practical conditions in the place, allowing Murray the chance to make a start on mapping the rivers that held Sarawak together.

I went with them. Despite his efforts, James was not yet fluent in Malay and could speak scarcely a word of the Dyak tongue. I had spent much of my time studying the language from those tribesmen who visited Kuching and was thus already able to understand enough to be of value.

We took the *Skimalong* and a crew of six, beside James, Mr Murray, and myself. We were away for weeks exploring the country. On the river Sadong we rode the bore, being carried ten miles in scarcely more than half a hour. By contrast, on the Skrang, the *Skimalong* had to push its way through the narrowest reaches of the river, where fallen trees and bolting vegetation almost blocked our path and we were lucky to travel ten miles in a day.

Here and there a branch would project from the jungle far into the river and we would see a huge lizard basking in the sun. Little *kera* monkeys peered out from the bushes beside waterfalls that dropped sheer down creeper-hidden cliffs; leaf monkeys, proud in their bright red hair, leapt easily from tree to tree, swinging their long tails for balance and never missing their landing; crocodiles scuttled nervously from their basking grounds, vanishing into the muddy brown water as the *Skimalong* approached.

And on every river we would find the homes of the Dyaks. I had heard of their longhouses where a whole tribe would live together under one roof but I was still astonished when I first saw one. It was on the one of the tributary rivers that ran into the Sarawak to make its way, eventually, through Kuching. The building was close to the water's edge and, like almost all the buildings of the country, it was supported on high timber posts. The posts were of hard wood and resisted the attacks of insects that would devour the bamboo used to make the walls of these places. Everything appeared to have been knocked together in the most casual manner imaginable. Yet, even without the use of nails or screws, the buildings survived for years, and their ramshackle nature produced dwellings that remained cool and pleasant even on the hottest and most humid of days.

Nothing about the construction, then, was out of the ordinary but, although the name 'longhouse' should have forewarned me, I was astonished by just how long it was. The building must have stretched twenty or thirty yards. All along the length of one side was a great hall, with little cells partitioned along it to provide what privacy the inhabitants might want. The other side was open to the air, forming one huge balcony where the women of the tribe were preparing food or busy at their looms (for the Dyaks are famous for their weaving). We were welcomed into the great hall, with the whole tribe joining us in that elongated space. The young men were decked out in their finery of war bonnets and loincloths while the women were wrapped elegantly in brightly coloured sarongs. The children—mostly naked—ran here and there through the crowd.

Despite the numbers, the hall provided room for all and enough space for ceremonial dancing. As day moved to evening, a feast was brought in and we all sat together, Englishmen and natives, sharing our food and toasting each other as if it were the most natural thing in the world.

As the days passed, we travelled further into the jungles that made up Mr Brooke's new realm. We met with Sibnyow and Bukar, Brang and Sabungo. On every hidden waterway, there was a longhouse, and every tribe we met was different. Here, none ever ventured from the longhouse without the sumpitan; there the blowpipe was never used. Here, the men all bore elaborate tattoos; there tattooing was unknown. Here the women went naked save for their sarongs; there a dress of bamboo was worn above it.

Everywhere their new Rajah travelled, his reputation travelled before him. Here was the man who had saved the lives of the rebels of Siniawan. This was the man who had brought down Makota. The Rajah Brooke would save the Dyaks from the oppression of the Malays. They welcomed him as a brother and took him into their hearts.

He would sit late with the chiefs, drinking the powerful rice wine of the longhouses and, as the liquor eased their tongues, they would tell him the nature of Makota's rule. In the tribe of the Sintah, the chief waved in the direction of his people's fruit groves, hidden in the darkness. The government, he said, was like a fruit tree. There was food on the tree for all the birds of the forest. He raised the calabash and drank deeply while James waited to see where this analogy was leading.

The old man put the drink aside and continued. "Under Pangeran Makota's government, the big birds pecked the smaller ones and drove them away and would not allow them to have food. We were little birds and we were pecked very hard. There is a saying—what is the pleasure of eating the plantain if you must sit on the thorn? So it was with Pangeran Makota—he gave us a little, which was the plantain, and he asked a great deal, which was the thorn. I want to eat no such plantains."

It was the one thing that never varied. Wherever we went, we heard tales of how Makota had impoverished the country,

sending useless items to the chiefs and demanding they be purchased for large sums. We heard how Makota's agents would
claim first right to buy the Dyaks' produce at a price of their
own choosing.

Nor was it Makota's greed alone that oppressed the people.
His power was upheld by a legion of officials and captains and
all demanded their share. The same boat would be seized by
three different officials claiming a right by the authority vested
in them, and the unlucky boatman would not only lose his vessel but have to find other goods to placate the men who's 'right'
to the boat had been pre-empted.

Each evening, as the tree frogs started their chorus and the
bush crickets set up their mechanical wailing, the men would
come and James would listen to them as the sounds of evening
gave way to the sounds of night—the pulsating, monotonous
buzz of the ground crickets, the scuttling of moonrats hunting
worms in the jungle litter, the tell-tale crack of timber as ele-
phants crashed through the forest.

It was in these conversations with the Dyak people that
James first came to realise the impact of piracy on Sarawak. Of
course we had known there were pirates in these waters. European vessels had been attacked and the *Royalist* was by no
means unusual in carrying cannon to defend herself. What we
had not realised was the pirates were also active inland…and
they were tolerated by the rulers of the country.

The clearest example of the hold these villains held over the
people came with a messenger from the Lundu people. He paddled alone in a primitive canoe hollowed out from a log and
caught up with us one night as we sat about the fire beside a
longhouse some five days journey from his tribe.

He had come, he said, that the new Rajah should hear the
story of his people. They could not invite the Rajah to visit
them in their longhouse for they had no longhouse that he
might visit. Yet their story, he said, must be told.

"Our home was a happy one; none who came to us wanted.

The fruit on the trees was saved, the fish in the river near us was never destroyed, rice was plenty. The fish, the fruit, and the rice were preserved that the Malays might eat of them; yet they had no pity on us. We were few, but the same demands were made upon us as though we were many. We begged for mercy but we were told if we did not pay all that was demanded of us, the pirates would come. We gave what we could, but it was not enough. Now our longhouse is no more. Our people are fled to the jungle. Many of our men have been killed and our women and children enslaved. We have heard you are a good man. Can you not stop this terror?"

The news of the level of piracy and the impact it was having on the country had the effect of depressing James' mood toward the end of this trip, but his spirits lifted immediately on our return to Kuching. Budrudeen had been true to his word and James' new house was already near completion. It had been built in the style affected by Europeans in India—built low to the ground, rather than on piles like most of the native buildings. It was also floored with wood, like Hassim's audience chamber, rather than bamboo, like most of the other houses in the town. The rooms were light and airy, the building surrounded by a sheltered veranda where the household could take the air spared from the worst of the sun.

James forgot the grand problems of rule in the immediate concerns of moving in. His cabin on the *Royalist* was stripped to the bare essentials as desk and chairs were shifted ashore. More furniture was ordered from the local carpenters. Colin Hart was driven to distraction as James ordered that the best of the crockery and cutlery aboard the *Royalist* be transferred to his house, while the steward pleaded he be allowed the means of presenting dinner properly aboard the ship. Bookcases appeared in the room James had designated as his library and a chest in his cabin was opened to reveal a score of books that was to be the nucleus of his collection.

The move into the new house was an important time for

me, as well. Since we had kissed that night, I had been unable to deny in myself an unnatural affection for Mr Brooke. The situation of the ship and the continual proximity of others as we explored the country in the *Skimalong* meant we had been unable to talk about our feelings. In any case, I do not know we would have spoken much. James has never been one for introspection and I was not, in those days, a great one for talking about my feelings. Indeed, were I able to express myself freely in conversation, I might not be driven to open my heart in writing as I do now.

Though we did not speak of these things, we both knew our hearts. I would watch him as he went about his business, still seeming so young in those days, his eyes so full of life—but so capable of tenderness when he caught me looking at him. He moved easily and had a grace that made him ever seem a more natural ruler than Hassim. He smiled often and whoever he smiled on would feel, for a moment, their lives had been touched by a special charm. He was the most beautiful man I ever saw.

Yet the Good Book says: *If a man also lie with mankind, as he lieth with a woman, both of them have committed an abomination.* Although I was not much of a one for church, I had always tried to live a Christian life. Indeed, I had congratulated myself I had not indulged in fornication, as have so many of my shipmates, not realising my nature, and they were tempted in ways I had not been tempted.

But I was tempted then. James offered me love and a security I had not known since my mother had died. I could move into his house with him and live in a luxury I had no other chance of knowing.

These temptations I could resist but there was more. James offered me a world I could never enter otherwise. He could read and write—and in those days, for all my skill in languages, I could do neither. He was a gentleman, the son of a judge. He had manners and learning and a way of talking—all superior in every way to mine. And yet he offered me an entrance way into his world. He did it because he loved me.

That, even, I might have been able to resist, except for one thing. I do not ask you to understand but I beg you will not condemn. For, in simple truth, I loved him, too.

So it was I joined him in his new home. Officially, I was to live there to be always on hand in case he needed to talk business at any hour and required my services as interpreter. Indeed, this was not so fanciful an idea, for his home was always open to the people of the country and the Dyaks would often slip quietly into his house to talk with their ruler. James sat cross-legged on his veranda, two or three natives squatting before him, and they talked of the country and the state of the crops and when the pigs might migrate from the mountains and whether, when they did, the hunting would be good. I usually attended and might translate now and again, when some grievance led a petitioner to talk heatedly and at length. Usually, though, James understood what was said and his ability to converse with people in the various dialects of the country grew apace.

I look around me now, at this fine room in a grand house in Singapore, and think with such longing of those first days. I remember the evenings looking out across the river, the sound of crickets in the dusk, and the smell of the bougainvillaea, heavy and sweet on the breeze. It was, I realise now, the best of the times we were to know. Then, though, it seemed but the opening of a new period that would see James Brooke the ruler of a prosperous and happy land and me as his favoured and devoted companion.

# Chapter 6

THE PIRATES WERE THE root of the problems.

Ever since he had learned of the predations of the pirates and the impact they had upon the country, James knew he would have to take some measures to stop them, though I think he would have delayed in any dramatic action if he could. The pirates of Sarawak were not isolated groups of individuals but organised raiding parties. Pirate attacks were often, in effect, inter-tribal battles. Any attempt to wipe out piracy would, he knew, take more than a few men in a gig breaking the odd native head. The country had barely ended years of civil war. James had no intention of involving himself in more fighting if he could avoid it.

Instead, he concerned himself with setting up an agency in Singapore to deal in the antimony that was the main mineral wealth of the country. He bought a new ship, the *Swift*, to carry antimony to its markets and had new quays built in Kuching to facilitate the loading of the ore. He sat up late into the night with Murray, putting the surveyor's studies into order and undertaking the first systematic audit of the country's resources.

He had books sent from London and built up a library of authors like Adam Smith and John Stuart Mill. I would watch him reading for hours on end, and he would tell me that in these books the great minds of our time and of the past had set down their thoughts for the enlightenment of all men. It was then I decided I wanted to learn to read and James, with all his other tasks and concerns, would yet put them all aside to teach me. So, alongside Malthus' *Essay on the Principle of Population* and a collection of seed catalogues was a copy of *Mother Goose* and an illustrated alphabet, such as might be found in a nursery.

At first I found it difficult to master the trick of reading. I had a good ear for language but could not take in words through my eyes. James would sit next to me, encouraging me with occasional hugs and gentle smiles, while he traced out the letters and taught me the sounds.

Sometimes he would lose patience and speak harshly to me, calling me dim-witted and a dunce. I had told him about my early life living on a farm and he could throw this against me, saying I was naught but a stupid farm boy. On occasion he could reduce me to tears, but then he would take my head in his hands and kiss me, telling me he was angry only because he loved me and wanted me to learn more quickly. Often this would be the end of our studies for the day as we would embrace and forget all about letters and reading.

Generally James was a good and kind teacher. I have a sweet tooth and he would keep a supply of the candied fruits the Chinese so enjoy. When I made progress he would feed them to me, one by one, and so my progress was swift and steady.

As soon as I began to read, James was anxious I learn to write, and I was introduced to the mysteries of quill and inkpot. Indeed, I was really taught with a quill, as steel nibs had to be shipped especially from Singapore and they were expensive while fine feathers were readily to hand. I found a pleasure in cutting and using a quill that I have never found in writing with a mechanical contrivance and I believe learning in this style accounts for my fine penmanship today, a quality often commented on by those who know nothing of my lack of early education. In those first days, though, I struggled to scratch out anything legible and, again, James would cajole and tease me, smiling at my successes and usually tolerant of my failures.

We could have gone on in this way for years, studying methods to improve the economy of the country and patiently implementing them step by step. Barely six months into his rule, though, I was in the town when cries from the riverbank made me hurry to the new quay to see what was the cause of the agitation.

It was a line of Dyak war canoes. They were more solidly built than the Malay *prahus*. (Later I was to learn each one would hold some seventy to eighty men.) Like the Malay craft, the rowers sat below a fighting platform. On each boat, warriors stood on the platforms, posturing and waving their swords.

The craft were pulling up the river line astern, their sweeps churning the water in time to the beat of brass war-gongs, silk pennants flying. From stem to stern the platforms were fringed with decorations that bobbed up and down with the motion of the vessels. At first I could not make out what these were but as they drew nearer, I realised with horror they were human skulls.

I ran back toward the house to join James. There I found him with a telescope to his eye, looking out at the approaching fleet.

"They're pirates, John," James said, without taking his eye from the telescope. "Sea Dyaks—mainly Sakarran, with some Saribas."

Even without the telescope, I could see activity aboard the *Royalist* as the crew hurried to their battle stations. "We should get to the gig."

"No, John. If they were to attack, we would achieve nothing in the gig and the *Royalist*'s gunners would fear to fire lest they hit us. We must stay here."

As we watched, the leading vessel turned, veering away from the *Royalist* anchored in the stream and heading to the shore. Behind it, the fleet slowed and stopped, wallowing in the tide.

"It's a peaceful visit, I think."

As James spoke, I saw a party scramble ashore, form up into a ragged group, and start toward our house.

"We can't be sure," I said. "We should bar the door and break out whatever weapons we have to hand."

"Which would give us a court sword, two dirks, and a shotgun." James smiled. "I think we had best assume they are friendly, John."

James cried out to the servants to prepare the house for guests. We had only two men about the place, not being used to keeping up any style, and all four of us rushed about to try to make it look less like an Indian bungalow and more like a Rajah's palace. I began to recognise the wisdom of receiving in an audience hall, as Hassim had done. Hassim's hall, though, had lain abandoned and growing thick with dust since James had taken up his position, so we had no choice but to receive our uninvited visitors in our home.

By the time the pirate delegation had formed up in front of the house, James was sprawled in an old armchair decorated for the occasion with a velvet cloth I remembered finding when we were setting up home and which I had consigned to store as too gaudy for use. We had arranged two tables along the sides of the room so as to delineate an area for those seeking an audience of the Rajah. Bowls of fruit were placed along these and one of the servants was busy brewing up some tea so we would be able to offer refreshment to our guests.

The pirates arrived before Mr Hart was able to get a squad of seamen up to form an honour guard, and it was left to Mr Brooke and myself to face our visitors alone for the time it took the crew to arrive.

Fortunately, the pirates' leader—a tall, well-built man called Surabada—made every effort to charm. He told us he had heard that Sultan Hassim had handed the rule of Sarawak to the Rajah James Brooke and he launched into a well-rehearsed paean of praise for the hero of Siniawan, the wise and benevolent ruler, the generous friend, the ruthless foe, etcetera, etcetera. I translated this with a straight face and James sat doing his best to look heroic (an easy task) and wise (which he found considerably harder).

Surabada produced gifts for the Rajah. There were some fine Chinese vases, a small chest of jewellery that we suspected had belonged to a merchant whose vessel had been ambushed by our guest, and spices, possibly stolen from the same vessel. We kept a supply of trade goods for dispensing to visitors and by raiding this we were able to provide a proper response—a Chinese vase which was fortunately slightly larger than the one we were given, bolts of cloth, and some European knives, the blades of which excited much curiosity, being forged of a piece and lacking the watering of local weapons.

By now the honour guard was in place, lining the tables which marked our impromptu audience chamber, and I was glad to have a few sturdy lads showing themselves as our guest regaled us with tales of his headhunting expeditions and accounts of battles on the South China Seas. He showed us the tattoos on his fingers that recorded each head he had taken and those on his arms and legs that celebrated some feat of valour on the high seas.

He was careful to set his stories in provinces far from Sarawak and, though all the vessels he attacked appeared to be native craft or, at worst, Dutch merchantmen, still we felt there was a martial theme we would ignore at our peril. So James casually recounted details of the damage the six-pounders had wrought at Siniawan and enlarged upon the excellence and courage of the Dyaks on the field of battle.

The discussions carried on along these lines for some two or three hours. A great deal of tea was drunk. Some sweet cakes were produced and consumed and then, as suddenly as they had arrived, the pirates smiled broadly at us, bowed their thanks, and withdrew to their vessels.

The fleet, though, showed no signs of moving off.

The presence of so many pirates, though they made no immediate threat, made us aware how vulnerable we were. We were also concerned that the lack of ceremony James had encouraged in his dealings with the local tribes might be taken as a sign of weakness by those less favourably disposed to him. Though there was not much we could do immediately, we made such preparations as we could. Budrudeen was away, having agreed with James that it was better the new Rajah establish his authority without constant reminders of the old regime. He had ostensibly gone to inspect the antimony mines and we did not expect his return for two weeks or more, but many of his household remained in Kuching and we were able to organise a native honour guard to supplement our own men. I commandeered his servants to put Hassim's audience hall into order and rounded up all the musicians I could find so we could provide entertainment if required.

Mr Hart, meanwhile, discreetly moved men and muskets to the house so we could at least present a show of armed force if necessary. James reasoned that, even if we had not enough men to make a proper defence, simply allowing Surabada to see we were not entirely unprotected would make him realise we were to be taken seriously.

Thus it was that when Surabada led his followers ashore on the next day, they were met by a neat file of Malays, armed with spear and *kris*, who shepherded them politely to the audience hall. Mr Brooke remembered our first experience of Kuching and kept them waiting outside the hall a full hour while musicians and servants filed in through the rear entrance until he was finally ready to receive the pirates in style.

As had been the case on the occasion of our initial meeting with Hassim, the band played vigorously enough to prevent the necessity of replying to any uncomfortable questions, but we were able to grasp clearly enough that the pirates, the exchange of civilities completed, were anxious to move to the business of their visit. This was to ascertain how much they were to pay for the privilege of pillaging some of the tribes furthest from Kuching.

I gestured for the band to play more loudly; James developed a sudden deafness and, shortly thereafter, expressed a desire to withdraw for his customary siesta. Those of us who had never known him take a siesta in his life kept our faces impassive while Surabada and his escort, happy to believe James was adopting the relaxed mores of the Malay court, returned to their boats.

As soon as they were gone, we convened at the house for an urgent conference.

We had drunk nothing stronger than tea that morning and when I arrived a pitcher of ale and a couple of bottles of wine made a welcome showing on the table. Mr Murray was there already, grimacing at the ale until James gestured to the cupboard where he kept his liquor, at which Murray liberated a bottle of whisky and appeared immediately more at ease. As I sat and poured myself a glass of ale, Mr Hart entered without ceremony and sat alongside me.

James started the meeting. "I take it there is no possibility we might have misunderstood Surabada's proposition, John?"

"None at all. He wants to know the terms on which he can operate inland and, for good measure, whether there are any particular areas where we would find it politic for him to attack."

Mr Hart, who had not been in a position to hear Surabada's proposition clearly, expressed his disbelief but Mr Murray was unusually silent, taking a good pull of his whisky and then opining it made sense to him. "I'd been wondering, in all our travelling about this place, how so many tribes reported predations by pirates when their homes would be accessible by water only if their enemy had passed through Kuching. I had considered the pirates might make a porterage or the accounts we heard might have been much exaggerated, but this simplest answer serves best. The pirates were allowed to pass by the corruption of Hassim and his court."

"And that," James pointed out, "also allowed Hassim to punish those tribes whose loyalty he doubted."

There was a silence while we addressed ourselves to the

drink and tried to absorb the unpalatable facts we had just been presented with.

James was the first to speak. "Colin, you're our naval expert. Are we in a position to stop so many vessels by force?"

"If the *Royalist* is prepared for action and is lying upstream as the tide turns, we could be carried through the fleet firing as we go. The wind has been upstream these last two days so we could make canvas and move up against the tide, albeit more slowly, giving us a second pass. On that pass we would be vulnerable to attack, but the pirates would already have taken casualties and would probably not be prepared to assault us *en masse*. If only one or two attack, they can be picked off with the swivel or with muskets."

"Is there any way to achieve the same effect other than by an attack without warning?"

Mr Hart walked over to the window and looked at the fleet lying in the river, a few hundred yards away. "It would be more dangerous, but it might be possible."

"If you failed, would we lose the *Royalist?*"

"The ship would be at hazard, sir," Mr Hart conceded, "but if the tide was with us, we might cast the anchor and stand a reasonable chance of escaping downstream, even if we had to yield the passage upriver."

"Then, Mr Hart, that shall be what we will do. I would avoid an unprovoked attack, for all that these pirates would show no such courtesy to the inland Dyaks were they to be allowed to pass. We shall attempt diplomacy but our efforts will be backed by force if need be."

James strode from the room, returning with one of Mr Murray's carefully drawn charts of the locality which he spread on the table, holding each corner down with a bottle or glass. I could see Mr Murray wince, as if in pain, as he saw his labours stained with spilt wine and beer.

"Gentlemen," said Mr Brooke, "this is how we will defeat them."

❋

THE COUNCIL OF WAR lasted through the afternoon and into the night. The leader of the guard at Budrudeen's household was summoned to contribute and the chiefs of two of the nearest Dyak villages joined us just before dusk. We worked through the night, planning how our one vessel could hold off the entire pirate fleet if Mr Brooke's attempts at diplomacy were to rob the *Royalist* of the advantage of surprise. Our efforts were further hampered by the necessity that all our preparations be made in secret, although the enemy lay in our midst.

Despite our lack of sleep, we were ready in the audience chamber when Surabada requested an audience the following morning. James had decided to adopt an approach radically different from that of the previous meeting and the pirates were summoned in immediately. There was no band, but we had dragooned twice the number of retainers into lining the walls and Surabada could not have failed to notice that all were fully armed.

Although he could well have made himself understood, James had elected not to speak but to have me make a statement on his behalf. He confined himself to sitting on a handsome armchair requisitioned from the *Royalist* and doing his best to look regal while I stood before him, reading from his script like some sort of court chamberlain.

I started by thanking Surabada for his gifts and apologising we had not been able to match their magnificence. At this point, a couple of servants entered carrying between them a chest with as many baubles and bangles as we had been able to find in a hurried search the previous night.

"We give you these poor tokens," I read on, "as a sign of the affection in which we hold you and as a symbol of peace between your people and ours."

By now Surabada could see things were not going the way he had expected, but protocol demanded he look pleased and even interrupt the speech to say how delighted he was with Rajah Brooke's beneficence and how unworthy he felt to receive it. He was about to say more, trying no doubt to return to the purpose of our meeting, but I held my piece of paper before me and read on over him.

"The Rajah is delighted that you should have favoured us with the honour of a visit. He will treasure the memory of his meeting with you. The Rajah is concerned, though, that you do him too much honour by remaining for so long away from your own homes. He begs you should return to your fields and your families."

I sat.

Surabada rose to his feet and looked around him. I saw no one move, yet a ripple of expectation ran around the edges of the room where the guards seemed to be holding their weapons with a little more care than they had shown before.

The pirate chief smiled, but it was the smile of a hunter, nearing its prey. "We thank Rajah Brooke for his fine gifts. We must, indeed, trespass no more upon his time. We will depart from Kuching and attend to our business in those fields which have so long sustained us."

And then, with a discipline and organisation that showed them as the well-organised body of fighting men they were, Surabada's retinue were on their feet and moving out of the hall almost before we recognised his parting words for the threat they undoubtedly were.

"They're going to move upstream. They've as good as told us."

As the last of the pirates left, James was already on his feet and crossing to the open side of the hall with its view of the river. All seemed peaceful, but one thing had changed. During the meeting, the *Royalist*'s boats had taken her in tow, and she now lay upstream from the pirate fleet, broadside on to the flow. James grabbed up a red cloth that lay at the edge of the hall and he waved it vigorously until an answering flag waved back from the *Royalist*'s deck. At once there was a flurry of activity on the vessel.

At the same time, two small boats that had been awaiting our signal set out slowly toward our ship, one from each bank.

Mr Hart marshalled the guard from the room to take up positions along the river, facing the *Royalist*'s prow.

James himself remained in the audience hall with its view of the river. For all his enthusiasm for a fight, he knew success or failure depended on the strategy we had planned the previous night and the valour of one man would make no difference. I stood alongside him, as anxious as he as to what the outcome might be and knowing he would need my comfort if the day went against us.

"There is still a chance they might leave peacefully, isn't there, John?"

I knew he wanted to believe it but we all knew Surabada's men were no farmers. "The fields that had so long sustained them," he had said. Those were the fields of Sarawak, the fields of the people James Brooke saw as his subjects and whom he had promised to protect.

Now there was activity on the pirate vessels: the gongs began to beat the rhythm of the rowers, the oars churned the water, and a score of boats started upriver.

From our vantage point we waved the red flag again. The two boats standing out toward the *Royalist* now moved further forward and as they did so, the chains anchoring them to the bank were drawn clear of the water. We had used the longest of the *Royalist*'s anchor chains to improvise these booms. Now the river was impassable from each bank to the boats and the only passage for the pirate fleet was the gap where the *Royalist* lay broadside on to them.

The pirate vessels bunched toward the centre of the river, save for a few which turned toward the banks to free the anchor chains from their moorings.

James waved a green flag. I saw the crew run out one of the guns and a single shot threw up a plume of spray ahead of the pirate fleet.

For a moment the rowers paused. I heard commands being cried out, the sound carrying easily across the water. The gongs resumed their beat and the fleet again moved toward our ship.

The red flag waved and, seconds later, the crash of a broadside rolled up from the river. Three of the pirate craft were hit. I could see some men slumped at their oars but the rest rowed on and the fleet kept moving forward.

Now the *Royalist*'s swivel gun opened fire. The new gunner had learned his art at Siniawan and each shot struck his chosen mark. More commands issued from the pirate fleet and they spread out across the river, making a harder target for the *Royalist*'s gunners. Their plan seemed to rely on their flank vessels removing the anchor points of the boom and allowing them to pass by the *Royalist* without engaging it directly.

It was a good plan, too, for the flankers were already approaching the ends of the chain. At that moment, though, there was a cry from the river bank, and the men we had secreted on the far shore rose from their positions and started a withering musket fire into the pirate boat, now mere yards before them. Almost immediately, the men Mr Hart had led from the audience chamber started firing from our side of the river.

The two flanking vessels were driven back toward the main fleet and the pirate's chance of destroying the boom was gone. Their attack had been broken.

No doubt they could have regrouped and pushed through against the *Royalist*, but they were taken by surprise and the heart had gone out of them. It was as we had supposed—they had little experience of coming under heavy fire from well-organised and well-prepared forces and were not prepared for the casualties they had taken. There were more shouted commands and the fleet stopped its advance on the boom.

I held out two flags toward James. One was red, the signal the enemy was to be pursued, the other white.

James hesitated.

"You could destroy them. The tide is still on the ebb. The *Royalist* can fire once more from her position now and then run down with the current. There are too many injured men among the pirates for them to make good speed. The *Royalist* can run among them, firing as she goes."

The pirate vessels were already turning, pitifully exposed to the *Royalist*'s guns. Faintly, across the water, we could hear the screams of the wounded.

James reached for the white flag and signalled we should disengage. The firing ceased and we watched in silence as Surabada's fleet started its long voyage downriver.

# Chapter 7

SURABADA'S VISIT HIGHLIGHTED OUR vulnerability in Kuching. Budrudeen, on his return to the town, admitted there was not much Hassim would be able to do to defend Sarawak. Indeed, this was part of the reasoning behind his allowing the pirates to travel freely on the river. It seemed, then, that if we were to be able to protect the people of the province, we would have to make our own arrangements for our defence.

Some of the immediate measures we took were simple enough. The doors to the house were reinforced and thick mahogany shutters were fitted. With the doors bolted fast and the shutters closed, the house would withstand attack long enough for reinforcements to be sent to relieve us. A flagpole was set on the roof and an agreed system of signal flags enabled us to communicate with vessels on the river and other key points in the town, including Budrudeen's compound. An armoury was installed and the servants, as well as James and myself, drilled with the muskets until we were confident we could give a good account of ourselves.

The other changes took longer to arrange. As the *Royalist* and the *Swift* voyaged to and from Singapore, they brought, in addition to their regular supplies, new armaments for our defences. Six months after Surabada had first arrived in Kuching, a battery of five ten-pounders was set up overlooking the quayside, defending the town against attack and offering a formidable obstacle to any fleet attempting to pass upriver. The temporary boom that had served so well in holding back the pirates was replaced by a massive cable and wood construction projecting from the far bank, forcing any vessels travelling upriver to pass close to the town, under our guns and through a gap that we could easily defend with one ship.

The artificial constriction of the river had an additional advantage—it made it easier to stop every vessel passing the town and thus to institute a tax on the produce being passed to or from our port. We already gathered a harbour fee that paid for the improvements to the quayside but now we could raise some small revenue from all those visiting the market. These measures, though resented by some, were generally seen as fairer than the predations of the Malay officials and we had no choice but to impose them for we were sorely in need of the money.

The trade in antimony was profitable but it did not yield as much as James had hoped. He decided he had to travel to Singapore and ascertain whether he could improve the terms on which we traded or, failing that, secure some of our immediate needs by an arrangement with one of the banking houses there. He would have had me travel with him but I knew my ignorance of Society could not fail to be an embarrassment to him. Indeed, though I know he did not mean to distress me, it was clear he was not anxious to have me known as a friend until I had more the manners of a gentleman. So it was agreed I should remain in Kuching to exercise a stewardship on his behalf while he was away. Even so, given that I was officially only an interpreter, Mr Hart was to have nominal charge until James' return.

This was to be our first separation since we had acknowledged our love, and the night before he was to leave I realised how much I had come to cherish him. I think he, too, realised how much we meant to each other, and he was especially tender with me. Before dawn I clung to him as a child to its mother but he, kissing me gently, slipped from my embrace and left me alone as he went about his business abroad.

It was lonely in that house without him. Singapore was but four days away with a fair wind but it might as well have been the other side of the world. The first evening after his departure, I sat looking out over Kuching and suddenly it struck me how alien was the land where I found myself and how far from the West Country of my childhood.

Such pining, though, could not help in doing all that was to be done and the work before me seemed likely to offer the best cure for any transient unhappiness I might be feeling.

Business took up much of my time. Mr Hart was, I think, sensitive to my situation and he took care not to impose his authority. I was therefore left to deal with the realities of administration which meant, as often as not, dealing with the antimony trade. The metal was mined by Dyaks from the interior of the country but the mines were owned by Malays. Many owed their allegiance to Makota and almost every day, it seemed, there would be someone of Budrudeen's faction petitioning on one ground or another that a mine should be transferred from its current control to his.

Although I would try to postpone these decisions until James returned, this was not always possible. On one occasion my petitioner told me there was already actual fighting at the mine, with some Dyaks insisting they represented the new owner and those already employed there defending the site against the usurpers at sword-point. It seemed they fought with more enthusiasm for their livelihoods than they had ever done in the recent war, and three or four men had already been killed. I had to make a ruling before there was more bloodshed and I deemed it politic to find for Budrudeen's allies, as they were most like to be our allies too. Thus did we find ourselves enmeshed in the coils of court intrigue.

At a more mundane level, problems would occur when several mines brought the ore to Kuching on the same day. They would all demand payment immediately and none was prepared to wait while other loads were weighed and tallied, a procedure that could take some hours. The labourers would be exhausted from their work upon the river and unprepared for a long wait, with nothing to eat or drink and the prospect of a long journey against the current before they would be back at their homes. Their overseers would worry about the cost of delay and the work left undone at the mines while men were idle at the docks. Mr Brooke had arranged a rota to avoid such delays and Mr Hart had his men travel from mine to mine, explaining the days on which ore should be transported, but the system was honoured more in the breach than in the observance. I would often be called upon to negotiate between three or four angry crews, all insisting their vessels should be the first to be unloaded.

Mr Hart had appointed a quartermaster, one Wilkins, who was responsible for ensuring there were sufficient provisions for all Mr Brooke's men in Kuching. This meant the crews of *Royalist* and *Swift* and a party of around a dozen who were seldom aboard either craft but ran here and there in the *Lily*. The *Royalist*'s gig was kept almost permanently busy on Sarawak's rivers by now, either surveying with Mr Murray or carrying messages to the various villages of the interior. Our own establishment had grown, too. We had hired a general factotum whose Malay name defeated most Western tongues and who was generally known as Freddy. On his recommendation we had also taken on a girl—some member of his extended family—who cooked for us. Both lived under our roof and Wilkins was responsible for our household supplies as well as those of the crew.

Wilkins had acquired a fair understanding of both Malay and the main Dyak dialects but when there was a dispute—and disputing was lifeblood of Kuching's commercial life—then I would be called for. I do not flatter myself that my diplomatic skills were so valued. Rather it was the presence of an official interpreter that would elevate their haggling into trade negotiations and by satisfying their pride, we were able to strike a better bargain than Wilkins would achieve, however shrewd his judgement.

Even with all these matters to attend to day by day, yet still I had time at leisure and I resolved I would make a garden around our house. This would offer a useful distraction and, I hoped, please my James on his return.

Murray had started to collect examples of the native flora on his surveying trips, and I asked him for such of his specimens as I thought would make an interesting and attractive display. He supplied me with a beautiful gardenia bush, just a foot or so in height and covered in pure white blossoms that yielded a powerful aromatic odour, filling the air with fragrance. Rhododendra grew in profusion around the jungle clearings and I was able to plant bushes along the side of the house so that, wherever the eye fell, their brilliant colours would lift the spirit. In a spot separate from the other bushes, I planted a yellow flowered cinquefoil, as high as myself, but Murray assured me it would grow to more than fifteen feet in a few years time.

These bushes, with their bold colours, seemed to reflect something of James' character, but I planted other flowers for myself. Here and there beside the house or nestling in the shade of their brash cousins, I set a variety of the native orchids. Mr Murray has already identified fifty or more of these delicate plants and I was able to grow five or six varieties around the house—some lemon yellow, some purple, some with spectacular blotched markings of orange and black, but all with the remarkable pendulous shape and powerful scent of this family.

So the time passed pleasantly enough, the mornings toiling at my stewardship, then a rest in the heat of the day before I spent some time planning the garden and arranging for the plants and shrubs to be laid out and tended. In the evening I might be visited by some Malays from the town or Dyaks visiting from the interior. They would sit and drink sweet tea or chew betel nuts, talking of nothing in particular until they were relaxed enough to let me know the real reason for their visit. Thus I would receive news of intrigues in Budrudeen's household or some story passed on from Hassim's court in far-off Brunei. The Dyaks would tell me of the latest swindle practised by the Malay mine owners, and which chiefs were loyal and which could not be trusted. I, in turn, passed on such stories as I thought fit about James Brooke's doings, news of the Empire and the movements of our British forces about the world, and accounts of the wonders of the age as reported to me from Singapore and the Straits Settlements. And so we spun our web of politics and innuendo and, when it seemed best to do so, outright lies, all under the brilliant tropic moon.

James returned at last, his enthusiasm buoyed by new funds to keep our venture solvent and new buyers for the produce of our country. I scarce had time to open my mouth, let alone show him the garden I had laboured on, before he was telling me how he had spent his time in Singapore.

"You should have seen me, John," he said. "I decked myself out in a new jacket and a fine beaver hat and I was quite the hero of the hour."

He must have discerned some hint of irritation in my face, for he cast his eyes down like a chastised schoolboy. "I had to do it, John. I don't seek glory for myself but if we are to keep this place going, the world must believe in Sarawak. And, as all the world sees of Sarawak is my poor self, they must believe in me."

I could not deny the truth of what he said. I smiled and kissed him, and for a while he was silent. But soon he was again describing his adventures while he had been away. He had, it appeared, not only charmed the traders into providing us with the commercial support we needed but had also spent much of his time at Government House, explaining to anyone who cared to listen that Sarawak could be a valuable British outpost and a check on Dutch expansion in the East Indies. The Governor of

Singapore himself was prepared to make time to talk with Rajah Brooke and James felt his activities had at least the tacit support of the British government.

He talked for an hour without pause and only then did he think to ask how I had occupied myself in his absence. Scarce had I drawn breath to answer him, though, than he pulled me to him.

"I've been too long away," he said. "Let's go to bed."

And so we did.

❈

THE BACKING OF THE Singapore merchants relieved us of our immediate concerns about the finances of the country. James even relaxed enough to enjoy the garden I had made for us.

The money he brought back with him allowed us to pay our men and buy hoists and cable to improve the docks. Until now every delivery of antimony had been loaded by men carrying it on their heads along a wooden gangplank. Once we were able to hoist a cargo net to load antimony a ton at a time aboard our vessels, we could clear the docks so much more quickly that the amount of antimony passing through Kuching more than doubled. Our main concern became to make the mines more efficient and produce more ore. All too soon James was back in Singapore to raise yet further funds so we could invest directly in the mining, bringing European tools and expertise to the business and improving the yield.

Strange to say, although it seemed sometimes my life revolved around antimony, I had never seen any of the mines, the nearest of which was a two days' journey away. It seemed to me foolish that James should invest so heavily in something neither of us had seen with our own eyes so, about a month after his second visit to his bankers, I set off upriver on a tour of inspection.

We started with the *Lily* heading for Siniawan. The journey was familiar from the days of the war but when we disembarked at Siniawan, all was very different. Although James had been able to save the lives of their leaders, the town of Siniawan had been razed to the ground and its population had drifted into the jungle to start their lives again at some more discreet location. Now the place was a small Chinese settlement with neat wooden houses facing onto carefully tended plots. It even boasted a small temple, from which the smell of incense carried to the river on the evening breeze.

Despite the evidence of agricultural activity, it was clear the Chinese lived mainly by trade. Facing the river bank, where the *Lily* scraped ashore, were a row of tiny shop-houses supplying the needs of travellers, be they the crews of the antimony miners transporting ore downriver or the native people of the region. Inside you could scarcely move for goods of all kinds: native medicines, tinned provisions shipped from Singapore or Java, clothes and clothing materials of every description, and the tall Chinese pots so valued by the native peoples here that they had almost become a currency. Why these last things should be so ubiquitous was a mystery to me but it was so. The Dyaks had neither potters wheel nor firing ovens to make glazed ceramics such as these and seemed overwhelmed by such items, valuing them far beyond their simple utility as storage vessels.

I had often had cause to deal with the Chinese merchants of Kuching who would come to James' house with one complaint or another as they saw his regulation of business in the town restrict their absolute freedom to profit from the place. I recognised their industry as allowing some progress in a country whose character might otherwise be determined entirely by the indolence of the Malays or the ignorance and backwardness of the Dyaks. Yet I think it was the sight of the Chinese settlement at Siniawan that first made me realise how tightly they had woven themselves into the fabric of Sarawak.

The next morning I woke early and, with an escort from the *Lily*'s crew, set off away from the river toward the Singè mountains and the antimony workings.

We skirted the jungle, climbing for several hours along a

path across rocky ground where grew just scrub and stunted trees. Ahead of us, the mountains drew almost imperceptibly closer.

Finally we arrived at a steeper slope where, all at once, we were surrounded by bustle and activity. Trenches had been dug into the earth and these ran into the hillside. Some were so long they ended up as tunnels, cut horizontally into the steeper ground ahead of us, propped up precariously by rough hewn trunks of wood.

In the trenches Dyak labourers were hacking at the ground with what looked for all the world like primitive hoes, leaving broken rocks to be shovelled into great woven baskets which could be slung on carrying poles to transport the rock to the river at Siniawan.

Malay overseers wandered here and there among the toiling Dyaks but, to my surprise, there seemed almost as many Chinese on the site as there were Malays.

I enquired as to who was in charge and a shortish Malay hurried over from the shade of one of the stunted trees on the boundaries of the site, where he had apparently been resting from the sun. He introduced himself as Anwar Ibrahim and he explained he represented the owner, whose name I vaguely recognised from Hassim's court and whom I was confident was now ensconced with Hassim in Brunei.

When I expressed interest in the workings, Ibrahim started to show us around, but as soon as I had any questions as to the mechanics of the operation, he would beckon to one of the Chinese to explain the details of the work. So Li Tun explained how much rock they would extract in a day, Lon Soo told me how many men worked on the site, and Tu Zo described the mechanics of grinding the rock and washing it in a spring half a mile away to separate out the ore. It was all too evident that, though the mines were owned by Malays, they were run by the Chinese. This fact, so obvious on the ground, had been quite concealed from me in Kuching and I felt this intelligence alone had more than justified the time and effort of the trip.

My visit to the mine not only gave me a better understanding of the place of the Chinese in the economic life of Sarawak but it confirmed James' belief that European investment in the workings would bring significant rewards. Simply replacing the rough tools with well-made picks and shovels would improve production, and if we installed tracks to move the boulders about the site by truck, rather than in baskets carried on men's shoulders, more ore could clearly be handled with less use of labour. These and a myriad other improvements were essential if James were to meet his commitments to his backers, for the Sultan had a nominal monopoly on antimony and any increase in production would enable us to renegotiate the terms on which the mine owners held the mines from us.

I returned to Kuching full of enthusiasm for the improvements we were planning to introduce. James was determined I should acquire such skills as would enable me to take my proper place as his man of business. I had always had a head for such arithmetic as was needed to buy and sell and keep our domestic economy afloat, but now James was determined I should learn to reckon like a clerk, keeping proper accounts in a ledger book. "For if you can never be a gentleman, John, at least I will have you fit for a decent place in the world."

It was unkind of him to remind me so often of the difference in our stations. In truth, when we were about the house no difference existed. We were equals then and he would be as likely to bring me a cup of tea, bestowing it with a fond kiss, as I might perform some small domestic service for him. When Freddy brought in dinner or prepared our clothes, he did not distinguish between us. Yet to the wider world, I was marked out as his inferior and, for all James would swear he had an honest admiration for my skills, I believe he was not himself unconscious of the difference in our status.

Still, any bitterness I felt about my situation was not allowed to fester into a canker but, rather, was diverted into a ferocious energy with which I pursued my education. Soon I was a competent bookkeeper, able to keep a decent record of the state of our Treasury. James applauded my success and I basked in his praise, but no sooner did he feel I fully understood the mysteries of his accounts but he had to explain to me the basis of economic theory and the works of such thinkers as Adam Smith. I had come a long way from *Mother Goose* and now sat up reading *The Wealth of Nations*, until James complained I was turning into a bookworm and a bore and, laughing, pulled me away from my library and into bed.

My studies were not wasted, though. I came to see how our efforts in Sarawak illustrated perfectly the arguments of the great economists. Surely there was no clearer case of the benefits trade could bring to the inhabitants of a country than we could show here before us. The Dyak labourers would benefit as their work would be more productive and they would not need to toil so long in the heat of the day simply to extract enough ore to pay for their subsistence. The mine owners, franchised by our government, would benefit from their share in the increased profit of the mines. We would be enabled to pay our debts and support ourselves, and the people as a whole would benefit from the improved governance we could impose with the surplus profit of our endeavour.

All would have been well had it not been for Surabada and the pirates.

We had thought Surabada's enforced retreat would have taught him a lesson and we would hear no more from him. Our mistake was to have underestimated the scale of piracy in Borneo and the lengths to which the pirates would go to maintain their hold over the country. When James Brooke forced Surabada to quit Kuching, he was, unbeknownst to him, declaring war on all the pirates of Borneo. So they gathered and plotted secretly with the aim of driving the British from Sarawak and demonstrating their power against us.

At first we were unaware of any organised campaign. Pirate

raids had been a fact of life for coastal settlements for as long as anybody could remember. We would send the *Lily* to the site of each reported outrage but this was just a gesture on our part. It might take days to reach some of the farther villages and, in every case, the pirates would be long gone. All our men could do was to search the smouldering ruins and bury the dead.

It was only as the months passed and we received increasing reports of attacks on isolated communities that we realised this was more than just the regular reality of life on the frontiers of civilisation.

By now, a dozen villages had been destroyed and we had yet to see a single pirate, let alone apprehend them. James called a council of war at the house, attended by myself, Hart, and Murray. James also asked Budrudeen to join us, as his knowledge of the history of the pirate tribes and their political relationships was likely to prove invaluable.

Budrudeen's presence meant the meeting had a certain air of formality. Though he was by now regarded by us all as close to a friend, still his status as a member of the Royal household meant the proprieties had to be observed. We all wore the jackets which had become almost our uniform for such occasions. Instead of lounging comfortably in the study, we sat in state around the mahogany table in the dining room. Servants, hired especially for the day, bustled in with tea and the sticky sweetmeats the Malays enjoyed so much, though James drew the line at introducing betel nuts into his residence.

Once all the proprieties had been observed, the servants were ordered to withdraw and we soon settled down to business. Budrudeen spoke first, explaining the realities of piracy with a brutal frankness that surprised us. "You think of these pirates as mere brigands but you do not understand them at all. The Dyaks are a warrior people and for the Sea Dyaks, piracy is the way of life of whole communities. Their fleets are the armies of their tribes. When you forced Surabada to turn away from Sarawak, you struck the first blow in a war. Now he has found allies—for the other pirate tribes fear if they are to be denied Sarawak then, in time, they will be driven from the rest of Hassim's lands. So they mass against you. That is why the number of attacks upon our land is increasing."

Murray, as ever, had to disagree. He did not care for the subtleties of politics. As far as he was concerned, a pirate was a pirate. The idea they might form alliances and develop strategies would be strange enough if they were Europeans. The thought that mere natives might plan like this was patently absurd to him. "If they have a grand alliance to attack Sarawak, why do we just see these few raids here and there? Why do they not attack the rich inland villages, as Surabada threatened?"

"Because you have closed the river to them at Kuching. They have been defeated here once—they will not try again. Therefore they attack coastal villages in force or march inland to mount smaller raids as and where they can strike."

Murray looked sceptical but, before he could respond, James spoke. "Mr Murray, your work has given us some splendid maps to work with. Why don't we use them?"

The flattery was effective. Murray pushed aside the plates littering the table and unrolled his maps. Budrudeen leaned forward. "You see. The pirates have struck here. And here. And here." Again and again he stabbed his finger at the charts and now the pattern of predation became clear. They had already destroyed the larger coastal settlements and were now working their way inland. With this understanding of their strategy, we could fairly predict where they would strike next.

We agreed nothing could be achieved from the approach we had taken to date. If we responded only to the attacks after they had happened, we would always be too late. Our only chance, it seemed, was to provide guards for those villages at most risk and thus to be able to put up a resistance to the attacks when the pirates first struck. Now that we saw the pirate strategy, we could identify the places we most needed to protect.

Our problem was we could not spare the men from our

crews to keep guard in three or four of the likeliest villages for as long as might be necessary. Nor did Budrudeen want to send the warriors of his own household away from Kuching on such a duty. The only solution we could see was to hire some of the natives to do the business and train and equip them at our own expense.

In contemplating such an expedient, we realised we were effectively setting up our own army. This was not a step we undertook lightly, as our exchequer had made no provision for such a measure. Yet James was passionate that as he ruled the country, so it was his duty to protect his subjects. The money must therefore be found.

Budrudeen declared firmly it would not be possible to raise the money by a levy on the Malays and if we were to take a greater share of the revenue from antimony, then the mines would not be profitable enough to persuade the owners to operate them. The Dyaks lived simply and the possibilities for raising money from them were limited. Our only choice, it seemed, was to levy an additional tax on commerce, taking one percent of our estimate of the turnover of every trader in Kuching and the major settlements.

Mr Hart protested that any such impost would fall heavily on the Chinese. "The Chinese live by trade and therefore will bear the burden of any such tax while the Malays will maintain their wealth and the Dyaks, whose defence will be the principal business of any army we form, will pay scarcely anything."

"In fairness," James responded, "the Dyaks do not yet have such an economy as will allow us to expect a contribution in cash."

Mr Hart could not accept this line of reasoning. "The Dyaks have no money because the interior is still scarcely opened to trade. You have said yourself, James, it is by trade that we will raise these people from savagery and introduce them to the benefits of civilisation. Yet when the Chinese trade, they are to be penalised for it."

I wished Mr Hart had not described the Dyaks as existing in savagery, for I considered there was a lot of truth in what he said. Yet James would turn against any argument that, as he saw it, denigrated their way of life. He loved the people of the jungle with a boyish enthusiasm as closed to rational debate as his dislike of the Chinese.

Unfortunately for Mr Hart, James's opinion was shared by Budrudeen. The Prince, like most of the Malays, felt no affection for the Chinese but tolerated them for the services they provided to the indigenous peoples of the country. "They are not *bumi putrah*," he said, using the Malay term for 'a son of the soil'. For him, only the Malays and the Dyaks, as *bumi putrah*, were worthy of consideration in planning the future of the country.

Murray, of course, disliked all foreigners on principle and, as the Chinese seemed to him more foreign than most, he was happy to subscribe to this view.

It seemed to me, at the time, that singling out the Chinese in this way would end badly and I ventured to say so, but James' mind was made up. Indeed, when I tried to put the argument more forcibly, he grew sharp and so I held my peace.

Thus it was we established our army. On the *Swift* we had one Patterson, who had served with the Marines before jumping ship in Hong Kong and then gradually worked his way through a succession of craft until he had ended up with us. He had a useful knowledge of matters military and was transferred from his regular duties and put in charge of training our new recruits. These were made up mainly of young Dyak warriors. It is a tradition among these people that a young man should travel away from his tribe and demonstrate his prowess in the wider world before returning home to settle down. James' army therefore appealed greatly to these people and we were soon able to recruit a force of some fifty men, which we armed with old muskets purchased from Singapore. After Patterson had drilled them to his satisfaction and we had established they had a reasonable skill with the muskets, the force was split into four groups and taken, each in turn, to the four villages we thought most at threat.

Barely a fortnight later, a young boy from one of the villages arrived in Kuching and demanded of the first person he met that he should, as he expressed it, "Have audience of Rajah Brooke."

It was early afternoon when he arrived at the house. James and I were in bed. We had separate rooms but there was a connecting door and our man Freddy was clear we should not be disturbed during our siesta. However, the boy was so agitated and his cries for audience so persistent that he knocked timorously on the door of James' room and asked if the Rajah Brooke might be roused. In fact James was already roused and cursed the servant fluently for a full minute while I shoved a sheet into my mouth and tried not to laugh. Poor Freddy! He knew perfectly well how much a disturbance would annoy James and, though he would die rather than admit it, knew why. But at the same time, he was a soft-hearted man with a particular fondness for children and could no more have driven away our visitor than could James himself.

Eventually, with much muffled laughter and the odd slap, I was driven back into my own room and James pulled on his dressing gown to go and find out what all the fuss was about. This splendid garment of red silk dressing gown was bought from a Chinese and the back was covered with an embroidery of the most magnificent dragon, so James in his dressing gown looked more the Rajah than most men would have looked in far more conventional attire. Meanwhile I had pulled on a suit of more unadventurous clothing to take up my position as interpreter, advisor, and *aide de camp* to Sarawak's ruler.

It was a glorious day. The rains were coming to an end and we had the benefit of brilliant blue skies without the desperate humidity that could make every move an effort until the weather broke. Through the windows came the sound of a woodpecker and, from the river below, the gentle splash of oars as a boat pulled toward the jetties. It was one of those days that made you feel glad to be alive and confident in the goodness of our Creator.

Waiting for us on the veranda was the Dyak boy.

He was about ten years old, naked except for a loincloth. His right arm hung loosely at his side and from that shoulder, downward across his chest, was an open gash, no longer bleeding but already showing pus around the raw edges of the wound. He was squatting on his heels with his good arm hugging himself across the chest while he rocked back and forth, as if to comfort himself.

We sent straight to the town to get a doctor while James knelt beside the lad to ask who had attacked him. It was clear that he had been attacked—the wound was certainly the result of a back-handed slash with a parang, one of the deadly jungle swords the Dyaks wielded. It was claimed the heavy blade of the parang could sever the head from the shoulders with one blow. Certainly I had seen it used to hack through vines as thick as a man's arm. The boy was lucky to have survived at all.

By the time the doctor arrived, we had heard the boy's story. In truth, there was little to tell. Patterson had dispatched his men—a dozen of them—to the village, where they had arrived safely and been welcomed at a feast. They had spent the next day at ease but their sergeant had established a proper routine by the second day, with the men divided into watches to keep guard and the men off duty resting or helping with chores around the longhouse. The village was responsible for feeding them while they were billeted there and it was natural they would be asked to help with the carrying of wood or the gutting of animals slaughtered for their meals. Even at such times, though, the men kept their weapons readily to hand and their ears alert for any warning from those on guard.

For just over a week, this routine was maintained. Then, an hour or so before dawn, the pirates arrived. There was, said the boy, no warning from the guards. He saw one of those who would have been on duty that night lying with his throat cut.

We reasoned the pirates must have crept up on the guards and killed them silently before the alarm could be raised.

The rest of the men had camped in two groups, four bivouacking on the ground outside the longhouse and four sleeping inside with the people of the village. It seemed one of those outside was able to raise the alarm before they were slaughtered. The four inside took up position to defend the entrance to the hut and, according to the boy, they may have killed one or two of the enemy who tried to storm the place. In any case, the pirates soon gave up any idea of seizing the longhouse by assault and, instead, set fires against the supports and burned the place to the ground. Those who tried to escape were either killed or taken as slaves.

A few made it to the cover of the jungle, but the pirates had pursued them. Some of the raiders appeared skilled in tracking—as many of the Dyaks were—and the trails left by the panicking survivors were easy enough to follow. Our informant had barely escaped with his life and he was, as far as knew, the only one to do so.

A doctor arrived from the town, a Malay with a good knowledge of Eastern remedies, and a man I trusted to do his best by the child. The wounds were cleaned and dressed and he was given a draught of honey and opium to help him sleep. A bed was made up in our guest room and he was laid there with the greatest care as Freddy appointed himself to watch over him.

James and I sat out on the veranda and looked out over the town. The scene was little changed from that of an hour before but I no longer noticed its beauty. We sat in silence for some time. Then, as if to himself, James said just one word.

"Keppel."

That was the moment the pirates' fate was sealed.

Of course I had heard of Keppel. Everybody had heard of

Keppel. Henry Keppel was everyone's favourite sea-dog. Although only in his early thirties, he was a bluff, 'hail fellow, well met' chap with a red face and a solid build—the very picture of a jolly naval officer. It was only as you got to know him better that you realised his easy-going manner disguised a ruthless ambition. He was already writing the diary of his voyages that was to be published in so many volumes of heroic tales, resulting in a grateful British monarch awarding him a knighthood.

But when Henry Keppel first came into my life, he was just starting his climb up the greasy pole. He was a Rear-Admiral, certainly, but as Commander of the South China Fleet, he was losing his way in an obscure outpost of the British Navy. We were not at war with the Dutch, the only other significant European power in the area, and none of the native rulers had anything remotely resembling a navy. So Keppel was reduced to sailing aimlessly around the islands of the archipelago looking for someone to fight. And now James offered him the chance to lead his ships into battle against our pirates. For Keppel, it was the answer to a prayer.

Barely a month after James had first sent word that we would appreciate the assistance of the British navy, Keppel's flagship was in Kuching.

The *Dido* was an 18-gun clipper, impressive even to our own crew, who were familiar with ships of the line. To the people of Kuching, she was a visitation from another world, and Keppel made the most of his chance to awe the natives. She came in under tow with her sails furled and 150 tars lining her yards. As she dropped anchor, the guns sounded out the salute—all eighteen firing in turn and then the first three firing again, having reloaded as the later guns discharged. For those who had any understanding of naval warfare, the lesson was not lost. These were gun crews who knew their business.

Nor was the show over with the salute. The decks were lined with a Marine band, at attention in their red coats, and as the echoes of the cannon died away, they regaled us with *Rule Bri-*

*tannia* and the National Anthem, all of us very still and sombre as that played. James did not generally play the Anthem in Sarawak, saying we were no part of the Empire but owed our allegiance to the Sultan who had given the rule to him personally and not as a representative of the British Crown. Now, though, we stood at attention as the band played and the White Ensign hung on the mast above our heads. I felt the arms of our Empire were reaching out across the thousands of miles of ocean between us.

Henry Keppel wasted no time in arranging a meeting with James. I had assumed he would call on us at the bungalow, but he specified a meeting aboard the *Dido* and on the afternoon of his arrival James, Colin Hart, Mr Murray, and I were rowed across to his flagship. We were shown into Keppel's stateroom, where he rose quickly and strode across to James, arm outstretched.

"Mr Brooke, I am so very pleased to meet you at last, sir. I have heard so much of your endeavours and am delighted to offer you every assistance in my power."

James and Keppel exchanged handshakes and then James introduced us. Mr Hart and Mr Murray were easily explained and, indeed, Keppel expressed particular pleasure in meeting our surveyor as he had a professional interest in Murray's work of mapping the coastline. When James came to introduce me, though, there was a perceptible pause. In Kuching I had at first been introduced as his interpreter and, as time had passed, my status had become so well known to all those of significance in our modest kingdom, it was no longer necessary to give me any title at all. But here 'interpreter' was an obvious nonsense and, faced with the uniformed splendour of the social order we had left in England, it was necessary I have some title.

"Mr Williamson is my…assistant."

Keppel bowed slightly in acknowledgement and, dismissing me in an instant, turned back to James and the business in hand. "My intelligence is that these pirates have camps both on the coast and in the interior of this island. From these lairs, they have preyed on merchant vessels travelling to and from Singapore. My efforts to deter them by patrolling the Straits are ineffective. The chances of our intercepting an attack are minimal. Our only course is to strike at the root of the evil and destroy them in their haunts. In this way, we can rid the British merchant navy of their present peril and, I hope, offer you valuable service."

James demurred somewhat, suggesting it would be enough to provide increased patrols with the aim of breaking up any attacking force moving into Sarawak.

Keppel, though, would have none of it. "Your coastline is long, the rivers innumerable, the tracks these vermin can follow through the forest near invisible to Western eyes. Our only chance, sir, is to destroy them in their strongholds."

And so it was decided. Mr Murray sat down with his charts and he and Keppel discussed where these strongholds might be and the best routes to them. Mr Hart was consulted as to the mechanics of navigating the rivers and James talked about the forces we might have available to assist with any military activity.

Meanwhile, I sat quietly, watched, and listened.

It was clear Henry Keppel had no interest in the people or politics of the country. His interest was solely in extirpating the pirates by military force, and James was swept along by the promise of action and excitement and a rapid conclusion of his troubles with the pirates.

So it was that, only a week later, we sailed East along the coast of Sarawak, heading for the mouth of the Saribas River. The *Dido* led our little flotilla, with the *Royalist* astern and then a dozen *prahus*, hurriedly assembled from Budrudeen's allies and carrying a force of some three hundred men. Several Dyak chiefs had also turned out, mainly those whose villages had suffered the depredations of the pirates and who eagerly welcomed this opportunity for revenge. Admiral Keppel apparently shared James' distrust of the Chinese and none of that race accompanied our troops.

The Sarawak River gives its name to the country because it runs through Kuching, which is not only the capital but easily the country's largest town. The Saribas, though, is a far mightier river than the Sarawak. We entered the estuary at midday and sailed until evening before it narrowed to the point where we were within cannon shot of both banks at once. Not that there was anything to shoot at on either shore, for the river wound through scores of miles of mangrove swamp before it reached the sea. The mangrove trees grew out from the banks, giving the impression the jungle was moving forward into the water. Their roots trapped the mud and, with it, the stink of the marsh gas. The smell was revolting, even in the middle of the channel. The dark ranks of trees, their twisted roots reaching out toward us, combined with the foetid stench to give an aura of menace I did not feel in other parts of the jungle.

Whether the others in our party were affected by the evil spirit of the place or whether they were more concerned we were moving steadily into the territory of the pirate tribes, the men had grown noticeably quieter throughout the day. By the time we stopped for the night, there was a perceptible tension about our force. The *Dido* and the *Royalist* dropped anchor, and the smaller vessels secured themselves to the clipper as best they could, clustering for protection beneath her 32-pounders.

The next morning we progressed only a few more miles before Keppel ordered a halt. Although the channel was still navigable, the *Dido* and the *Royalist* were too big to manoeuvre in the limited space available. This would leave them vulnerable to fire from the shore, where the trees were thick enough to provide useful cover for any attack. We therefore transferred ourselves from our ships to the *Skimalong* and the *Dido*'s boats to continue our journey upriver.

As the river narrowed, the smell from the banks worsened and mud spits reached out toward the channel. Often we would scrape perilously onto swampy ground before swiftly reversing our strokes to push clear into the swirling tide. By now we were well into hostile territory, far beyond any point where Kuching's rule had ever been acknowledged. Those of us who were not at the oars nervously scanned the jungle, hands gripped firmly on spears and muskets.

Again, as night fell, we rested as best we could in the river. By now the mud had given way to firmer river banks but the possibility of attack meant we did not dare venture ashore to make camp. Sleeping in the boats was difficult at best, but added to our physical discomfort was the nervousness that had us start awake at every nocturnal cry from the creatures of the jungle. By morning we were tense with fatigue, yet we still had to row another three or four hours to our destination.

Eventually the order was given to ground our craft on a narrow beach formed in one of the many bends of the river. In planning our expedition, Mr Murray had met with anyone I could find who had any knowledge of the territory where the Saribas Dyaks had established themselves. He was confident their longhouses were near the river and only a few miles upstream of our present position. Small groups of Dyaks, each representing one of the pillaged villages, slipped silently into the jungle to reconnoitre. We remained on the beach, the Redcoats mounting a picket in case of surprise attack.

It was some hours before our scouting parties returned, but they came to report success. The Saribas pirates were, indeed, based some five miles upriver. They lived in two longhouses of conventional design, but their warlike mode of life had encouraged them to defend their homes with a palisade some eight feet high, which ran along the riverbank and extended around them, demarcating the clearing they inhabited from the surrounding jungle.

Mr Murray set out his charts upon the ground and I interpreted, explaining his maps to the Dyaks and their excited comments to him until we were all sure we understood the lay of the land and the fortifications we would have to overcome. At this point Mr Murray took his charts to the Admiral, and Mr

Hart and James joined him to plan the details of their attack.

It was by now late in the afternoon but Keppel was determined we should see action as soon as possible. He was anxious not to spend the night encamped where we were. The beach was crowded with our men and an overnight camp, with the practicalities of cooking and ablutions, would be difficult. There was also the danger that, so close to our enemy, our presence would be detected. Even if the pirates did not take the opportunity to mount a night attack, we would still lose the element of surprise. Keppel was also determined an attack late in the day would have practical advantages. The enemy would be relaxing, for the Dyaks typically ate at dusk, and the evening shadows would protect us in the shadow of the trees while the pirates, caught in the open, would still be clearly visible to us

We had expected some measure of defensive work around the pirates' homes so Keppel had brought with us a six-pound carronade, which was normally mounted on the fo'castle of the *Dido*. Smaller and lighter than the cannon we had used at Siniawan, the carronade was still a fearsome enough weapon deployed against an enemy whose heaviest artillery would be a musket, and its design made it especially suitable for the destruction of a wooden palisade. Keppel had had the weapon mounted in the bow of one of his boats and it was resolved that this vessel, commanded by the Admiral himself, would lead the attack by water. At the same time, James infiltrated his own force into position on the landward side of the settlement, so any pirates fleeing from Keppel's Marines would fall into the hands of our Dyaks and Malays.

In the event, the plan worked perfectly. Hidden among the trees, we looked out toward the pirates' palisade as we listened to Keppel's carronade open fire from the river. Then came the cries of the Marines as they stormed ashore through the wreckage of the village's defences, and minutes later, the pirates fled into what they thought was the safety of the jungle. As they ran toward the trees, our force emerged to meet them.

Unprepared for our attack and already running for their lives from the British, they could put up no effective resistance. Scores fell to the heavy jungle swords of the Dyaks, while the wavy blades of the Malays' *kris* were soon coated in the blood of the dead and dying. Those who escaped our first attack made no effort at resistance but fled into the jungle, where we did not pursue them. Instead our men clambered over the palisade to meet the Redcoats in the village.

We found the Marines rounding up the women, children, and old people of the place who had sheltered in their homes as the fighting men had fled. James made a speech, which I duly translated, explaining our invasion of their country was not for the purpose of pillage or gain to ourselves but as punishment for their repeated and aggravated acts of piracy. Our followers then herded them away from the two great longhouses which, with all their material possessions, were ceremoniously put to the torch. We seized their chickens and drove their pigs with us as we set off back to our boats and, despite Keppel's previously expressed concerns about a night camp, we disposed of the livestock in a great victory feast on the river bank.

The *Dido*'s crew formed a separate group from the rest of us, organised with military precision around their own fire, on which they were roasting a pig. The Admiral swaggered around his men with a handshake here and a comradely buffet there, and as soon as he saw James, he called for him to join them. James was more than happy to do so. I think that in that martial band he relived his youth with the irregular troops of the East India Company. Also, it was plain the younger officers, especially the midshipmen, idolised him and he was vain enough to enjoy this.

I did not begrudge him their company for I was more than happy to have some time quietly sitting among the Dyaks, trying to come to terms with what I had just seen—what, indeed, I had been party to. For that evening I had seen a different James Brooke from the man who had gone almost reluctantly to war at Siniawan, who had seemed to understand Dyak ways and had pleaded with the Sultan to minimise the deaths that followed his victory. Instead, in the company of a British Admiral, surrounded by British troops flying the White Ensign from their boats, he seemed to act instinctively as a British officer, clearing the natives from their village as an act of cold calculation, having already killed any who might resist.

Yet for all my doubts about the wisdom of this course, the Dyaks I feasted with that evening were more than happy with the day's work. Many had taken heads and they boasted of their prowess, holding their grisly trophies by the hair and recounting details of how they had made their kills. Others sat quietly, wiping their parang swords clean of blood, smiles playing quietly on their lips. I remembered the boy who had arrived bleeding in our home, what had happened to his people and to the troops we had sent to protect them, and I understood how the Dyaks around me felt. I resolved not to judge James but to wait until we were quiet and safe at home, where we could talk together of all that had been done in the Rajah's name.

Avoiding James as we rowed our way back was easy. The natives in our force, both Dyak and Malay, were happy to talk to me about what had happened and to speculate as to what actions we might take against piracy in the future. I stepped precariously from boat to boat, exchanging a few diplomatic words with all the captains and chiefs as our fleet made its way back to the *Dido*. James, by contrast, concentrated his attentions on the sailors and their officers and, even had we sought each other out, it was likely we would not have exchanged a dozen words together on the journey.

On the *Royalist* we were inevitably thrown closer together but James was full of himself, congratulating each of the crew and interfering abominably with Mr Hart's running of the ship, until Colin practically ordered him to get to his cabin and stay there. I, on the other hand, went quietly about my business, taking the opportunity to discuss with Mr Wilkins the economics of his provisioning the ship and making some suggestions as to which of his suppliers might perhaps be encouraged to reduce their charges. I spoke to Mr Hart about the general costs of the venture, which he considered minimal, the *Dido* having contributed the artillery and the *Royalist* being in port in any case. We discussed what arrangements we should make for loading the ship ready for her next trip to Singapore and whether we could do any of the loading at night to have her the sooner back in commercial service. I even managed to exchange a few civil words with Mr Murray, who was delighted to have had the opportunity to extend his maps of the Saribas.

With such conversations and the natural bustle of a ship under way, I managed to avoid any serious discussion with James until we were back in Kuching. There, I had resolved, we would talk over what had happened and what were to be our plans for the future.

When we arrived in the house, though, James seemed quite unaware there was anything untoward in my manner. Rather, he was so excited, he seemed to notice very little. He greeted Freddy with a breezy "*Salamat pagi*" then, though it was still morning, practically dragged me to the bedroom.

Normally James was very gentle in the physical side of our relationship. Indeed, when I think of his loving caresses, I cannot wholly believe what we did was absolutely wrong in the eyes of a forgiving God. But that day he seemed almost like a stranger. Though he professed his love, even in terms more extreme than he was wont to use, still he took me without any gentleness at all. And though I know he intended me no harm—and, indeed, gave me much pleasure—yet he was rough with me and hurt me.

Afterward he held me in his arms and we lay for a while together. In time, when he seemed calmer, he spoke of his feelings about what had happened. "It is a terrible thing to say, John, but—God help me—it was such fun. They were wicked men and they had done so many foul things, and then to have them at our mercy and to cut them down..." His voice trailed off and he held me again, his arms gripping me until I thought my ribs would crack.

Despite the earliness of the hour, we slept for a while after that and when we woke, his wild exuberance was gone and his dark eyes seemed darker than usual, as if the events on the Saribas had left a mark upon his soul.

# Chapter 8

OR THE NEXT FEW weeks, James would alternate between brooding in the house and rushing about the place for conferences with Mr Hart, Mr Murray, or Admiral Keppel. I was not invited to these conferences and I cannot pretend this was not hurtful. Perhaps it was that James was conscious I was not entirely happy with these schemes, but I fear he was ashamed of me before Admiral Keppel. For there was no doubt the Admiral had a presence to him we were not used to in our little country. And, on the *Dido*, James was surrounded by adoring midshipmen whose youth was untainted by any association with poverty. Certainly none of them had ever woken before dawn to milk a cow. Before this, I would have thought my early struggles made me the better man but, watching James bask in their adulation, I wondered if this was how he viewed it.

Whether, in the end, he would have acquiesced in the series of attacks Admiral Keppel planned, I do not know. In the event, the Admiral received orders directing him back to the waters off Canton and the *Dido* and its crew vanished from our lives as suddenly as it had entered, though not without many promises to visit Sarawak again.

With Keppel gone, a campaign against the pirates was no

longer possible and our lives moved slowly back onto their accustomed path. With no midshipmen to impress, James was mine again. He took care to spend as much time as he could at home with me, as if to make up for his previous neglect.

It was a happy time. We made some visits to a few of the nearer Dyak longhouses, dispensing gifts and trying, by our behaviour, to show we considered the days of bloodshed could be put behind us. Even so, we did quietly undertake some additional measures for the defence of the populace. Our trip up the Saribas had shown the value of the shallow-draft *prahus* in negotiating mud banks and sand spits. They could also be more easily beached when landing men against an enemy ashore.

The *Skimalong* was on hand only when the *Royalist* was in Kuching, and James decided we should have a boat ready at all times so we could respond to news of pirate attacks. Thus the decision was made to build a boat in native style but fitted with rowlocks and oars such as our men were used to handling. Mr Hart deputed a couple of his men to work with a tribe whose craft we had admired when they visited the market in Kuching. The work was swiftly done, and less than a month after the *Dido*'s departure, James proudly took possession of the latest addition to his fleet. Colin Hart, Mr Murray, and I escorted him to the quay where a bottle of rice wine was ceremoniously smashed against her prow and the *Jolly Bachelor* was officially christened.

Our experience on the Saribas had also convinced James we needed to have more men under arms, readily available if another expedition were called for. To that end, Patterson was given the title of lieutenant and told he was, henceforth, in charge of Sarawak's standing army, which was doubled in size to one hundred men. James had learned from our previous mistakes. The force was not split up and billeted among the various villages but maintained as a single unit in Kuching, from where it would be despatched hither and yon as we heard reports of pirate activity. The plan was not to capture the pirates in the course of a raid but, by showing ourselves prepared for battle, to serve as a reminder of what had been achieved on the Saribas and as a warning we could repeat the lesson elsewhere, if necessary.

The cost of maintaining such a force fell heavily on our exchequer. Although James' trip to Singapore had resulted in some improvement in the revenue from the antimony trade, still the country barely covered its costs, even before the expenses of war. Now James was forced to borrow to keep our economy afloat.

Paying the interest on these debts and making Sarawak cover its expenses became our major concern over the months ahead. There was no real prospect of increasing our income from antimony and the fees for using the port were already as high as we felt could be sustained.

At first, we were reduced to such small economies as any householder might indulge in when money was tight. For some time we had accepted mail at the house and this was despatched to the mine workings or Chinese trading outposts or wherever, as and when any of our boats were making the journey. Now James decided this business should be put on a more regular footing and a postage service introduced so people might pay for the delivery of their mail.

Unfortunately, as many a householder has discovered, the inconveniences attendant upon such an economy were out of proportion to the benefit obtained. We had to have stamps printed and then had to arrange with some selected merchants to sell them, and that meant myself having to institute an audit to ensure we did not pay commission on stamps that had not actually been sold. Then we put up a proper post box, with a lock, so the mails could be posted in decent form. After all this, many of the letters in the post box would not be stamped, the idea of paid postage being a novel one. James would worry some vital message might be delayed, so he would insist it be carried anyway…thus encouraging the populace to view stamps as an optional addition to the envelopes, making the whole exercise even more fatuous.

Overall, I would guess the paid postal service cost us several guineas a year to run, while the free service had at least not been an actual burden on our finances.

Such 'economies' were clearly not sufficient to save us from financial ruin, so a higher strategy had to be developed.

James was, as were we all, convinced of the merits of free trade as a thing good in itself. It had the additional benefit, though, that as goods were traded, so the possibility of taking a small percentage of the trade value as tax could generate revenue for us without impoverishing the population. Indeed, the benefits that should inevitably accrue to the people through the exercise of such trade should serve to increase their wealth and happiness. So it was that James determined we should encourage trading between the villages of the country.

The main problem with this grand design was that the Dyaks had scarcely any interest in such a way of life. Nevertheless, James directed much of our efforts to encouraging the tribes in commerce with the settlements around them. Besides exhorting them as to the benefits that might attend such a change in their economy, we took practical measures to make such intercourse between neighbouring tribes more practical. Our tiny army spent days at a time pursuing not pirates but small groups of head-hunters who, for reasons of personal gain, petty pride, or historical enmity, would prey on strangers and hence add to the natural perils of travel in the jungle.

Often James would lead such expeditions himself, leaving me to deal with the more sedentary aspects of the administration. He would return with tales of epic pursuits through the jungle and desperate fights when they would finally fall on one of the pillaging bands. James would always dwell on the bravery of the Dyaks—both those he was fighting alongside and those who were, on that occasion, his foes. Yet the stories I heard from others always put James at the forefront of the fighting. Though he might have a pistol at his belt, he was far more likely to be seen swinging at his adversaries with his old cavalry sabre—hardly the most sensible weapon for close fighting on foot.

One day, to his immense delight, one of the tribal chiefs presented him with a *mandau*, the traditional jungle sword of the Dyaks. The blade was not flat but thick, giving it much more weight than a European sword. The edge, though, was ground to razor sharpness. James insisted I take a walk with him and his new plaything and we strolled through the woods with him hacking at every branch and vine we passed. His enthusiasm was only slightly dimmed when a misjudged blow led to the blade kicking in his hand and coming dangerously close to taking his leg off. Later I was to learn these swords would often behave in this way—a result of the curve their design put on the blade. Among the Dyaks this reaction was ascribed to a malicious spirit, rather than the mechanics of the swing, and some swords were regarded as cursed and dangerous to the user.

James had greater luck in mastering the blowpipe or *sumpitan*. His own specimen of this native artillery was regarded as a mere toy by the Dyaks as it was only about a yard long—a heavy wooden tube with a hole bored precisely down the centre of it. We would practice together, rolling little balls of clay and taking turns to blow them at leaves. I had little success but James was soon an expert and the trees nearest our home had leaves so riddled with tiny holes it looked as if they had been struck by a plague of caterpillars.

James had always been popular with the native tribes, who saw him as a protection against the Malays. As he spent more and more time in their company, their appreciation and respect grew into love. He became more fluent in their tongues than I was myself and would take every opportunity to escape his labours in Kuching to spend a night or two in the interior. He slept on the floor of the longhouses and spent his days hunting with the young men or just sitting peacefully on the balconies of their homes, watching village life proceed around him.

As his efforts to stop headhunting and warfare between the tribes began to bear fruit, so the different tribes would seek each other out to exchange goods rather than simply for the purposes of warfare, as had all too often been the case in the past. People began to understand it was safe to travel between the villages and trade such surplus commodities as they might have available. The principal beneficiaries of these improvements, though, were not the Dyaks but the Chinese.

"I would see my Dyak friends benefit more," he would complain to me. "But what have they to trade? They hunt for the meat they need; they grow a few crops in their mean fields. They do a little weaving. Where are the goods they can sell?"

The Chinese, on the other hand, were consummate traders. Junks began to appear regularly at our wharves. They carried ironware, pottery, bolts of brightly coloured cloth, beads and bangles and bracelets, spices and pickles, and tinned goods of every sort. Under Makota's sway, they had already established rudimentary trading links with the native villages. Now, as our new policies were put into effect, their activities increased.

Such were the benefits of free trade to the Chinese that those already established in the country sent for others of their clans to join them. The population of Kuching was swollen by a score or more Chinese families who built themselves simple wooden houses in an enclave to the south of the main town, on the opposite side of the river from our bungalow. I would often venture there to admire the bright reds and golds of the temple they had constructed in their midst and to enjoy the sight of their colourful lanterns swinging in the evening breeze during one of their many festivals. But James avoided the Chinese quarter, as he termed it. He would often complain of the noise from their firecrackers and, indeed, placed strict limitations on the use of fireworks—ostensibly for the protection of the town, which was predominantly of wood.

As we struggled to develop our small country, word of what was happening in Sarawak spread about and we received letters from young gentlemen in Singapore—and even one or two in England—who asked if there were any opportunities for a younger son to join our enterprise and, perhaps to rise in fortune or, at least, in rank.

At first we dismissed such letters out of hand. As I journeyed in the *Jolly Bachelor* to parley yet another agreement between neighbouring villages, sleeping on the hard ground at night and spending my days struggling to find a compromise between two proud chiefs with a thousand years of history and accumulated grievances I could not begin to understand, it was difficult to see why any European would want to join our enterprise. We seemed often the servants of these people, rather than their masters—rushing hither and yon to deal with rumours of piracy or adjudicate over an unpaid debt. And the idea there was a fortune to be made was ludicrous. Every month saw us spending more of James's dwindling funds and it was only his increasingly desperate negotiations with the Singapore banks that kept our country solvent.

Eventually, though, we came to realise the administration of a country—even with so small a population as Sarawak—was too great a job to be handled by those of us who had started on this adventure. Colin Hart was seldom to be seen, spending much of his time at an office James had established in Singapore to represent our interests. Murray, though often passing through Kuching, was forever dashing about the country, surveying this or measuring that. Besides, his naturally irascible temper showed no signs of improving and we had no desire to draw him closer to us than necessity already required.

Thus it was we decided the time had come to recruit fresh blood to our administration. From those who had written to us, we selected Simon Corkerdale, late of Oxford, and George Willetts, who had spent three years in Singapore and now sought employment in less civilised surroundings.

George Willetts was the first of the two to arrive, being to hand, as it were. He was a tall man and would be a big man when he was older, but he was just five and twenty when he arrived in Kuching and still had the look of youth about him. Yet he had seen something of the world, spoke fluent Malay and, like the chap in the play, knew a hawk from a handsaw. He hailed from Liverpool and, though his father was a gentleman and he had an education, yet he had a solidness to him that impressed the men and they were happy to follow him despite his youth. He generally moved slowly, but with an easy grace, and when the occasion demanded, he could shift himself like lightning.

Soon after he arrived, I was showing him the loading of the *Swift* with ore when a hawser parted and a net full of rock was deposited on the deck. We had but a moment's warning, from the sound of the snapping cable, but Willetts spun about, sweeping me into his arms before throwing us both to the timbers of the deck, safely out of harm's way. I will not say he saved my life, for the great bulk of the stones fell safely away from where we had been standing. Still, his instinctive response boded well for his future inland, where he would be almost solely dependent on his own resources for months at a time.

Willetts had already left Kuching—sent away to mediate between two tribes in a dispute over a girl who may or may not have consented to her marriage and whose family may or may not have been insulted and whose brother may or may not have resolved this in the time-honoured way of lopping off the head of his sister's paramour. It was trivial, impossibly confusing, and about to lead to a small scale war that would kill a dozen or so warriors and twice that number of women and children, besides making trade in the area impossible for the next couple of years. I wished him luck…he was clearly going to need it.

Simon Corkerdale was as different from George Willetts as one could imagine. Just a year or two younger, he yet gave the impression of being little more than a lad. Where Willetts was slow yet graceful, Corkerdale was always in edgy, impatient movement. In his company I did not feel the calm assurance Willetts radiated, yet there was no questioning the sharpness of his mind. He was full of ideas for improving the local economy. He proposed changes in our port fees that encouraged captains to bring their vessels in at times when we were best ready to service them, reducing the clutter of shipping that could block the approach to the docks and keep our own vessels waiting, and losing money, while others jostled for position ahead of them. He had read the latest works on the prevention of disease through public works and proposed a system of trenches and bamboo piping to ensure the effluent of the growing township was discharged below the point at which water was drawn from the river.

He also introduced me to the wonders of double-entry bookkeeping. I had thought my accounts were already smartly enough presented and I found these new ideas difficult to master but master them I did, to his great satisfaction. "Why, John," he would say, "we'll have Sarawak solvent yet." His energy seemed unbounded and after his day's work, he would spend his evenings in recitation. He loved poets like Alfred Lord Tennyson, then a new and strange voice and certainly a change from the readings from Shakespeare and "The Rime of the Ancient Mariner," which were the nearest James ever came to high culture.

Corkerdale was obviously clever—much cleverer than I and cleverer, I think, even than James. Even so, I was not sure how he would cope when left alone to administer a chunk of territory on our behalf. Because of my concerns, I arranged that he would be kept not too far from Kuching and I would make some excuse to call upon him every few weeks. In the event, he proved a very able administrator and, although he never excited admiration or love amongst those he was sent to govern, still his district was always smoothly run. He arranged for regular patrols by our small army and set out to administer justice in a more systematic way than had been the case heretofore. He would even arrange court hearings where he would preside in a frock coat and a beaver hat, arguing the dignity this costume added to the proceedings was well worth the discomfort of wearing such attire in that climate.

The growth of our little colony was beginning to attract more interest, both in Singapore and in England itself. Several Singapore merchants wrote, suggesting they might set up their own houses in Sarawak. Most expressed their interest in terms of the assistance they could afford to our own enterprise by being readily to hand, without the problems of transport and communication that inevitably resulted from our remote location.

However, as Corkerdale was quick to point out when he learned of these approaches, almost all our income derived, directly or indirectly, from our monopoly of trade on the island. We therefore decided no other European merchants were to be allowed to set up in Sarawak. James would have liked to extend this ban to the Chinese but this was, frankly, impossible. So many Chinese merchants were already established and they were always bringing in relatives from their vast clans, enabling them to establish sizeable trading empires under the guise of family firms. We decided we should take what action we could to limit the expansion of Chinese mercantile activity and to tax what we could not control. However, the extirpation of Chinese trade was not to be attempted.

So it was that we imposed additional port taxes on goods we knew to be destined for Chinese traders and limited the number of new trading posts they could establish. Instead we set up new outposts manned by agents of our own who traded on our behalf. At the same time, we sought to buy for ourselves all the antimony mines in the country. Whilst we could not confiscate these from the Malays who held them by the authority of the Sultan, we could—and did—prohibit their transfer to others. As the owners grew older or needed to realise the capital in their investments, they were given no choice but to sell to us and thus, little by little, our monopoly was extended.

With the influx of mine managers and traders operating under our aegis, the size of the European population of Sarawak was growing fast. While James remained nominally in charge, I now found myself responsible for the administration of what was, in effect, a growing British colony—and growing not just in size but in prosperity. For, finally, our finances were edging into surplus. By recruiting men with a background in engineering, we were able to introduce modern methods to the antimony mines. The new tools I had foreseen when I visited the workings were, at last, introduced. Machinery was improved. Roads began to replace the rough tracks to the mines, so the ore could more easily be transported to the rivers.

Although James still affected contempt for the East India Company's approach to the management of its colonies, he understood their managers knew all the ways revenue could be extracted from a primitive economy. So he had Mr Hart sound out about Singapore for a man with experience in the Company and send him to us.

The gentleman who arrived was Mr Johnson. He was a great, round fellow, much given to sweating and with very little hair. He wore a waistcoat, even on the hottest of days, and was continually wiping his face with a yellow handkerchief. He was intelligent enough and could make pleasant conversation when the occasion warranted it, but neither James nor I liked him and there was no question of his joining our establishment. Nor do I think he would have wanted to. He had no interest in the place or the people, beyond the possibilities of converting their skills and resources to money.

"Cash, Mr Brooke. Gold, *gelt*. Commodities are not valuable of themselves but solely in terms of the income they can generate."

He would stride up and down our veranda of an evening, smoking a foul cigar—he had brought a supply with him from Singapore—and lecturing us on what he called 'the practical application of economic theory.'

"You have done well to limit the activities of the Chinese." He gestured disdainfully across the river, presumably intending to indicate the Chinese quarter of the town. "They are not honest or straightforward in their dealings. Too much is done through family connections."

I could see James nodding. His time in Kuching had brought him to the point where he was better able to conceal his dislike for all things Chinese, but he was happy to agree to any argument that bolstered his prejudice.

"Replacing Chinese merchants with your own agents means there can be a proper record of trading activities. Thus not only do you increase profit but you are in a position to extract revenue by taxation of such activities as yield that profit. As trade is increasingly conducted through outposts manned by your own servants, so we are able to take a small proportion of each transaction and thus generate income for your treasury."

He smiled complacently, no doubt envisaging the possibility of our growing rich on the plunder of our country, and we did not disillusion him. We smiled and offered him more drink and paid him—paid him well—for his advice and then, when the *Royalist* was next on its way to Singapore, we despatched him back to the counting houses that were his natural abode.

We took his advice on taxes, though. But rather than increase our overall income, we could use this money to finance activities that had been previously supported by levies on the Dyaks. For example, our army had been fed by those they protected: to wit, the Dyak tribes on which they were billeted. The Chinese, though benefiting from the peace they brought to the country, did not contribute to their upkeep. Now, with all paying taxes, we could use the money to buy food from the tribes people who, in turn, could spend that money on trade goods from the Chinese.

My reading of the great economists, and my conversations with Simon Corkerdale, demonstrated clearly that this change could not but be for the good of all. The benefit to the Dyaks was clear and immediate but the Chinese also gained advantages from the increase of trade that followed the introduction of a money-based economy.

With so much going on, I found myself more and more kept in the house, working on my ledgers like any clerk or poring over new regulations to ensure they were workable and fair. I had less time to spend at leisure and, when I did, I naturally spent as much of it as I could with James. His black moods had passed and Keppel's name was never mentioned between us. He was boyish and gay, spending, it seemed, ever more of his time off in the *Jolly Bachelor*, exploring his kingdom.

After a trip to one of the Dyak tribes, he informed me he had felt it necessary to introduce a woman into our ménage. I was not a little surprised at his news, for James, though easy with women, had no desire to be on closer terms with them than society demanded. Indeed, he had firmly forbidden the introduction of any ladies into our colony and the European population of Sarawak was composed entirely of bachelors. Fortunately, he had not gone so far as to prohibit fornication, so this proscription was not generally viewed as onerous.

James saw the unease on my face and raised a warning hand. "I'll hear nothing against Betsy, so you needn't start to say anything, John."

"Betsy!"

I confess—I squawked. The idea of James introducing a local girl to our house was almost incredible. Admittedly we had the cook, but we scarce saw her from one month to the next. And how had he found a "Betsy" in Sarawak? And why was he referring to any woman so informally?

James response to my cry was to burst into laughter. "Come in, Freddy!" he called. "Put Mr Williamson out of his misery."

The door opened and our servant entered hand in hand with Betsy.

She certainly wasn't human but she was too big for a monkey—about three feet tall. Most of the creature was covered in long, orange hair, but the face was bare, and from it two large brown eyes gazed soulfully up at me.

"It's an orang-utan, John. A gift from Urdisa." Urdisa was the chief he had been visiting. "She's young yet but I want to keep her and see how she grows."

Betsy had, by now, moved away from me and was seating herself at the table, as if she had spent her life in polite society…except that she seemed uncertain what to do with her legs. She tried them this way and that, eventually folding them in her lap and picking at her toes.

"It's all right, John. She's frightened of water, so I've arranged a sort of kennel for her on an old boat. She'll be quite safe there."

A loud crash brought our attention sharply back to the beast's activities. She had left her seat and was sprawled on the floor, clutching a sextant which, moments earlier, had decorated one of the shelves of the room. She was apparently unsatisfied with the effects of the fall, as she was trying to reduce the larger pieces of the device to their component parts.

I decided it was time to dress for dinner. As I left the room, James and the ape were sitting on the floor together, her long arms wrapped around him. The Rajah had, it seemed, made yet another conquest.

BETSY'S ANTICS SEEMED TO reflect James' own simple pleasure in life at Kuching. While she roamed about the house, exploring from below the floorboards to the peak of the ridged roof, James ranged around the countryside. He would follow Betsy's wild cousins as they clambered from tree to tree, sleeping in nests in the leaf canopy and hardly ever descending to the ground. He listened to the ear-splitting dawn chorus of the gibbons and heard the maniacal laugh of the helmeted hornbill whose huge ornamental beak was valued at twice the price of ivory by the Chinese traders.

Looking back, it is clear the two of us were too wrapped up in our own affairs…and in each other. I should have spent more time in the town, listening to the talk among the Chinese traders. James should have spent longer with Budrudeen's friends, keeping in touch with Malay gossip.

As it was, the blow, when it fell, caught us quite unawares.

We learned afterward that Surabada and his agents had been active around Kuching for months. He had opened negotiations with the Chinese, promising them freedom to trade as they had in the past and a reduction of taxes. To the Malays he promised a return to the old ways, offering them a free hand in the exploitation of the Dyaks. Even some Dyak chiefs had been approached—those who had fallen foul of our efforts to stop headhunting or who felt that their interests had not been properly reflected in the rulings of our officers.

They had plotted subtly, approaching only those they knew to be disaffected by the changes we had brought in. Their allies were few but they were powerful…and we were not prepared for their assault.

IT HAPPENED ON A Sunday night. I remember it had been a quiet day. James was not a religious man—indeed, he had earned the enmity of the Bishop of Singapore by refusing to allow a missionary station in Kuching. Nonetheless, we would attend a service on board the *Royalist* or the *Swift* when they were in port, but both were at sea that day and we had spent the Sabbath relaxing. James had played with Betsy. He allowed her at my library and I complained she had torn the covers from one of Mr Dickens' novels. We dined early and retired to bed soon after dark.

I was wakened with a hand upon my mouth. To my astonishment, I saw Freddy standing beside our bed, his fingers to his lips. As soon as he saw I was awake, he roused James in the same way.

James moved to light a candle, for the room was illuminated only by moonlight shining through the open shutters. Freddy, though, signalled urgently he should not do so. "They must not know you are awake," he whispered. "Your only chance is to flee."

Then what confusion followed! We both wanted to ask Freddy a multitude of questions, but he whispered we must be as near silent as possible.

"The house is surrounded by your enemies." This into my ear and relayed by me to James. "If they hear us, they will kill you."

We dressed ourselves as best we could in the moonlight and, following Freddy, tiptoed through the sitting room to the doors that opened to the veranda. The night being warm these, like the shutters, were ajar, and we were able to nudge them slowly wide enough to creep out.

Outside, the moonlight showed a scene as innocent as any other of the nights we had slept peacefully in our bed. Yet as I lay flat upon the boards around the house, I heard a whispering that was more than just the breeze in the bushes. Then I saw a shadow move, beyond my little garden. A moonbeam caught, for an instant, a glint of metal. Freddy's warning was true—we were about to come under attack.

While I still hesitated, wondering how to escape the trap I found myself in, Freddy—who had remained behind in the house—opened the doors on the other side and ran from the building. From all around him, figures moved silently from the darkness, hustling him away. Yet we heard no sounds of violence, so we supposed—correctly as it turned out—that our besiegers had no quarrel with our servant but only with ourselves.

Later we were to learn Freddy had been warned that evening that he should leave the house. His courage in waking us and warning of the plot was all that saved us from the assassin's knife.

James' martial instinct took over while I was still trying to work out what had happened. Recognising Freddy had distracted attention from our position, if only for a few seconds, James rolled across the boards and slipped to the ground underneath them, pausing just long enough to beckon me to follow.

There was no possibility of escape across the open ground around the building, so we retreated further under the veranda and waited to see what would happen next.

From our hiding place we could just make out shadowy figures moving closer until, all at once, there was a yell and our home was surrounded by armed men rushing to the doors. We heard their feet on the boards overhead. Then James was dragging me out and we were running for the trees.

Behind us, we could hear the cries of our attackers as they searched the house and the crash of furniture being wantonly destroyed. So eager were they to tear apart our home in search of us that we had almost gained the shelter of the trees before anyone looked in our direction and set the enemy in pursuit.

We were two and unarmed. We had no choice but to run, relying on our knowledge of the area and the cover of darkness. We made the trees, a few shots sounding ineffectually behind us. Then we were plunging through the jungle, branches tearing at our clothes, tripping on roots and sprawling every dozen or so paces in the litter of the forest floor.

Fortunately, we had spent many an hour exploring in these woods and knew the lie of the land better than our pursuers, who were more acquainted with the alleys of the town across the river. We made for a creek that ran through the woods some half a mile from the house. As soon as we arrived upon its bank, we pulled off our boots and, without any further preparation, plunged into the waters and swam for the farther side. There we sat shivering in our wet clothes and listening as the sounds of our pursuers drew away from us.

Sitting in the dark beside the creek, we reviewed our resources. We had water at our feet, but no bottle to carry it in. We had no food, no arms, no map, no compass. The *Royalist* and the *Swift* were at sea. Our army, such as it was, was scattered about the country, the nearest force some two days upriver, if we had a boat…which we didn't.

James decided our first step should be to reconnoitre the town, to establish whether this attack was a part of a larger rising or an isolated attempt on his life. This was easier said than done. The river at Kuching was wide and the current strong—swimming it was hardly possible. We resolved instead to work our way upriver, away from the bungalow, until we could find some craft small enough to manage and then to use that to make our crossing.

We made our way to the river by moonlight but decided against travelling farther in the dark. We were moving steadily away from the parts of the forest we knew and the risk of carrying on by night was too great to hazard.

We rested as best we could. I slept but fitfully and what sleep I had was disturbed by dreams. I saw the dark shapes of men attacking our home but they were Keppel's tars and, as we fled, we stumbled across the bodies of the dead on the Saribas.

I woke the next morning more tired than I had been when we stopped for the night. Forcing myself to wakefulness and remembering the danger of our position, I fell in behind James as he set off along the river. We made as good a speed as we could, trying to put as much space as possible between us and any pursuit.

After about an hour, we came upon a canoe pulled out of the water near some fields. Pausing only to ensure there was no watch being kept on it, we seized the opportunity to get ourselves upon the water. This not only meant we could move more quickly, but we were no longer as immediately threatened by pursuers on foot, as we now had the protection of the river.

Bobbing in comparative safety on the stream, we reviewed our options and decided on our strategy. The first thing we had to do was to establish the scale of the trouble and find out what support we could still draw on in the town. This we could do only if we returned to Kuching. Our first move, therefore, had to be back in the direction of the horrors of the previous night.

Reluctantly we set off downstream, paddling cautiously and staying close to the bank, taking advantage of such cover as was provided by the branches hanging out over the water. About a mile north of Kuching, we left the canoe and again made our way along the river's edge, slipping into the trees as we came toward the town.

Even from the shelter of the jungle, it was clear all was not well. The docks were deserted and there was a smell of burning on the air. Smoke could be seen rising from some of the buildings.

James looked at me. "Budrudeen is away, but if we can get to his compound, we can seek shelter and find the extent of this revolt."

Our adventures so far had left us wet, dirty, and bedraggled. Our clothes were torn and our faces bruised from falling in the dark. We decided our best chance was to walk through the streets, keeping to the side alleys as much as possible and hoping not to be noticed, but relying on being mistaken for a couple of drunken sailors if we were.

The streets were almost deserted, which made it the easier to walk through the town without notice. James clearly hated it, slinking from shadow to shadow instead of striding proudly through the streets acknowledging the greetings of his subjects.

In the event, we did not have to make our way directly to Budrudeen's compound. As soon as we were within sight of it, the clouds of smoke billowing from behind the compound walls told us all we needed to know. We turned and headed back toward the jungle.

KUCHING WAS CLEARLY NOT safe for us. We decided our best chance was to head upriver, in the canoe we had appropriated. We reckoned if we pushed ourselves to our limit, we could reach Corkerdale's post in two days. We would have to trust to the water of the river to satisfy our thirst, and we would not starve in two days.

"Think," said James, with grim humour, "how much effort we shall be saved by not having the necessity to carry provisions for the journey."

In the event, we passed a grove of sugar cane soon after we started our journey and crept ashore to break off some stems. With not even a knife to cut them, breaking the canes was harder than we had expected, but we were able to snap off sections we could chew the ends of, sucking out the sweet sap to stave off the pangs of hunger. Nevertheless, the absence of any solid food sapped our strength and we had made much less progress than we had hoped when night forced us to stop paddling and try to rest. Without any weapons and with nothing we could use to start a fire, the fear of wild beasts meant we were forced to sleep in the boat. With no anchor, we moored by driving ourselves hard into the branches of a fallen tree, the boughs of which projected some way into the river. The constant wash of water and the scraping of the dead branches against the hull invaded our dreams, and neither of us slept well.

James' old chest wound began to trouble him. By noon, he was visibly weakened, and well before nightfall he was coughing in a way that began to alarm me. As his condition deteriorated, we paddled even more slowly and were still far from our goal at the end of the second day.

Another night sleeping on the boat in clothes we had worn continuously since our escape meant flesh rubbing into evil sores which, in turn, attracted all manner of biting insects. We were stiff and hungry and cold, and in fear for our lives. Every real or imagined sound on the bank would have us reaching for sword or pistol…before remembering we were unarmed.

The thin dawn light found us pale and haggard and almost totally unrested. We decided we must reach Corkerdale that day. If we spent another night on the boat, hunger, wretchedness, and fatigue would mean we would make barely any progress the next day—and we knew every passing day made it more likely the revolt would have spread throughout the country, leaving us with no place of refuge.

All that day we paddled. Around noon, it rained. The water fell as if in solid sheets, battering us with its force. We had no cloaks to shelter under and could not afford the time to pull to the bank and wait out the storm under the trees. So we paddled on, our wet hands blistering, the sores on our bodies a constant dull pain.

Eventually the rain stopped. Our clothes steamed but did not dry and we travelled in silent misery until the sun fell.

Fortunately, the storm had left clear skies behind it and the waning moon provided enough light for us to see our way. We paddled in a sort of torpor, aware of nothing except the effort of raising and lowering our arms and the moonlight on the water, marking out the way upstream.

Suddenly we were roused by shouts from the bank. Too tired by now to care if these were the cries of friend or foe, we turned toward them and soon willing hands were pulling at our tiny craft and helping us as we staggered ashore.

"Who's there? What's going on?"

Corkerdale's voice sounded clear on the night air and there was the man himself, hurrying toward us, surrounded by armed men.

He pushed through the crowd that had gathered around us, stopping as soon as he realised who we were. "Heaven be praised! You're safe."

James turned and stepped toward him but almost immediately swayed uncertainly on his feet and had to be caught by the men who had helped us ashore.

Corkerdale started to issue urgent orders in the native tongue and men moved forward to carry us toward the longhouse.

I heard someone say, "He's a lot better at the language than I ever thought he would be." I had just time to realise the speaker was myself before I passed out.

I RECOVERED CONSCIOUSNESS TO see James' face looking down at me, concern in his brown eyes. As he saw my own eyes open, there was a flicker of a smile at the corners of his lips and he bent forward quickly and kissed me.

I was lying on the ground near to the longhouse, wrapped in a blanket. The reason I was not in the house itself was clear—I was resting alongside a fire that brought relief to my shivering bones. The Dyaks did not need to heat their houses so fires were used only for cooking, which was done well away from the dry wood of their dwellings.

James sat cross-legged alongside me. "Are you well enough to talk?"

I nodded.

"The others are sleeping now. I said I would stay here with you. We're safe enough. There are sentries posted."

He coughed gently, but his chest was clearly troubling him much less already. His hand went to his throat and he fiddled with the collar of his shirt. He was wearing clean, dry clothes, and I realised he must have borrowed them from Corkerdale, a rather smaller man than he was.

"Word has already spread of the revolt. Surabada is behind it, of course. But the Chinese are backing him. It is their treachery that has lost us Kuching." He grimaced. "Some of the Malays have taken the opportunity to advance themselves by joining the revolt. Most of the Dyaks are loyal, though."

He leaned forward toward the fire, stretching his hands to the warmth. "Corkerdale's called the local chiefs together and put the villages on a war footing. The warriors are ready for a fight. The trouble is..." His voice tailed off and he turned to look at me.

"John, you know how many men Surabada can command. He's been planning this for months. If we face him without even the *Royalist*, we'll be destroyed. We need firepower. I need my ships."

He was right, of course. On our own in the jungle, we could no more help the Dyaks defend themselves against pirates now than they had been able to defend themselves in the past. Our only chance was to reach one of our ships and then fight our way back to Kuching with all the power we could command. But how to reach our vessels? The River Sarawak was closed to us, as there was no way we would be able to pass through Kuching. If we sailed back down the river and abandoned our boats above the town, we would be in the same situation as we had just escaped—trapped in Kuching with no way of reaching the coast.

The alternative was to make our way overland to another river, negotiate a vessel from one of the tribes that lived there, then head out to sea. The nearest river where we could be reasonably confident of finding a friendly tribe was the Rebu, which lay fifteen miles to the northeast…but that fifteen miles was solid jungle.

The next morning James, Corkerdale, and I met for a council of war with the village chief, Dinda. He was accompanied by three of his warriors, magnificent young men, their arms and legs decorated with elaborate tattoos, their heads wrapped with scarves.

Corkerdale took charge of the meeting. James seemed diminished in his too-small borrowed clothes, but Corkerdale had a clear authority with these people and they listened carefully as he explained the situation.

Dinda seemed concerned about an expedition to the Rebu. Although Corkerdale's efforts had almost eliminated headhunting, a journey of fifteen miles would take them far away from their traditional hunting grounds and was not to be entered into lightly. The young warriors, though, seemed excited at the prospect of travelling to another settlement and they urged their chief to let them go.

In the end, it was agreed that James and I would be escorted by a dozen warriors. Corkerdale was to remain at the village to reassure the tribe that Rajah Brooke's authority was still to be respected.

We rested for the rest of the day. I relaxed on the long veranda of the great hut that housed all the people of the tribe. The women had taken their handlooms out of the gloom of the communal hall and were weaving in the sun. As I watched, war bonnets, tunics, and carrying sacks formed themselves beneath their busy fingers, while inside the hut I heard a woman singing to her baby as she ground tapioca for the evening meal. All was as it had ever been, here in this clearing by the river—and the plotting and planning that occupied our lives in Kuching seemed an illusion.

Alas, the next morning I had to leave that demi-Eden to set off on the march that marked the first stage in James' battle to regain his kingdom.

We started along a well-trodden path leading from the village to the fields where sugar cane, tapioca, bananas, and pineapple were grown to provide the basic requirements of the tribe. Then we started away, striking into the jungle on a narrower path almost hidden beneath the long rank grasses and tangled creepers. Soon we were deep in the forest. The path had vanished and without the tracking skills of our companions, we would have been hopelessly lost within a hundred paces.

Despite the absence of a path, we were able to move easily. It is a myth that moving through the jungle is a constant battle through the vegetation. Here, where the trees grew old and tall, the dense canopy of leaves left the ground in a perpetual twilight where little vegetation grew, and we moved swiftly across the carpet of dead leaves and twigs.

From time to time we would come to places where the trees grew thinner. Here, scorch marks showed lightning had struck one of the trees, starting a blaze that left a clearing a mile across. There, the slope was too steep to hold enough earth for the taller trees to grow. In these places, the jungle was the stuff of adventure storybooks, with bushes and scrub fighting for the light, covering every inch of the ground. We had to either go around—perhaps travelling a mile or more out of our way—or we had to cut our way through, our escort's swords rising and falling in an easy rhythm with every step we took.

After a few hours our route led us uphill and the nature of the ground changed, becoming steadily rockier. The jungle gave way to a low scrub, which was much harder to make our way through until we came on a path some two metres wide. It was a pig-track, marking the route of the annual migration of the boar which form a valuable addition to the natives' diet. We were able to follow the track for a full mile before we had to branch off and again hack our way, step by gruelling step, through the scrubland.

All at once, the scrub gave way to woodland. Here, the trees grew shorter and farther apart than in the jungle proper. You could almost imagine yourself in a beech forest back in England, pushing through bushes and scrambling over roots. Suddenly our guides motioned us to silence and then, slowly and with evident caution, started to edge back the way that we had come. Only after we had, with painstaking caution, worked our way a good quarter of a mile did one of them whisper, "Tiger!" before setting off in a new direction.

Such delays and detours meant we made slow progress. As when James and I had travelled from Kuching, we carried no provisions, but now we had gourds to carry water and weapons so we could kill our food on the way. Indeed, in the late afternoon, our guides insisted we sit and wait beneath a particularly tall and stately tree while they vanished with their blowpipes into the forest. They returned some thirty minutes later with two small deer, which they carried slung over their shoulders until we made camp some two hours later.

Sitting by the firelight, sniffing appreciatively as the deer cooked above the flames, I was struck again by the timeless peace of the place and I slipped easily into a dreamless sleep.

THE CHATTERING OF MONKEYS woke us with the dawn.

The day passed much as the previous one. Our progress was slow but steady, and toward the end of the afternoon we came upon the River Rebu. Our guides started downstream, urging us to hurry. They wanted to be safe in the village by dark. In part, this was because of a natural desire to spend the night in the safety of human habitation, but they were also anxious that the inhabitants of the place should not find strangers coming upon them after the sun had set. For all that the land was safer now than it had been, still the people harboured real fears of assault and would likely attack any travellers they found in the dark rather than risk strangers in their vicinity by night.

As it was, we arrived just as the last rays of the sun were lighting the river and we were greeted as friends by the people of the village. Our warriors had killed two more deer that afternoon, though they had always planned to eat in the village. Their quarry they now presented to the chief, it being customary for travellers to bring some sort of gift. James and I had nothing to present, our circumstances having rendered us destitute, but the deer served as a gift from all and the excuse for a welcoming feast.

That evening being given over to eating and drinking, the object of our journey was not mentioned until the following morning when, as we had done three days before, we sat with a Dyak chief and his warriors to plan our next step.

Word had already reached the village that Kuching was fallen to the enemies of the Rajah. It is a constant source of amazement to me that these things are known so quickly, with no semaphore, no telegraph, and little in the way of everyday communication. Yet it is rare that a traveller carrying, as he thinks, the latest intelligence, does not find that his news has run ahead of him to every tiny village that he visits. Indeed, there was news for us—Surabada and his pirates were already in Kuching.

We explained we needed a vessel to take down the river and out to sea. There we hoped to link up with either our own ships or those of Keppel's squadron which, we believed, were again on patrol in the South China Sea.

The Chief was clearly nervous at the turn events had taken. Surabada would not stay long in Kuching. With James deposed, he could return to his principal interest: raiding the tribes of the interior. Our hosts reasoned, with justice, that Surabada would first turn his attention to those tribes most loyal to the Rajah. By assisting us in the way we asked, the whole tribe would be put into danger. Yet these people remained loyal to James, even in his present state. He was stripped of his power and sitting among them in borrowed clothes, begging their assistance— and, for the love of him, they gave it.

Our friends were not prepared to risk too open a confrontation with Surabada. They could provide us with a vessel—a boat not unlike the *Jolly Bachelor*—and they could provide a crew. But they would not take us beyond the mouth of the river. The boat, they argued, was not really fit for the sea and Surabada might well have vessels patrolling the coast, which would be bigger and designed for naval warfare. The Chief was not prepared to risk his men in such a one-sided conflict. Nor could we blame him, given that the pirates would show his people no mercy if they were caught aiding us.

We explained that without a vessel we could take to sea, we had no chance of rejoining our forces and mounting any sort of a counterattack.

In the end, the Chief agreed to a compromise. He would provide the vessel and a crew to the river mouth. We would be escorted by another craft carrying provisions. Once we reached the sea, we would be provisioned for a long voyage and the crew would return in the second craft. We could jury-rig a sail to our boat and, provided the weather remained calm, we would be able to set out into the shipping lanes and hope to meet up with a European vessel.

It was a desperate gamble. To manage any vessel on the open sea with just a crew of two would be difficult in the best of circumstances, and impossible if a storm blew up. We would never make it to Singapore. Our one hope would be to fall in with another vessel before our provisions ran out or the weather changed. Yet the alternative was to rot in hiding in the jungle, watching as all we had achieved was destroyed.

James rose to his feet and bowed graciously at his hosts. "We thank you for your kindness. Your offer is most generous. We will leave tomorrow."

❋

WHAT CAN I SAY of that journey? We were carried to the coast in just one day, our crew paddling lustily, leaving James and me silent and idle in their midst, each lost in his own thoughts. That night we camped together. No fires were lit and we posted sentries all about but there was no sign of pirates.

The next morning dawned fair. There was a mild breeze carrying out to sea. Conditions were as good as they would ever be. We transferred our provisions and rigged a crude mast amidships from which we hung a sail improvised from the same sort of cloth I had watched being woven only a few days before.

We clambered aboard our frail craft and willing helpers pushed us from the shore, through the lazy breakers, and out to sea. We turned and waved, but already our escort were launching their own craft, hurrying to return to the comparative safety of the interior.

I am not a praying man but I confess I prayed that day. I prayed no patrolling pirate would see our craft. I prayed the weather would hold. And I prayed that somewhere, on the measureless horizon, we would see a friendly sail.

At first, it seemed all our prayers were to be answered. No pirate patrol intercepted us. (Later we were to learn that Surabada's men were too busy pillaging Kuching to have mounted any patrols at all.) The weather remained calm and the wind, as far as I could judge, favourable.

As the long day wore on, though, our most urgent prayer remained unanswered. We saw no other vessel.

We had no charts and no compass to use them if we had. I had not thought to grab my pocket watch as we fled Kuching and James' was destroyed by immersion in the course of our adventures. We could estimate time only by the height of the sun, and our direction by its position at what we judged midday. For all that we would trim our sail to hold the breeze or take a turn or two at the paddles, we were essentially adrift on the ocean.

By nightfall, we had seen nothing. Our supplies had seemed plentiful when we set out but a day in an open boat under the tropical sun had seen our water supply dwindling faster than we had expected.

We sat in the starlight and chewed the dried monkey meat we had been given and resolved that we would drink less the next day.

Morning came and with it the sun. The clear and cloudless sky that had seemed such a blessing when our greatest fear had been storms was now our enemy. The sun blazed down and we had no escape. We contemplated taking down our sail and rigging an awning but decided against it. Lost as we were, we knew every mile we could move north put us further from Surabada and nearer to the shipping lanes. And, probably more importantly, the sail made our little craft more likely to be seen should we pass within sight of any vessel.

Desperate for shade, we tore off our clothes to rig a tiny shelter amidships. Yet even in this patch of shadow, the heat was nigh unbearable and we were plagued all day by thirst. That evening we discovered that, despite all our efforts, more than half our water was gone.

The third day was like the second, and the fourth like the third.

On the fifth day, our water ran out.

The sixth morning I woke to what I supposed was to be my last day in this life. The two of us were near delirium. Our sole comfort was each other and we clung together for most of the morning. Every hour or so—as far as I could judge—one of us would clamber laboriously to his feet and scan the horizon for a few minutes before collapsing back into the bilges. Even to stand was exhausting and squinting into the glare for a sail that was never there...that destroyed our souls.

When I did see the ship, I thought it was a hallucination. But then I pulled James to his feet and he saw it, too. We waved and shouted and at first we thought it had not seen us but then, slowly, she came about.

She was the *Van de Meer* out of Utrecht. She was engaged by the Dutch East India Company. Her captain spoke not a word of English and his mate, who did, loathed our race in general and, in particular, those who traded in what he saw as Dutch territory. He saw two near naked, bearded men, half delirious, adrift on a native boat, and he did not care to disguise his contempt.

The crew were surly and the ship's doctor, who pronounced us fit, an ass.

They saved our lives.

# Chapter 9

THE *VAN DE MEER* was headed for the Dutch colonies in Sumatra, but their course through the Straits of Malacca took them past Singapore and, with a great deal of grumbling as to the inconvenience, they were eventually persuaded to put in there so we could be disembarked.

We made our way to the office where Mr Hart represented our interests in the colony. Fortunately, it was no distance from the quay where we were landed for we had no money and, in the cast-off clothing we had been given aboard the Dutch ship, no litter bearers would have given us credit, so we were compelled to walk.

Luckily, Colin was there when we arrived and we were shown quickly to his private office.

His first reaction was to hurry from his desk and embrace James and then, scarcely less warmly, myself.

"Good God, you two," he said, releasing me and holding me at arms' length while his eyes took in our ragged appearance. "I had feared you dead."

He already knew of the revolt. The *Royalist* had arrived in Sarawak just three days after we fled the bungalow. It had started up the river toward Kuching but retreated when it found the river full of Surabada's fleet. Fortunately, the Master had had the sense not to try to fight his way through but had returned to Singapore.

Colin had already been to see the Governor of Singapore, asking him to offer James the protection of the British flag, but the Governor had refused to take any action, arguing that Sarawak was not a British possession and James should look out for himself.

When Colin explained this, James slumped into his chair with his head in his hands.

"I had little hope I would see my country behave honourably," he said, "but that they will allow all British influence to be driven from Borneo is even worse than I could have anticipated."

Since the night of the revolt, I had seen my friend grow more morose. The boyish confidence and easy command he held over those around him—things that were usually the essence of his character—these had been slipping from him. Yet, safe in Singapore with the worst of our trials surely behind us, only now did he allow himself to collapse into despair.

"England has abandoned me. We have achieved so much. We have established a British outpost in an area dominated by the Dutch. Yet we are abandoned." He paused, apparently close to tears. "For God's sake, Colin, it was the Dutch who saved us!"

Colin moved over to him and bent to put his arms around James' shoulders, comforting him like a child. "The Governor is a fool. He's a political and not to be relied on. I have sent messages direct to Keppel for his personal attention. There is a man who will stand by his friends."

Without releasing James, he looked up at me. "I'll arrange a carriage to my lodgings. Get him there and keep him there. I don't want anyone seeing him in this state."

COLIN'S QUARTERS WERE SIMPLE, reflecting the straightforward nature of the man himself, but they were comfortable. And, importantly, they were private.

James' outburst was caused by the black mood that had seized him again but there was some element of truth behind it. He could hardly blame the British government for giving less than whole-hearted support as Sarawak was his private fiefdom, subject in theory to Hassim and independent of Queen Victoria. Yet James was clearly British and his rule in that country extended British influence in a part of the world where the Dutch were fast establishing a dominance that could hardly be in British interests. So James might have expected some formal assistance from his own country.

Yet in Singapore he was treated as just another merchant, struggling to make a profit alongside all the rest of them. We had mocked Mr Johnson behind his back, but his attitudes were the predominant ones. James had expended his own fortune and whatever credit he could get, not in the hope of profit but in an attempt to improve the lot of his people. And to show what Britain and British values stood for.

Keppel, I think, had understood something of this and had helped us as much as he could. But when he was given orders to patrol elsewhere, he had gone and left us to our fate. In the end, our saviour had been Dutch. James Brooke, English gentleman adventurer, had been saved from rebellious natives by the true colonial power in the region.

Yes, it was far from the whole truth, but there was enough truth in it for me to understand why he said it. And it was true enough for it to be imperative that no one know of his condition now. With no support from the Governor of Singapore, Sarawak's credibility as a trading partner was entirely dependent on James Brooke's credibility…and anyone seeing the wretched creature curled up on the bed in Colin's rooms would have been looking to withdraw from trade with Sarawak as quickly as they could.

JAMES REMAINED IN HIS black mood for three days—longer than I had ever known him in such a state before. While he lay abed or sat silently staring ahead of him, Colin and I prepared for the battle to retake Sarawak.

The *Royalist* and the *Swift* were both in Singapore and the crews ready and anxious to return to Kuching and reclaim what was as near a home as they had.

In the months since Keppel had left us, we had all grown unused to battle so the crews were kept busy rehearsing gun drill. Muskets were bought and issued and the men practised until they could load and fire at least two shots every minute.

Ball and grapeshot were procured and stored ready near the guns. Powder barrels were rolled up the gangplanks and stowed carefully below deck.

And we hired a surgeon. Colin thought we would likely need one.

✳

BY THE TIME KEPPEL arrived in Singapore, James had recovered. Knowing him as I do, I am not sure he was ever again the confident youth I had so loved but if there was a change in him, it was subtle enough that no one else remarked on it. Certainly Keppel gave no sign of seeing anything amiss. He greeted James with real enthusiasm, pumping his arm and congratulating him on his escape.

"You did the right thing," he assured him. "Withdraw and regroup. We'll have them now." And he rubbed his hands together, like a glutton anticipating a feast.

Although I knew Keppel was genuinely fond of James, I could not at first understand why he was so anxious to enter into battle on his behalf. It was Colin, who had been living a while in Singapore and better understood the politics of the place, who explained it to me.

"Keppel has been sailing round in circles for months," he said. "He knows there are pirates out there but he can never catch them. Just three months ago, two pirate vessels attacked a junk standing in sight of the docks here. By the time help had rowed out to them, the crew was dead, the cargo looted, and the pirates halfway to the horizon. When he does manage to sink a boat or two, there's no glory in it. He's anxious for promotion and he's realised he'll never get noticed patrolling the sea-lanes like a parish constable looking for burglars. He wants a battle that will show him as the scourge of piracy in the South China Seas. He thinks James will give him the chance."

Watching Keppel unfold his plans, I could well believe this. He would not only take the *Dido* to Sarawak but also planned to press the *Phlegethon* into service with him. Named for the Hellish river of fire, the *Phlegethon* was a steam-powered paddle ship owned by the East India Company. She was ideally suited to working in the rivers and estuaries of the archipelago and her manoeuvrability in such waters more than made up for the fact she carried only four guns. With these two vessels, he was confident he would be able to retake Kuching and then use the town as a base for anti-piracy operations throughout North West Borneo.

James, on the other hand, was not convinced. He absolutely vetoed operations in any of Hassim's territory other than Sarawak, explaining such actions would jeopardise British relations with the Sultan and James' own position at Kuching. Nor was he entirely happy at the idea of the British navy having the free run of his country.

"We can make an example of the insurgents in Kuching and then show mercy elsewhere. I have established control of the country in the past with scarce a score of men. I'd as soon not rule over a ruin maintained by bloody force."

Keppel would nod, as if indulging a favourite nephew, but he would still huddle over his charts which, thanks to Murray's efforts, now marked every inlet and river along the coast.

"And how is Mr Murray?" Keppel asked one morning, tracing the coastline with a stubby finger.

"Well up the Ranga River—and if he's any sense, he'll stay there until this is over. But you can never tell with Mr Murray." James gave a quick smile and then, at once, his face turned grim. "For God's sake, Henry. I've men all over the country. We have to get to them soon or Heaven only knows what their fate will be!"

❈

KEPPEL WAS ALREADY QUITE aware of the need for speed, but I suppose James' continual urging that we start the expedition as soon as humanly possible could have done no harm. Anyway, our squadron was quite ready only four days after the planning began. Keppel sailed ahead in the *Dido* with the *Phlegethon* sailing close behind while the *Royalist* and the *Swift*, carrying our own men, followed at a distance. Colin Hart forsook his office and was back in command of the *Royalist*, where James and I kept him company and made our plans.

James held fast to the idea we should try to restrict the fighting to Kuching, although he expected we would need to be prepared to conduct raids throughout the country if the rebels refused to yield any other towns they might have taken. He was optimistic, though, this would not be necessary.

"You know the Malays, John. They'll all fall in with whoever they think is winning. We see Surabada off and they'll come back in line. Most of the Dyaks will have stayed loyal. We can deal with the Chinese easily enough. It's just the pirates we have to fight and they will still be based in Kuching. They have no interest in holding any of the inland towns—pillage and move on, that's their style."

So our tiny armada force sailed eastward toward home. If Keppel still had his own ideas of what we would find at the end of our journey, he stayed aboard the *Dido* and kept his own counsel.

❋

OUR VOYAGE WAS SWIFT and uneventful, and only four days after leaving Singapore, we lay at anchor at the entrance to the Sarawak River. We were just a dozen or so miles from Kuching but there were hours of winding river between us and our home. James and I leaned on the rail, looking toward the jungle, grey in the fast fading light. The bo'sun called up that signal flags were unfurling on the *Dido*'s mast.

"D-I-N-E W-I-T-H M-E," said the first string. Then another: "P-L-A-N A-F-T-E-R."

So Colin, James, and I found ourselves together in the *Lily* being rowed across to dine with the Admiral. It reminded me of our first days in Borneo, when we had forever been together in that little craft, yet one look at the melancholy in James' eyes was enough to remind me how much had changed.

An admiral's stateroom is very grand compared to the accom modation on a craft such as the *Royalist*, but it was still too small for over-much ceremony. Our dinner that evening was an informal affair, though the food was good and a fine claret was served.

During the meal, Keppel kept us entertained with a string of stories about his life in the Service. He told a good tale when it suited him to entertain his listeners and was clearly concerned to keep our minds from dwelling on the battle planned for the next day. It was only after we had eaten and toasted the Queen, God bless her, that he turned to business.

"I intend to leave the *Dido* here," he said. "I will take the *Phlegethon* upriver alone. It is a smaller vessel and with no need to rely upon the wind, we will be better able to navigate the river."

James sat forward to interject but Keppel raised a hand to silence him. "I know you would like to take up the *Royalist* but this is purely a tactical decision. Manoeuvring in the river will be difficult. It is that which lays us most open to hazard. One ship is easier to manoeuvre than two. Thus one ship, alone, will make her way to Kuching. The *Phlegethon* is the best suited to this task, so the *Phlegethon* it will be. She will make her way through Kuching. She will not seek to engage the pirates until she is upriver of them. Then we will turn broadside across the river and endeavour to drive the enemy out."

He smiled without humour. "As they reach the mouth of the river—that, gentlemen, is when you will have your chance."

※

WE SAT A WHILE longer, deciding exactly where to moor our ships to provide the best opportunity to fire into the pirates as we ambushed them at the river mouth. There was some discussion about tides—it was best to take the *Phlegethon* upriver with the tide but to arrive when the tide was on the turn.

James wanted to sail aboard the *Phlegethon* but Keppel vetoed this. James could do no good there, he argued. James, in turn, forbade Keppel from taking any action ashore until the *Royalist* had brought him back to Kuching.

They agreed the *Royalist* would remain with the other ships blockading the river mouth but that, as soon as the pirates were clear of her position, she would start upriver. James would return to his capital, escorted by his own men. Only after he had landed would Keppel's Marines, if required, start operations ashore.

Keppel and James rose to their feet and shook hands with a formality unusual between them. Keppel bowed to Colin Hart and myself and accompanied us to the deck. As we clambered down the ladder to the *Lily*, he leaned over the rail and waved down to us. "Never fear, Mr Brooke. We'll see those villains beaten yet."

Then he was gone and we were rowing back to the *Royalist* to spend the night restlessly anticipating the events of the next day.

In the end, we had nothing to worry about. Keppel's plan worked perfectly.

Of course, I did not see the initial action myself, as I remained aboard the *Royalist* with James, but I heard about it when Keppel reported the details of his success that evening. For all that he loved to tell a story—especially one where he was a principal actor—on this occasion the admiral simply summed up the way the strategy he had outlined the night before had been put in place that day.

"We ran up to the town easily enough—steam power certainly has its uses. Surabada was still there, as we had surmised. There were boats everywhere.

"I had my concerns we did not carry enough guns to do the job but I need hardly have worried. The smoke and the noise of the paddles had them in a panic before we started firing and once the shot began to fly, they couldn't get out of the place fast enough."

Keppel hadn't relied on the four cannon of the *Phlegethon* but had packed the ship with as many Marines as it could hold and they kept up a withering musket fire on the pirates. Some of the enemy tried to put up a fight and a few got near enough to hurl their throwing spears. Two sailors and a Marine were killed. Several others were hurt but not so as to incapacitate them, although one was reported near to death by the evening as his wound was apparently infected.

The *Phlegethon* cut straight through the fleet, her paddles churning the muddy water white. One of the pirate canoes, approaching too closely to the vessel, was caught up in the flow of water to the paddles and dragged into the wheel. The boat was destroyed and the crew lost, while Keppel swears that aboard the *Phlegethon* he felt barely a shudder in her timbers.

The steamer's guns kept up a steady fire as she moved remorselessly upstream but Keppel did not attempt any serious engagement until the ship was almost level with our boom. On the shore, all was confusion. Groups of pirates and Malays rushed here and there but, clearly unprepared for attack, their frantic activity lacked purpose. Some did try to get the guns into action but, never having used these weapons before, they struggled to load them. Others ran to swing the boom into place—a wasted effort, as Keppel's plans did not involve moving beyond Kuching.

Now *Phlegethon* swung about and her broadside engaged the shore battery.

"I was watching through my glass," reported Keppel, "but at first I could see nothing for the smoke and debris that hid the scene. When it cleared, there was no sign of life within twenty yards of the guns. We fired once more, to be sure, but that was it, really."

Keppel did not fire on the boom. He had no need to clear it and did not wish to damage our defences more than necessary. Instead he concentrated on the pirate fleet, firing again and again directly into the mass of boats.

The *Phlegethon* was a small ship but, with her steam engines and her guns of the latest design, she represented the power of the European world. Faced with a force so outside of their experience, the native sailors took the only sensible course of action. They fled.

The *Phlegethon* followed lazily on the ebbing tide, lobbing broadside after broadside into the retreating foe.

On the *Royalist*, the crews were ready at their own guns. We were the closest vessel to the shore, ready to lead our victorious fleet to Kuching as soon as the battle was over. So it was that we were the first to see the retreating pirates as they broke from the river, heading for the open sea.

Even as our guns opened on them, there was chaos in their fleet. There must have been forty or fifty of their boats filling the river. As our shot fell amongst the first of them, they tried to retreat. As their vessels turned, they ran into those behind them. With the river full of craft desperately trying to manoeuvre around each other, our little flotilla was able to close toward them, firing repeatedly into the melee.

Fortunately for Surabada's men, the entrance to the Sarawak is dominated by great mangrove swamps, through which smaller channels cut their way to the sea almost like a river delta. Although we must have sunk a dozen or more craft, the enemy were nothing if not good sailors and soon they broke for the tiny channels where our craft could not follow.

The *Dido* attempted to pursue those who had managed to run our blockade but, watching her clumsy attempts to turn, we knew they would have no success in catching their nimble prey in the enemy's home waters.

James turned to Mr Hart. "We've done enough here," he said. "I'm anxious to get to Kuching as soon as we can. Take her in, Colin."

"The tide's on the ebb. We'd have to tow her up now and it's no easy run."

James didn't even look at Mr Hart as he replied. His eyes were fixed on the jungle.

"Get the *Skimalong* in the water, Colin. We're going home."

IT WAS STRANGE TO find ourselves moving slowly up the river, by now so familiar to me, yet not knowing what we would find at journey's end. Everything was as it had been the last time I made this passage—the mangroves, the jungle, the chatter of monkeys in the distance—yet all was changed by our knowledge of what had passed in the weeks since we had last been here.

After some hours of slow progress against the tide, we came to the first cultivated fields that marked the beginnings of what had come to seem to me like civilisation. Soon after that, we rounded a bend in the river and Kuching came in sight.

At first it seemed nothing was changed. Yes, the *Phlegethon* was lying at anchor and the river was strewn with the wreckage of the pirate fleet, but the town was still there. Then I noticed above the smell of powder that lay still on the air the smell of old fires that had burned out but left their charred stink long afterward.

Here and there were gaps in the buildings of the town.

Smoke still smudged the air where Budrudeen's compound had been. The quayside had a desolate air and the doors of the offices hung open, off their hinges.

I turned to look at the other side of the river, at the home I had built with the man I loved.

There was nothing there but ruin.

James looked like a man in a dream, his face devoid of any flicker of emotion. He boarded the *Skimalong* and, at his command, was rowed first to the town.

Where normally there would have been the bustle of commerce, there was an eerie quiet. We were conscious of eyes watching us from the cracks of doorways but saw no one abroad. In one narrow alley where I had often haggled for supplies, I thought I saw someone sitting at their old stall. I started toward him but James caught at my sleeve. "Best not," he said.

I realised then why my old acquaintance had not moved and I turned away. Hart, who had accompanied us ashore, nodded to a couple of the men of our party and they went to do what was necessary.

"I'll organise a fatigue party for such work," he said. "We can't have bodies left unburied in this heat."

James, his face still a mask, said nothing.

We arrived, as if our feet were guided by a remembrance of our first visit to the town, at Hassim's old audience hall. It was undamaged but deserted. Within, there were the remains of a feast interrupted by the *Phlegethon*'s arrival.

"I've seen enough here," James said. "Let's see what's left across the river."

He led his sad procession back to the quay and the *Lily* set off for the far bank.

We took no escort with us this time. The two of us walked alone up to the remains of our home.

My little garden had been trampled. Our furniture had been scattered all about the place and the building itself had been burned.

In the centre of the ruins, someone had set up a crude cross. Nailed to it was the corpse of Betsy.

When James saw it, for one moment the mask of his face slipped and beneath I saw a glimpse of something I pray I may never see again. Then he turned away expressionless. "We must see Keppel," he said. "The man is right."

He started back toward the river and had walked a hundred yards before he spoke again. He said just five words before silently resuming his steady pace.

"I will kill them all."

I THANK GOD I was kept busy in the days and weeks that followed our return, for James was like a man possessed. We needed to contact our agents in the country to discover how widespread the revolt had been and what losses we had suffered. We had to bury the dead and ensure the security of the living. The normal commercial life of the place had to be re-established, for without money nothing else could be achieved. The buildings that had been destroyed had to be rebuilt. And all the time I had to reassure our people we were truly back in command and they could trust us not to desert them again.

James left all this to me. At first I was flattered that by now he was so confident in my stewardship, he did not feel he had to concern himself with the details. As the days passed, though, I realised he simply did not care. He was concerned solely with revenge.

Budrudeen was sent for and arrived with fifty of his followers equipped for war. He and James drew up a list of every Malay who had been involved in the conspiracy or who, they thought, might have been involved. Budrudeen's men then went from house to house to search them out.

They found only a few old men, the younger rebels having fled, but the old men were humiliated, being beaten in public and driven from the town. Most, I imagine, would have quietly slipped away to Brunei but those without friends to provide a boat and supplies for the voyage…well, they were old men and I suppose their time was almost done.

Those Malays who had been loyal to Brooke returned to their looted homes. Now, with our own followers, they were in their turn looting the households of our enemies. So it was that I spent much of my time supervising the rebuilding of our town while James watched his companions destroying the parts so far undamaged.

The Malay community suffered, but we knew many had remained loyal and Budrudeen ensured that his friends were protected. The Chinese, though, had no such champion. James had been suspicious of them from the first and his suspicions had eventually created the very treachery he had feared. As far as he was concerned, the revolt was an act of betrayal by his Chinese subjects and he turned on them with a fury.

Extra taxes were demanded to pay for the rebuilding work, and the bulk of these taxes fell directly on the Chinese. Money was to be raised not only on their trading activities but on their actual property, and I was required to go about the town with a squad of Budrudeen's troops, forcing my way into Chinese businesses and confiscating goods until I judged their taxes had been paid. On occasion, I was even required to break into private homes, and it was only after my special pleading that their temples were spared from this legalised looting.

I had thought, during the revolt and on our return to a ruined town, that I had plumbed the depths of misery, but this was worse. These were people I had been doing business with since the day we first arrived. I knew them. I knew their children. Some were scoundrels but many were honest by their lights and I liked them. Now I had to oversee our men breaking into their homes, searching their valuables, seizing whatever could be sold and, as often as not, destroying the rest by carelessness or just from malice.

The Dyaks fared best. They had a terror of Surabada, based on long experience of his piratical antics. They were also fiercely loyal to Mr Brooke. One by one, our agents among the Dyaks sent news of their continued safety. Even Mr Murray, not famed for his tact, had survived the whole time as the reluctant guest of a tribe far inland where he was surveying at the time. Whether he was the happier to be able to return to Kuching and a regular supply of whisky or whether they were happier to be rid of him, we never knew.

James sent for the tribal chiefs and, over days and weeks, they would emerge from the jungle to re-pledge their loyalty and to tell what they knew of Surabada and what measures they could take against him. Every meeting ended with James embracing the native chief, pressing vases newly looted from the Chinese stores upon them, and accepting promises to provide armed men at his command.

While James plotted revenge on his enemies by land, Admiral Keppel was not idle. The *Phlegethon* patrolled ceaselessly around our coast while Murray checked their charts and supplemented his existing observations so Keppel's craft had precise knowledge of the main channels of all the rivers of the country.

With so much activity and so many calls upon my time, I was hardly aware that Admiral Keppel's efforts were already beginning to show results. News came back from the *Phlegethon* that pirates had been engaged and enemy shipping sunk. The *Dido* took up position off some coastal town where many of Surabada's supporters had been based and bombarded it until nothing was left standing.

Encouraged by the presence of the British Navy, the loyal Dyak chiefs organised their own raids on those villages that had supported the rebels. Harried by land and sea, the pirates began to be forced back toward their heartlands on the river Batang, toward the northern borders of Sarawak.

This, though, remained a background to my own activities.

My greatest concerns related to the plans for a new home to replace the bungalow from which James and I had run the affairs of the country before the revolt. James was determined our new headquarters should be more secure and it seemed politic it should be a grander affair—a true *istana*, or palace, to symbolise the strength and permanence of the Rajah's rule. So the replacement of our airy bungalow was to be a solid fortress facing onto the river. Inside, a courtyard provided a place to sit in the cool air, but there were to be no more evenings on the veranda, looking down on the town below.

Often when I came to James with my ideas for the new building, Keppel would insinuate himself into our discussions, claiming that his training in warfare gave him a special insight into building for defence. The wide windows I had planned were to go, replaced by mean openings that could easily be protected by thick shutters. The balconies were decried as posing a risk should an enemy storm our home or in case an assassin might claim ingress like some malicious Romeo. The open arch, welcoming our subjects to their ruler's home, was to be sealed by great wooden gates, which should be opened only on ceremonial occasions, and the frontage should incorporate sentry boxes so guards could watch over us day and night.

In such an atmosphere it seemed natural I should, with increasing frequency, see armed men swaggering in the streets of Kuching, or that the nearest fields should have been tramped flat by the feet of soldiers practising for war.

When James at last summoned me to his great council of war, the die was already cast. Surabada had been driven back to his last great stronghold and Brooke and Keppel had, between them, decided the pirates, and all they represented, were to be, for once and ever, wiped from our world.

The meeting was held in the Sultan's old audience hall, where we had assembled on our first day in Kuching. I remembered the music playing and the servants plying us with sweetmeats. Tonight there were no such distractions.

James sat on a small dais with Keppel beside him. I joined Mr Hart and Mr Murray on one side of the platform, glancing across to where Willetts sat with Budrudeen and some of our truest Malay allies on the other. In the open space of the hall before us, other Malays and Dyak chiefs jostled for position while their supporters, many attired for war, stood warily around the walls.

There was no discussion. James addressed the room, reminding us all of the evils the pirates had brought to the country. He spoke in English and I passed on his words in Malay. "It is our firm conclusion that only the final extirpation of these villains will serve to bring us peace. Together, we can proceed against them. We have with us soldiers and sailors of Queen Victoria, who stretches her hand across the ocean to protect those of us who are her friends and to chastise our enemies. With their aid, we shall succeed once and for all in ridding ourselves of this menace."

His words were received in silence but, as I looked about me, I saw many of those in the hall nodding in sombre assent.

Admiral Keppel then stepped forward. Murray had unfurled a map of the country behind him but the Admiral recognised that most of the audience were unfamiliar with cartography and wisely chose to address them without its aid.

"Our enemy is driven back to his bases on the Batang, two days sail north along the coast. Their capital is at Beting Marau but it is protected by forts near the entrance to the river and, we expect, by palisades at those villages we will have to pass as we move toward Beting Marau. There will be fierce fighting at all these points and many men will die. Yet I am confident that with the power of the British Empire at your side, we shall see victory and the final end of piracy in Sarawak."

He paused and looked around the room. "We will sail in two days. It is not for me to command your assistance but any who sail with me will have many opportunities to show their valour in combat."

Many in the great hall cheered and the armed men around the walls beat their spears against their shields. Then a voice in the crowd called out, "And many opportunities to seize their treasure!" This was followed by laughter and more cheering and James, sensing the mood of the crowd, called for pigs to be slaughtered in the street and fires to be lit. The council of war turned into a celebration—an excuse for feasting and drinking.

I stayed a while, watching the warriors tearing at the meat and laughing together as some started war chants and others danced waving their swords around the fires that had been set up in the street. Then I made my way back to the *Royalist* and my temporary home.

As I walked through the deserted streets, I saw a Chinese face peer from a doorway, searching toward the sounds of the feast. Her eyes showed all too clearly the perturbation of her soul. And as I listened to that savage chanting in the night, I too feared what the future might bring.

THE EXPEDITION STARTED WELL enough. The *Dido*, the *Phlegethon*, and the *Royalist* headed the fleet as we moved up the coast toward the estuary of the Batang. Behind was an armada of native boats, among them the *Jolly Bachelor*, ready to do service further upriver, where the Navy's ships would be unable to penetrate.

Our first target was the fort at Patusen. This was a solid piece of work, constructed by Surabada when he had free sway over the area and reinforced and expanded since. From its walls projected the muzzles of more than fifty cannon pillaged from the ships his pirate fleet had captured. Standing almost at the water's edge, it presented a formidable obstacle to any attempt to attack upriver.

Even so, the walls were but palisades of timber, however stoutly made, and Admiral Keppel was confident our firepower was more than sufficient to breach them.

The *Dido* moved into the estuary and swung broadside on to the fort. As her guns fired, there was an answering cannonade from the fort. Although I would guess only half of the guns in the fort were actually discharged, still the water around *Dido* was white with the spray of falling shot.

This was the sort of conflict the *Dido* had been built for and we shouted ourselves hoarse cheering as her guns sounded for the second time, but our jubilation turned to horror as a lucky shot hit the mizzen mast and we watched it tumble to the deck, dragging rigging and sails with it.

The *Phlegethon* came swiftly to the *Dido*'s aid. She fired one shot toward the enemy but then lay to without making any further move to attack. While we looked on in puzzlement, another burst of fire from the fort threatened to disable her alongside the *Dido*. At this, we saw a burst of activity on the *Phlegethon*'s deck and ropes were thrown across to the larger ship. The *Phlegethon*'s paddles started to churn the water and she came about, towing the *Dido* away from danger. They were barely in time, as the pirate gunners had their range by now and their third round took some timber from the *Dido*'s flank and came close to hitting her saviour.

Ten minutes later, a furious Keppel boarded the *Royalist*. With the deck of his flagship a chaos of men clearing the wreckage of canvas and ropes and carpenters busy with repairs, he was transferring command to our ship.

"It's a damn disaster," were his first words. "A ship of the line bloodied by a bunch of natives with stolen guns. One man dead and half a dozen wounded. The *Phlegethon* useless—all her new fangled weaponry and the priming tubes are faulty. The damn guns won't fire."

As a naval man, Hart felt best placed to reassure. "I'm sure it's nothing that can't be fixed, Admiral. If we work through the night, the *Phlegethon* and the *Dido* will be ready for action at dawn and the *Royalist* can go in as support. The three craft together can wipe out the fort and we're on our way."

Keppel looked disgusted. "That's as may be, Mister Hart. I'm sure *we* will be on our way—but what of them?" His sweeping gesture encompassed the ragtag armada that followed us. "Do you think they will wait for us to proceed at our leisure?"

James' face was thoughtful. He understood his people and the importance they attached to keeping face. The withdrawal of the Navy's two ships would already have cast doubt on Queen Victoria's effectiveness as a war leader. The enthusiasm with which this crusade had been taken up could just as quickly fade and then the forces we would need to fight our way upriver might well melt away into the jungle.

"Admiral Keppel is right. We have to act decisively to maintain our momentum. The fort has to fall—and fall today."

Colin was already on his feet. "I can have the *Royalist* in position in five minutes. Our bombardment will start in six."

Keppel plucked at his sleeve. "Sit down, man. Don't be so hasty. You've seen what they did to the *Dido*. Do you want the same thing to happen to the *Royalist*?"

There was a silence while we imagined the scene on the *Dido*'s deck—the wreckage of the mast; men lying screaming, limbs shattered by falling timber, and one lying silent and still, never to speak or move again.

Keppel looked at Murray's charts on the table in front of him and closed his eyes in thought. When he opened them, he spoke with the conviction of a man who had seen in his mind's eye exactly how he would dispose his forces and what the effect would be. "We need an attack and we need it before the natives have time to dwell on our failure this morning. It must be led by the Navy so that we may restore confidence in ourselves. It must draw our followers into the action. It must show boldness, and it must be successful."

He paused and looked around at us all. "Gentlemen, we must storm the guns."

After the first stunned silence came a storm of protest. The fort's gunners had already shown they were well trained and competent. Surely any direct attack must fail. Yet the Admiral's plan showed how he had risen so far in his chosen service, for it was both simple and effective.

Keppel reminded us of what we all knew. The greatest difficulty of gunnery is gaining the range of the target. A target moving rapidly toward the guns, especially one low in the water, is the hardest for a gunner to engage. Further, a boat sailing directly at the guns presents a narrow target, while bombardment necessitates the vessel swinging broadside on, which is obviously easier to hit.

The frontal attack Keppel proposed also took advantage of our particular strength—the sheer weight of numbers we could bring to bear. The native forces at our command numbered more than a thousand men. Even were the guns to take down a score or more of their attackers, the fort would still be overwhelmed.

So it was that at midday our forces massed for the attack. The *Dido* and the *Phlegethon* lay well offshore, out of range of the batteries, but the Navy was nonetheless well represented. The *Dido* carried two cutters and a pinnace, as well as the Admiral's gig, and these four vessels were in the forefront of the assault. Of course, the *Jolly Bachelor* was there as well, alongside Budrudeen's war *prahu* leading our mixed fleet of Malays and Dyaks.

We were joined aboard the *Jolly Bachelor* by John Ellis, the captain of the maintop on the *Dido*. He had been seconded to us to handle a light cannon that Keppel had insisted we fit as a bow gun. Mr Ellis, we were assured, would prove his worth as a gunner, though I thought the Admiral detached him mainly because Ellis had been hit hard by the damage to his men that morning and Keppel had determined he deserved the chance to be in the thick of the action. The day would offer him ample opportunity for vengeance.

Whatever the reason for his presence, it proved an unlucky choice for him. As the boats rowed full out for the shore, the enemy gunners fired as best they could but, as the Admiral had foretold, they could not find our range. Only one vessel was hit and that was our own. A shot came directly at us and Mr Ellis, who was stood in the bow reloading our gun, was cut in two. His upper body fell into the water while his lower half, the legs still jerking spasmodically, collapsed into the boat.

The effect of this horror, which I would have expected to make us rigid with fear, simply drove us to increase our efforts at the oars. It seemed only seconds after Ellis had departed this world that the *Jolly Bachelor* grounded on the muddy foreshore in front of the fort.

For a moment, ready to leap out into the assault, I felt again the fear that had gripped me before the attack on Balidah. Though I knew now I had the sort of courage I needed to face the enemy, I wondered how I would acquit myself. I seemed to have seen so many battles, yet I remained no warrior but almost an accidental observer and did not know how I would manage if, today, I was called upon to fight an enemy who did not flee.

I had scarce time to consider this possibility before I found myself charging with the others, throwing ourselves upon the fort. There was no order or science in our approach. We were little more than an armed mob. I heard my own voice screaming with the rest of them as we beat upon the palisades. The fort had been designed to resist a naval onslaught rather than a direct attack of this sort, and the embrasures where the guns were mounted were barely four feet from the ground. Already our men were scrambling through these gaps and throwing themselves upon the gun crews who took one look at the mass of their assailants and turned to flee.

Too late! We fell on them, spears, swords, and Naval dirks all rising and falling in a frenzy of killing. Some few of the enemy escaped to the small town behind the fort but they were pursued and hacked down together with any who came forward from their dwellings to protect them.

In a very short time, it was over. The fort and the town were given over to pillage and that night we feasted on the enemy's supplies in the ruins of their stronghold.

James was in the best of humours. He had led the charge from the *Jolly Bachelor* and, though he made no boasts of his own, those around him claimed to have seen him strike down no less than three of the enemy by his own efforts.

"And was that true?" I asked, when I was finally able to sit with him in some sort of privacy.

"Maybe. Does it matter?"

I shrugged. I truly didn't know what to think. On the one hand, I loved James for his gentleness and kindness. On the other, there was something about his martial valour that, I cannot deny it, excited me.

"And you?" he said. "Went your day well?"

I blushed. "I did my best," I said. "I was there. I did my best."

"Don't worry, my angel." He ruffled my hair, smiling at me. "I do not love you for your strength in battle."

Then someone shouted from among the Marines and James rose, moving to Keppel and those young midshipmen with their dirks and their songs of war. I could have wept that I would never be like them.

I watched him laughing with them in the light of their fires and swore that the next time I saw battle, I would make James proud of me.

THE NEXT MORNING, WE set off upriver.

The Batang is narrower than the Sarawak that runs to Kuching, and even the *Phlegethon* was too big to manoeuvre safely if, as we were sure we would, we had to fight our way to our destination. The *Dido*'s pinnace—itself a fair-sized vessel with two masts as well as oars to manoeuvre in the river—therefore led us on the next stage of our journey. We had, altogether, nearly two hundred men from the Royal Navy in addition to around forty officers and men under Mr Brooke's personal command and the horde of natives under their various captains.

Late that day, we came upon a village by the riverside, abandoned by its inhabitants. We camped there for the night, knowing the enemy would be preparing to meet us at the next township, Silabas.

We arrived at Silabas in the early part of the next morning. A cluster of longhouses sat on one bank and a palisaded fort on the other. Just below the township, the river narrowed. Huge stakes had been hammered into the riverbed to slow navigation at the very point where our boats would be most exposed to the guns of the fort on one bank and fire from the village on the other.

Such, at least, was the grand strategy of our opponents but Keppel, in the lead boat, ordered his men to push forward. Instead of slowing, he increased his speed, the men rowing like demons, until they rammed hard against the stakes. Some gave way, allowing the boats to move onto the next row of defences as the rest of our fleet packed in behind until the river was filled with craft.

Taken off guard by such a bold assault, minutes passed before our foes could react, but now they poured fire down into the boats and I saw men falling, clutching as blood poured down uniform tunics or naked chests. The sailors and Marines fired back while our Malays and Dyaks leapt from those boats nearest the shore and sought to engage the enemy in hand to hand combat.

I had thought any attack against such obstacles as we faced would be perilous indeed, but I had underestimated the advantages we had on our side. Although our attack was expected, the enemy was taken by surprise in facing such a direct frontal assault. Mr Brooke's own men and those of the Navy fired modern weaponry, vastly superior to the pirates' flintlocks, and we fired in disciplined volleys. Most important, though, was the sheer weight of numbers we threw into the assault. For every man of ours that fell, three more would rush to take his place. Our followers were fired with the memories of their victory at the river mouth and convinced James Brooke and Henry Keppel would, between them, lead to inevitable triumph.

In less than half an hour it was all over. The warriors who were not killed fled into the jungle, pursued by our Dyak troops with orders to ensure none escaped to carry intelligence of our progress. The women and children, knowing their homes must inevitably be destroyed, salvaged what they could carry and fled in their turn.

As the place was abandoned by its inhabitants, so Marines, Malays, and Dyaks moved in, looting anything of value left and destroying all they could not steal. Within an hour, the longhouses and the fort were in flames. Once again, we feasted in the ruins of our enemies' defences.

That night, James and Keppel sat apart from the rest of us. From time to time, Murray was summoned to join them, and from him I learned they were planning the details of the final assault on the pirate stronghold at Beting Marau.

Had I known then the details of their design, I might have objected. As it was, I did not know but, even so, I went uneasily to my rest.

As I lay on the hard earth, I looked over to where the two men were still talking. A lantern threw their shadows upon the ground, resembling the demons I had seen in the shadow puppet displays of the Malays.

Then the light was put out and I slept.

WE MADE GOOD HEADWAY the next day and were within two miles of Beting Marau before noon.

The first I knew that our strategy was to be completely different here was when our fleet pulled to the shore and the greater part of our Dyak forces disembarked. James moved among the chiefs, speaking earnestly and quietly to each, then the warriors slipped away into the jungle.

Rather than move forward, our fleet lay still until the middle of the afternoon, when the Admiral gave the order to set out once more.

We arrived at Beting Marau with only an hour or two of light remaining. As the *Jolly Bachelor* emerged from the thick jungle and I saw Beting Marau for the first time, I was astonished at the size of the place. Although I had known Surabada led a significant tribe, I still thought of his men as renegades. It was only the sight of his capital that made me realise Surabada led a nation, smaller than Sarawak but nonetheless significant. I estimated there were two to three hundred dwellings ranged along one bank of the river. Opposite was thick jungle, but Beting Marau was encircled in a loop of water. By now the river was only some fifty yards wide and very shallow, but it still formed a useful defence. It was, however, almost the town's only defence. There was no palisade and only a small fort. Presumably, the people relied on the fortifications down river to protect them from attack.

The curve of the river meant there was a beach of sand along the front of the town and here we saw scores of Surabada's boats. Our attempts to stop the refugees from Silabas escaping to warn the enemy had clearly succeeded, for scarce a dozen of the vessels were in the water, the rest being drawn up on the beach and hence not available to use against us.

Those few pirates who could do so moved out to engage us with a bravery that verged on recklessness, but they were outnumbered and outgunned. Within minutes, we had control of the river that cut the town off from the jungle on three sides.

Keppel's gig turned toward the fort, now all that stood between Surabada and disaster. Followed by the two cutters, he ran ashore directly below the palisade. Seamen and Marines swarmed out of the boats and started their attack on the fort.

Here there were no low embrasures, as had doomed the fort at the river mouth, but neither was there much in the way of artillery with which the inhabitants could defend themselves. The guns they had presented no threat to the men immediately below the walls, as they were arranged to command the river and any shot would pass straight over Keppel's men. Some of the defenders tried to use their muskets or even their spears, but any who showed themselves above the parapet were despatched by sharpshooters positioned on the beach below.

The seamen had brought grapnels and they swung these into the fort, clambering up the ropes with an ease bought of long experience climbing rigging. Before James could bring the *Jolly Bachelor* in to support them, the Navy was inside the fort and Beting Marau's last defence had fallen.

At this point, I expected things would follow a similar course to those I had witnessed at the other pirate defeats, but this was not to be.

The pinnace, which had remained distant from the action until now, took up position opposite the town. I saw a flurry of activity on her deck, then there was a sound of rushing air, and the deck was wreathed in smoke.

It took me a few moments to realise what I had witnessed, for I had never seen a Congreve rocket launched before. These missiles were like the rockets that might be used at a Guy Fawkes show or to signal distress at sea, but they were launched in a low trajectory like cannon balls and, fired in batteries, they were an instrument of terrible destruction against any flammable target.

Now rocket after rocket flared into the undefended town, starting fires among the thatches wherever they fell. In minutes, Beting Marau was burning.

The town was still full of warriors as most had been unable to launch their ships and few had stayed in the doomed attempt to defend the fort. Now, with their town burning around them, they recognised the futility of resistance and prepared to flee to the jungle, ready to fight us on a more propitious day. Their escape, though, was hampered by the panicked flight of their women and children. Beting Marau was, as I have noted, a large enough town for there to be a significant population who were not warriors, and they had been as surprised by our attack as were their menfolk. As I watched from the river, I saw figures running through the smoke in all directions and the screams of the women could be heard above the crackling of the flame.

Now Keppel ordered his men to take positions along the beach. As the enemy fled, they fired volley after volley. Keppel himself joined the firing, his coxswain standing alongside him, loading and reloading his muskets.

As one man after another succumbed to the ruthless firing from the beach, the inhabitants of the pirate capital fell back, away from the river and toward the jungle. It was then the full murderous intent of Keppel and Brooke's plan became clear.

From the jungle came the cries of our warriors who had moved to Beting Marau while we rested on the river and who now cut off any retreat from the burning town.

James stood in the bows of the *Jolly Bachelor*, urging the men to pull for the beach. As we grounded, he leapt ashore and ran toward Keppel. Seizing one of the Admiral's muskets, he stood alongside him, picking off any targets he could distinguish in the smoke.

All around me, our men rushed toward the town, firing as they ran. I could see their mouths open and I knew they were screaming and yelling for vengeance, but I could not distinguish their words. My ears were filled with the crackling of the flames, the crashing of falling buildings, and the cries of those trapped in the burning town.

For a moment I stood, paralysed by the horror before me. Then I felt a shot pass by my head and remembered my promise to myself. I would no longer allow others the glory. I would join the battle in earnest so I could face my comrades as an equal in valour.

I saw a warrior step out of the smoke and stand to face us,

his spear raised, waiting for an enemy to step within range. I ran toward him, sword in hand, only to see him fall to a shot from a sailor standing twenty yards away.

I ran on. A figure leapt at me and my sword arm swung. I felt the impact and the warmth of his blood soaking my sleeve. I looked at the face of the man I had slain and the face staring back at me with empty eyes was that of a youth barely old enough to fight.

Another figure came at me, a warrior for sure. He threw his spear and I ducked aside before rushing at him, my sword swinging wildly. The first two blows he parried with his shield, then he staggered and my third attempt slashed open his belly.

By now I was in the narrow alleys that had once made up the town, but all around me was fire and ruin. Another figure lurched toward me and I lifted my arm to slash again before recognising the man as a European. We ran forward together, seeking desperately for someone who was not already dead or dying. All I wanted was to kill.

Someone leapt screaming from the conflagration, his hair burning. The man beside me rushed at him and struck his head from his shoulders.

A woman carrying her child fell and, before she could rise, the buildings around her collapsed and where she had lain there was nothing but flame.

I saw a Dyak warrior hold a child by the arm and swing his sword, taking off the infant's head.

The noise of the fire, the screaming, the smell of burning flesh, distinguishable even over the smell of charred wood—all these things filled my senses, rushing in on me. Then, as quickly as it had come, the blood lust left me, panting in the midst of ruin, blood dripping from my sword. I fell upon my knees and, leaning forward, spewed until my stomach was empty.

After that, my memory is mercifully vague. I moved through the killing fields. I felt the blood spatter on my arm as a man died beside me, my skin blistering from the heat of burning buildings, yet I saw the whole scene as if from a distance. A woman, screaming as three men violated her; a child running, streaked with flame; an old man, sitting, weeping, until a passing warrior, almost casually, stabbed him through the chest.

In time, I found myself back upon the beach in a crowd of cheering men. But that night we could not feast on the spoils of our victory. Every pig, every chicken had burned. Every food store was destroyed. Nothing had been looted. Where Beting Marau had once stood, there was desolation. Not even the rats survived.

# Chapter 10

I N THE MONTHS THAT followed the massacre, I willed myself
to forget. Now, as I write this, it is as if I see it all again. My
mind recoils from the horror and I remember it as if it happened long ago and to someone else. Which, in a sense, it did. I
am not the John Williamson that stormed ashore at Beting Marau. Part of him died there in the horror and the bloodshed.

The attack achieved its purpose. The pirates were a threat no
longer and Keppel was able to leave Sarawak with a clear victory to advance his career. Our Dyaks went back to the jungle
and we returned to Kuching and tried to resume our old lives.

There were changes, of course. We no longer spent the evenings on the veranda of our bungalow, receiving visits from
whoever passed by. Now our meetings were in the *istana* and
visitors would have to present themselves at the gate to be approved before they could obtain audience. Yet the atmosphere
in our courtyard remained relaxed and anyone with legitimate
business was admitted without any real difficulty.

Many of the changes that followed the Revolt were for the
better. As news of our success against the pirates spread among
the Singapore merchants, so they favoured our waters over
those where they could travel less safely. Kuching's trade grew

and, with it, the revenues that accrued to the government.

Trade between the Dyak villages was easier too. The action we had taken proved to the chiefs we were serious about the enforcement of order within our borders. Battles between rival tribes became a rarity and headhunting was virtually stamped out.

With the free movement of travellers about the country came some degree of industry. A tribe famous for its textiles would trade with another where a smith had established a reputation for the strength of his spear tips. So the economy, which had been based on simple survival and the crudest barter, developed into something more sophisticated.

For all James' prejudice, the Chinese were amongst the greatest beneficiaries of these changes, travelling about the country, setting up trading posts, and exporting to their associates in Singapore.

The suppression of the Revolt had also sent a clear message to the Malay nobility. Rajah Brooke would not tolerate treason and had both the means and the determination to destroy utterly any who plotted against him. Hence their loyalty was ensured. Budrudeen's compound—rebuilt now on an even larger scale than before—became a centre of political activity and every month found more of the great men of the place visiting to lay their talents at his service.

This era of peace and prosperity saw the finances of Sarawak put on a secure footing for the first time. From being forever concerned he would be unable to meet his debts, James became a potent force in the merchant community of Singapore. Colin Hart was forced to buy larger and more elegant premises from which to conduct Sarawak's business and, from being a constant borrower, began to invest in all manner of enterprises in the region.

Between James and myself, things could never be quite as they were. I could never forget what I had seen him do. And somehow I blamed him for the fact I had joined in the killing.

Yet such was my love for him that I did all in my power to put aside my revulsion. He, too, sought to recapture the happiness that had been ours. We treated each other with an especial care and often, as I lay in his arms and he whispered endearments in my ear, I could believe all would be well.

Yet, if all Sarawak united to veil the memory of what had occurred, the events were such that the wider world was sure to become aware of them.

The first suggestion anything might be amiss came with letters in the *Straits Times*. Mr Woods, the editor of this publication, considered himself a person of influence in Singapore society and resented the attention James' success was bringing. He was more than happy to publish suggestions that the dangers of piracy in the South China Seas had been exaggerated and our actions against the pirates had been disproportionate.

These stories circulated in Singapore. They found a ready audience amongst those merchants whose own prosperity suffered as our commercial success grew. In time, the stories spread to England and there they were taken up by those of the Liberal persuasion who found in them a ready stick with which to beat the government. Was it true, they demanded to know, that the British Navy had been involved in a massacre to protect the commercial interests of a private individual?

In vain did Keppel send home urgent messages about the scale of the pirate problem or his success in dealing with it. The Admiralty could do nothing, for the matter had become political and the voice of reason went unheeded. The London papers began to carry stories of 'The Massacre of Beting Marau,' accompanied by illustrations as fanciful as they were lurid. Mr Cobden, the Radical leader, arranged a public meeting in Manchester that condemned the massacre as "a gross outrage on all the rights of justice and humanity." An Inquiry was demanded and, in time, an Inquiry was commissioned.

On 11 September, almost exactly three years after the battle of Beting Marau, the Commissioners sent a ship to Kuching to carry Mr Brooke to Singapore to face the Inquiry. While he was treated with every courtesy, the summons, and the provision of a vessel for his transport, seemed more appropriate to a man being placed on trial than to a witness at a neutral investigation.

I accompanied James on the journey. He was in a dark mood, which was not lightened when we arrived in Singapore to discover Mr Woods ensconced with the Commissioners. Indeed, when James arrived at Government House, expecting to give his evidence, he was told his presence was not required until the evidence of Mr Woods and his companions had been heard.

That first day we sat and watched Mr Woods perform before the Inquiry. He was a good-looking man, though short, and he squinted slightly as if his eyesight were imperfect.

What, asked the Commissioners, did Mr Woods know of piracy in the region?

Mr Woods, it appeared, knew very little. He had hardly heard of any pirates. Questioned about the reports of piracy carried in his own newspaper, he admitted there were, indeed, *some* pirates, but they had not attacked British ships.

"These are native vessels, gentlemen," he said, addressing the Commissioners. "They prey on other native craft in their tribal wars. It is no concern of the British Navy to interfere in such private quarrels. If Mr Brooke had taken the inhabitants of Beting Marau under his protection, our Navy would doubtless have been bombarding Kuching."

James rose to his feet, his face reddened with rage and shame, but the Commissioners would not hear him and he stormed from the hearing in a fury.

We did not visit the Inquiry for another week. Colin had rented us apartments near the new offices and we retreated there. The place was very fine, with high rooms that stayed cool even on the hottest of days. Yet I was ill at ease there. Propriety meant James and I could not share a bed. James, in any case, was not fit company, being plunged into the deepest of depressions and refusing to speak for hours on end. I found myself sitting alone, wondering how we had come to this and what would become of me.

Each evening, Colin Hart would bring us news of the day's proceedings. A procession of merchants gave evidence. They had seen no pirates; their ships had never been threatened by pirates; they had lost no goods to pirates. Keppel's activities had been designed simply to strengthen the territorial ambitions of Mr Brooke.

James would rouse himself to listen to these accounts. Indeed, on some days his mood would shift suddenly from the deepest despair to a furious activity in which he would hurl abuse at his persecutors and stride about the room, threatening terrible violence on those who slandered him.

"For it *is* slander," he insisted on one such occasion. He had dressed in his formal uniform as Rajah and I looked on uneasily as he reached unconsciously for the hilt of his sword. "No one ventures to support the monstrous lies which have been perpetrated save those whose commercial interests are clearly served if my own activities are curtailed. The Commission is a farce—a farce of justice and a farce of enquiry when there is nothing to enquire about."

At last, he was invited to address the Commissioners with his own side of the story. Mr Wood was still present but only in his capacity of a reporter for the press, and his continued presence was conditional on his taking no further part in the proceedings.

James explained how he had come to a position of power in Sarawak and how he felt a responsibility to those of the native population who looked to him to protect them. He described the suffering Surabada had brought. He emphasised that Surabada's followers *were* pirates.

"If they have not been reported as attacking British ships, it is because easier pickings are available from their attacks on native craft which are less well armed. Yet, even so, I do not accept that no British ships have been attacked. Every year sees a score of vessels lost in these waters and it would be unlikely if none of these were the victim of piracy."

James turned from the Commissioners and addressed his next remarks directly to Mr Woods. "We found scores of guns of European manufacture when we destroyed the pirate fort at Patusen. Can we honestly believe none had come from British ships?"

It was clear James had impressed the Commissioners and his evidence was followed by that of several merchants who asserted that piracy was, indeed, a serious concern and a threat to trade in the region. Although he did not give evidence himself, I saw Captain Kennedy, my old Master from the *Lady Irene*, amongst the delegation of merchants who appeared in support of their comrades. He saw me, too, sitting with James and the other gentlemen, and frowned slightly, as if trying to recollect if he had met me before. Then there was a call for another witness and in the general confusion, I lost sight of him. I did not see him again.

Ironically, James' strongest supporters were the very Chinese merchants he despised. Their craft were the most likely to fall prey to the pirates and, one after another, they rose to testify that Rajah Brooke's efforts to rid the seas of this menace was of general benefit to the region.

The merchants were followed by Admiral Keppel, who gave his evidence arrayed in his full dress uniform. He was an impressive figure and his assurance that the pirates were a genuine danger to British interests seemed to settle things in our favour.

Even with such convincing evidence on our side, the Inquiry did not easily reach a conclusion. Representatives of the Aborigines Protection Society gave evidence as to the horrors of the massacre. The strength of their testimony was diluted by the fact it was entirely hearsay, but those of us who had been there knew what they said to be true and the absence of any evidence refuting their view presumably weighed with the Commissioners.

We had thought after all the evidence concerning piracy had

been heard, the Inquiry would be over, but this was not the case. Lawyers and government officials now took to the stand to argue about the legal status of Sarawak's forces and whether or not Keppel should have commanded an action in which the majority of those participating were not directly subjects of Her Majesty. The delay drove James near to distraction.

"This Inquiry drags on with nothing to inquire into. I should go back to Kuching." He would send for Colin and start to issue orders for return but then change his mind. "I must stay here and see this through. I have been deeply wronged and I distrust the Inquiry. I cannot in any way relax my endeavours to advance the real interests of Sarawak and therefore I have to remain."

So James stayed, prey to every doubt and uncertainty. Although I stayed to be with him, we hardly seemed to speak. Some days I would wander the streets of Singapore, losing myself in its noise and bustle, for the town was growing fast. Here, in this outpost of Britain, I felt remote from the jungles of Borneo.

Together we had built a new world for ourselves and for the people of Sarawak, but now all we had achieved was under scrutiny. I shared James' distrust of the Commissioners. They did not know our country. They heard no evidence from Dyaks or Malays. Theirs was a world of Empire, where the rules that governed London were thought to govern the world. I did not fear their judgement. But their Inquiry probed into matters where I had to judge myself, and I feared the Commissioners of my soul might bring a verdict that would damn me.

James had achieved so much and I had my part in that. Yet I had my part also in the murder of Makota. I had stood by while the village of the Saribas Dyaks was put to the flame. And then, at Beting Marau, I had joined the killing myself. If, after this Inquiry, I returned to Kuching, with what memories would I lay down to sleep in our new palace? And, when I recalled them, would I then sleep at all?

✳

THE INQUIRY FINALLY CLOSED at the end of October. The
report, we were promised, would be published in November.

James took to his rooms, avoiding all society. Colin and I
would visit every day, but he was plunged into one of his black
moods and would barely speak to us. Then, around the middle
of November, his mood changed and he was suddenly the
James Brooke of old, anxious to be out of the town, seeking
diversion in wild activity. He hired two horses from a livery stables near the port and insisted I join him in a day's riding across
the island.

Singapore is not an ideal place to go riding. Much of it remains marshland and that which is not boggy is thickly forested.
The man who hired us the horses doubtless expected we would
use them only for trotting decorously about town. Instead, James
headed for the centre of the island. We galloped recklessly
through the forests, covering ourselves and our mounts in mud
from the primitive tracks that were all the roads we could find.

We had no horses in Sarawak. In all my years with James,
this was the first time we had ever ridden out together.

I think it was an afternoon that reminded us both of our
pasts, before we had met. Looking at his face, flushed with excitement as we careered between the trees, I imagined him leading his troop into battle during his ill-fated service with the East
India Company. And I, too, was remembering my youth, exer-
cising the horses on the farm.

We stopped where the path ran alongside a river. The
ground was rocky and there were few trees. The water was unusually clear and we stripped off our muddy clothes and
plunged in, splashing and shouting and ducking each other like
schoolboys.

James had packed a picnic in his saddlebag. I remember bread
and cheese and quail's eggs and ham and pickles but I'm sure
there was more. And there was wine. We ate and drank while the

hobbled horses explored the river margins for fresh grass.

After our meal, we lay together for a long time and James held me, as he used to when we were at home together and the day's tasks were done and all was at peace in the world. And we kissed.

It was late in the afternoon before we stirred from that spot and made our way back to the city. We rode slowly now, and darkness was falling when we returned our mounts to their stables. We tipped the ostler to clean off the worst of the mud before their owner should see them.

James returned to his rooms and I to mine, agreeing we would arrange a similar adventure soon.

The next day, the Inquiry announced its report would be published within the week. All thought of recreation was abandoned. Colin busied himself with tidying our accounts and putting all in order for whatever decision the Inquiry would come to. James spent his days in meetings with his supporters, discussing the rumours of what the report would say and how he should respond to it.

I had no heart for any such activity. As the day of the Inquiry's report drew nearer, I found myself dwelling more and more on the events that had led to it. I wandered the streets of Singapore, full of Europeans and their carriages, their noise and self-importance. I went into a church to escape the noise and the heat. I needed to think.

It was years since I was last in a church. It was cool there. The air seemed to be the air of England, fresh and clean, reminding me of things I had not thought on for so many years.

I thought of my youth, the person I had hoped to become, and the person I was now. I thought of James and how dear he was to me, and how happy we had been. And I thought of his coldness when he was angry and the distance that could still suddenly seem to be between us.

I thought of Sarawak and the life that we had built there.

And I remembered the screams at Beting Marau and the smell of the blood of those I had killed.

It seemed to me I had come to a crossroads in my life. I thought about how James had taught me to write and I had asked what purpose there was in writing so much down when my memory had always served me well enough.

"Your memory is excellent, John," he had said. "Yet when we come to review a matter, to decide what course we should take in the future, why then it serves us well to write things down. For when we set it all out upon the page, then we can often see the course we should take."

It was then I decided to start writing this account. I returned to my rooms and straightway started upon this task.

I have sat since, at the table in this fine chamber, and have scratched my pen upon sheet after sheet of paper. That first day, I wrote for the rest of the day and into the night. I have written every day since.

I had not finished by 23 November when James, Colin, and I sat in Government House with a great crowd of Singapore society and listened as the Commissioners read their report.

The Inquiry exonerated James. Surabada's men were pirates. James was the lawful ruler of Sarawak and had acted properly in suppressing them. Keppel had made a proper use of his discretion in providing assistance.

The loss of life at Beting Marau was "greatly to be regretted" but was "mostly caused by native volunteers" and therefore no direct concern of the Crown.

At the conclusion of the reading of their report, James rose, bowed to the Commissioners, and left the room.

❋

I am my own Commissioner and my Report is now completed. I must make my judgement on James Brooke and abide by my recommendations.

It is given to few people to move in the orbit of such a dazzling star as James Brooke. He has lighted my life and the lives of so many of his people. Sarawak now is peaceful and prosperous. The Dyaks are like his children and he is the most loving of parents. Yet that Eden is haunted by the dead of Beting Marau. And we, who have grown beneath his care, must learn to care for ourselves.

Tomorrow, James returns to Kuching on the *Royalist*. I will stand on the shore and watch as my love is carried away from me. It will be unbearable.

THE MAN I AM today is the man James Brooke made me.

If I am ever to be more than that, I must seek my own path.

# Afterward

JAMES BROOKE RETURNED TO Kuching alone. He was to spend the rest of his life as ruler of Sarawak but, although the Inquiry had cleared his name, he was never as happy in Kuching again. He spent increasing amounts of time back in England, where he died on 11 June 1868. He is buried in Sheepstor churchyard on Dartmoor.

Williamson disappeared from history after the Inquiry. In 1861, a John Williamson is recorded as having bought the Grange, a substantial house in the village of Bickleigh, just north of Plymouth. The parish records show no trace of him in the years before that and whether it is the same John Williamson, we have no way of knowing. He seems to have been a well-respected member of the community, as he was churchwarden from 1863 until his death in 1872.

# Author's Note

JAMES BROOKE WAS A real person. Many of the characters in this story existed and many of the incidents really happened. It is, though, a work of fiction. Anyone who wants to know the real James Brooke can read his published journals or turn to one of the many biographies such as *The Burthen, the Risk, and the Glory* by Nicholas Tarling.

For those who enjoy separating fact and fantasy, a good rule of thumb is if it seems totally implausible, it's probably true. And many of the bits that aren't have been written down to make them more credible rather than exaggerated to make them more exciting.

The real James Brooke had a brief but distinguished career with the East India Company army, distinguished himself in battle, was invalided home, and resigned his commission, all much as described. He returned to the Far East in the *Findlay* in 1834 and the account of her voyage and his disagreement with Kennedy is substantially accurate. The storm scene, though, is a complete fiction.

He returned to England and remained there until the death of his father left him with the money to buy the *Royalist* in which he sailed to Singapore. The incident with the *Napoleon* had, indeed, drawn Hassim to the attention of the Singapore community and that was why Brooke sailed on to Sarawak. I have seen the name of that country transcribed phonetically in various ways. For what it's worth, I prefer *Sa-ra-wa*. Malay enthusiasts will end with a throaty sound, not dissimilar to the Welsh *a*.

I have given Raja Muda Hassim, the Bendahara of Brunei, the title of Sultan, as the gradations of the Malay court are impossibly confusing to the European reader.

The *Royalist* sailed from Singapore for Borneo in July 1839. By then, Brooke was 36. Nowadays he would be regarded as impossibly old, so I have made him younger.

His interpreter was of mixed British and Malay descent. He certainly wasn't my protagonist, who is an entirely fictional creation, but he does share the name Williamson.

Hassim invited Brooke to help in quelling the rebels and Brooke's tiny force was eventually decisive in the rebel defeat at Balidah. The plotting in the court, the judicial murder of Makota, and the details of the 'coronation' are, though, almost complete inventions. Hassim did, indeed, attempt to renege on his promise, but the resolution of the struggle was the result of immensely long and tortuous negotiations rather than the drama of a novel. Nor was Makota killed. He survived to be an irritant for years after.

Brooke devoted his life to developing Sarawak and his rule is still respected in modern, independent Malaysia. Many of the details of his attempts to bring Sarawak into the 19th Century, such as the setting up of a postal service, are historically accurate.

Henry Keppel was a real person and his visit to Sarawak in the *Dido* was as impressive as described, although the ship did not actually moor in Kuching. He was an ambitious sailor and did become an Admiral. At the time, though, he was Captain Keppel. As commander of the Straits Naval Squadron, he probably had more personal responsibility than most modern

Admirals, which is why I have given him an elevated rank. He did publish his adventures to considerable popular acclaim but as to the rest of his character…it's pure imagination. The expedition against the Saribas Dyaks happened too, although I have taken liberties with the details, and it really did end with a noble speech about punishing piracy, after which the village was burned to the ground. James Brooke's excitement is also a recorded fact.

James really did call his boat the *Jolly Bachelor*. You couldn't make it up!

The Revolt was a real event. James fled through a bathroom window and, as described, swam a creek to escape his pursuers. His adventures thereafter, though, are entirely imaginary.

Brooke felt betrayed by the British government, as outlined in the story. Keppel, though, came to his aid with the *Dido* and the *Phlegethon*. The various events described combine actual incidents from several different actions and a deal of artistic licence.

The massacre at Beting Marau was on an even larger and bloodier scale than I suggest. It led to questions in Parliament, and Cobden described it in the terms used in the story. There was significant public agitation about it. The Aborigines Protection Society, for example, was a real organisation that condemned the massacre.

Many of the details of the Inquiry, including Brooke's tirades against it, are a matter of record. Brooke did not, however, remain in Singapore for the outcome. His exoneration arrived after his return to Sarawak. The emotional impact of the events, though, was much as described.

James Brooke finally returned to England and is, indeed, buried on Dartmoor.

# About the Author

TOM WILLIAMS' WRITING CAREER started at about the age of 10, when he won a book in a national competition organized by a tea company. But, despite the student magazine publishing a piece of his at Oxford, there was no serious creative writing for decades after that. Instead, he wrote books for business covering everything from the gambling industry to new developments in printing technology.

It was on a trip to Sarawak, visiting Dyak longhouses, that Tom discovered James Brooke, and he spent far too much time in libraries over the next few years until he felt he had some understanding of the man. He also started collecting South East Asian weapons and now knows an unhealthy amount about how to behead someone with a parang. These interests combined to produce *The White Rajah*.

Tom lives in London. His main interest is avoiding doing any honest work and this leaves him with time to ski, skate, and dance the tango, all of which he does quite well. He is also working on another novel, again a historical story, but this time set in Argentina during the Napoleonic wars.

Lightning Source UK Ltd.
Milton Keynes UK
UKOW031050210513
211020UK00007B/195/P